The Dungeons

....

Charlotte Spielberg

Contents

Chapter 1: Promise

- -

"Now, name the kingdoms of Asterin. Tell me about their history."

"Soleil has been the most powerful kingdom in Asterin for three-hundred and fifty five years. It is also known as the land of the Sun people, who are believed to have descended from the Sun God himself. They have the strongest army in all of Asterin and occupy the biggest area of land."

I sat back a little more into my chair when my mother started to braid my long hair. Everyday after breakfast, she sat me in a chair by our small table and tested my knowledge on various subjects while brushing and braiding my locks. Today, it was history.

She taught me everything I knew, from art and medicine to history and politics. I learned how to fully read and write at age six, but I still enjoyed listening to my mother read me stories at bedtime as a child. She has given me a lot, despite our circumstances.

"Poseidon is the second largest kingdom," I continued. "The Sea people have the most powerful Water Force, and they have controlled the sea for centuries. Then there is Typhon..." I trailed off. My mother sniffled, making my heart break for her.

"I can move on to the next kingdom," I said softly. I did not want to bring up horrible memories that came with that name. Although I have never met him, it still made me sad to know his fate. I could only imagine how it affected my mother.

"No, it's all right. Go on." I turned around to see her face and she gave me an encouraging smile. Her eyes shined with unshed tears, which made my heart squeeze in my chest. She nodded when I gave her a questioning look. I turned forward again.

I cleared my throat and continued in a whisper. "Kingdom Typhon is the third largest kingdom by land. Its border is separated from Soleil and Poseidon by The Dark Forest. King Cerius and his people died when the Twin Volcanoes erupted nearly two decades ago. A fire started on the kingdom's land, which ignited most of the forest, leaving only ashes of trees and land behind."

"That's correct. And the other two kingdoms?" I heard my mother's quiet and shaky voice ask. She was now finishing off the intricate braided hairstyle on my head. She learned how to do it from Rose, a kind servant who secretly helped us all these years. I had seen an illustration of a princess in a book I was reading at the time and fell in love with her pretty hair. I wanted to have the same beautiful braids as her, so my mother asked Rose to teach her to do it on me. It was the happiest day of my life.

"Kingdom Gora and Kingdom Pesok. Smallest kingdoms in Asterin. The Mountain people of Gora are known to be most generous and kind. Despite their small land and resources, they welcome newcomers and offer shelter to anyone that needs it."

I smiled, knowing that good people existed in this world. It gave me hope in humanity. Then I continued. "Pesok is the land of the Sand people. Not a lot is known about them, because their king is very secretive and has never travelled outside of Pesok's border nor tried to communicate with its neighbouring kingdoms. History books have little information about Pesok."

"Yes, many historians could not access any information about Pesok, but..." My mother let go of my hair and walked around me to admire her work. Looking satisfied with the end result, she allowed me to feel my hair. I carefully ran my fingers over the soft ridges of each braid, imagining what I looked like. "I knew the king."

"You did?" I widened my eyes in shock. "You've never mentioned that."

"I wanted to tell you this as a surprise." She smiled at me, stroking my cheek. I grinned, thrilled to expand my knowledge. Mother always saved the most exciting bits of knowledge to tell me on my birthdays in order to make them more special.

"Please tell me, mother! What was he like?"

She chuckled softly at my eagerness, leaning against the table beside me. I got more comfortable on the chair and looked up at her, ready to listen.

"The king was a fair ruler, and his people loved him. He believed that knowledge was power, so he refused to let his enemies learn anything about his land. It kept them safe. Their enemies did not wish to risk their lives by entering unknown territory. He, however, knew everything about the other kingdoms."

"What did his land look like?"

"The kingdom was surrounded by sand. It was difficult to see anything when strong winds blew it in every direction," she said, smiling a little.

"King Serkan's palace was beautiful. Possibly the most beautiful place in Asterin. I wish you could see it."

I painted a picture of Pesok in my mind, imagining the palace, the king on his throne, as well as his people. My daydream was interrupted when I heard footsteps coming down the stairs and toward our cell.

Mother heard them too, as she started to gather all of our belongings and hastily shoved them under our small bed in the corner. If patrol guards saw our books and papers, among other things, they could be confiscated, which could cause a lot of trouble for us and especially Rose, who snuck them in for us.

For years, the guards didn't see anything out of order in our cell. We hid it out of sight, cloaked by darkness. They always only passed by the gates and did not bother to enter and search through the room. As mother put a hairbrush under the thin pillow on the bed, a small figure appeared outside of our cell door.

I exhaled in relief when I saw Rose's face under the hood of her blue robe. She was alone this time. Whenever she brought our meals, she was accompanied by a guard who opened the door for her and closed it when she was done with her duties. Servants were not trusted with keys to the dungeon cells.

"I'm alone," she assured us when I hesitated to speak. I nodded in response.

"What are you doing here?" I whispered. I did not wish to be overheard by anyone. There could very well be a guard lurking in the shadows.

"I brought you something," she responded in a low whisper. Her eyes glowed with mischief as she stuck her hand in the pocket of her cape and presented me with a cloth-covered object. "I took this from the kitchen. They made these for the princess, but I highly doubt that she would notice two of them are missing."

She rolled her eyes and knocked on her head a few times with her knuckle, a gesture that meant to say how dull the princess was. I laughed into my palm to muffle the sound. It was no secret to us that Rose disliked Princess Athena. According to Rose, the princess was an absolute nightmare.

She unfolded the cloth and brought two steaming apple cakes through the metal bars of the cell door. I took them in my hands and inhaled the sweet scent of apples, sugar, and cinnamon. "Rose! Thank you so much."

"I know they are your favourite." She winked at me. I grinned happily and offered one to my mother.

Mother also inhaled the delicious scent of her apple cake and bit into it, thanking Rose for these treats.

"Happy birthday, Emilia!" she sang, then adjusted the hood on her head. "I have to go now or they'll notice that I'm gone. Enjoy your cakes, darlings!"

She waved at us and rushed out.

"I don't know how we could have survived here without that wonderful woman," my mother sighed. She was looking at the wall outside of our cell gate, where Rose was standing moments ago. The woman who helped my mother deliver me in this very place. The woman who brought us bigger portions of food than customary for prisoners and even snuck in sweet treats whenever she could. The woman who updated us on current events in this kingdom and some news from other kingdoms as well that'd she'd hear from other gossiping servants.

She kept us sane and healthy. I don't know how she did it, but we were able to get clean clothes and water to wash ourselves every evening. Another luxury no other prisoners experienced. We were grateful for Rose and loved her like family.

~~~
~~~

The bell rung loudly throughout the castle and reached the dungeons, indicating that it was noon. Our lunch would be brought soon, which meant that a guard was making his way to our cell with Rose. I gathered my paintings and placed them under the bed. I have been painting the map of Asterin through memory, but did not complete it yet. Hopefully, it didn't get damaged when I moved it.

Mother and I walked closer to the cell door when we heard footsteps approaching. It was a guard, and he was alone. Rose was nowhere in sight.

I could not ask the guard where she was, since it would raise suspicion, but I was worried. Something was different today. I could feel it. That uneasy sense at the back of my mind that something wasn't right. My mother felt it too, because she moved closer to me and pulled me slightly behind her.

My heart rate sped up when I saw the guard wordlessly take out a big set of keys -- there must have been around one hundred of them -- and try each one on the door. He cursed when the third key did not fit into the lock then fumbled around with his keys again.

I took this opportunity to look at my mother, feeling panicked. We have never seen this guard before. He was much taller, more muscular and scarier than the usual two guards that alternated every other day. Rose was always with them too. Where was she?

I heard my mother's breath hitch and her eyes widen when she looked into my eyes. "It can't be." She whispered, looking shocked.

"Mother?"

"Emilia," she whispered, her voice breaking. Her eyes filled with tears. "I didn't know."

"What is it, mother?" I asked, quickly glancing towards the guard outside of our cell. He was still struggling to find the right key. I looked back at my mother.

"I thought you wouldn't have it since I'm not... I was foolish to think —" She was interrupted by the sound of a key clicking in place. The guard found the right one.

"Bloody morons, couldn't organize these keys," he cursed as he turned the key to open our cell door. The door creaked open as he stepped into the small space. His big frame made our cell look even smaller in size.

"What do you want?" my mother suddenly said to him in a strong voice, pushing me behind her completely. I tried to do the same with her, but she squeezed my arm, telling me to stay where I was. My heart was thudding loudly in my chest.

The guard looked down at her with one brow raised. He ignored her question and looked directly at me. His deep voice boomed in my ears. "You. You're coming with me."

He made his way toward me, but halted when mother stopped him by putting her hand on his chest. "You are not taking her anywhere."

The man backed up one step and crossed his arms. "We could do this quietly, or I could take her by force. Your choice. I don't have all day."

"You are not taking her anywhere," she repeated. "Gods know what you are planning to do with her. She stays with me."

"Woman." The guard rubbed his face in frustration. "I don't think you realize who you are dealing with."

"I don't care. You are not touching my daughter."

"Mother, don't. He could hurt you," I whispered to her and tugged on the sleeve of her shirt.

She ignored me and continued to stand her ground. The guard sighed.

"James!" he barked out. Another guard rushed into our cell. "Restrain her." He pointed at my mother.

James easily got a hold of my mother, moving her away from me, despite her struggles. My attempts to pry him off of her became completely useless when the big guard grabbed me and held both of my wrists in one large hand. They were much stronger than us physically. We could not escape them no matter how hard we tried.

"No!" I screamed, trying to kick the guard behind me. "Let go of her!"

I was kicking air as the man behind me lifted me off the ground and threw me over his shoulder. I started punching his back. That had no effect on him at all. My fists probably hurt more than his back of steel did. He started to walk toward the cell door. I lifted my head to look at my mother. James was simply holding her back and easily dodging all of her attacks.

"Emilia!" she shouted. "Don't look at the king! Keep your eyes down at all times! Promise me!"

I didn't know what she was talking about. She looked serious when she said it, her teary eyes never breaking away from mine, as my guard took me away from her.

"Promise me!"

"I promise!" I cried out as the big guard carried me away from our cell. The only place I knew for eighteen years.

Chapter 2: Sunlight

"Put me down!" I punched the guard's back with as much force as I could muster. He carried me down dimly lit stone hallways of the dungeon and went up the stairs toward a large metal door. He put me down, holding my wrists firmly in one hand as he fumbled with his keys again.

"Bloody hell, why are there so many," he muttered as he looked for the right key again.

"Take me back to my mother! What is he doing to her?" I yelled at him. He ignored me.

"Let go of me! I need to get back to her!"

He grunted and continued to thrust each key into the metal lock. None of them fit so far. His grip on my wrists loosened slightly while he concentrated on the door, allowing me to wiggle one arm out of his hold.

I punched his arm to her his attention. He kept ignoring me. I punched it again. Same reaction.

"My Gods!" I groaned in frustration. "Just let me see if my mother is okay."

"P-please," I added through clenched teeth. I hated begging him. I hated him. He left my mother all alone with that guard.

He halted and turned to face me. "No." He caught my free arm and joined my wrists together in his giant hand, this time squeezing them tighter. I couldn't get out of it. Then he continued to try some more keys. My skin was getting heated from anger.

"How many of those do you even have? By Gods, we will be here forever! You might as well let me go see my mother while you try your luck here," I tried to reason with the imbecile that had hundreds of keys, which all looked the same. If he was the key keeper, he was not a very organized one.

He went back to ignoring me. I switched tactics. "You know, it would be much easier if you marked your keys."

"You don't think I know that?" he bit out. Finally, one of the keys went in. He tried to turn it, but it wouldn't budge. He tried to turn it the other way, still it didn't move.

"I don't think it's the right one."

The guard clenched his jaw and turned to me again. "You don't say?" He went for another key, grinding his teeth together in frustration when that one also didn't fit.

"Oh, that one didn't seem right either."

He exhaled forcefully through his nose. "You're an irritating one, aren't you?"

I'm trying to irritate you, so you'd let me see my mother, you brute.

I kicked the keys out of his hand. They fell on the stone floor with a loud clank. He separated them as he went through each key, so he could keep track of the wrong ones. Now all of them got mixed up again.

He closed his eyes and inhaled deeply. When he exhaled, he opened them and shot me a glare, which would have scared me if I wasn't angry with him as well. I was definitely playing with fire, but I did not care. I had to make sure that my mother wasn't hurt by the other guard. Was he still there? Why did they only take me?

"Now will you take me to my mother?" I shot him a glare of my own. It would take him forever to sort through those keys again and he knew it.

He ground his molars in anger, as his eyes bore into mine. He tugged down on my wrists, bringing me down with him while he bent over to pick up the keys. Then he shot upwards and pushed me in front of him, maintaining his painful grip on me. "Walk."

I did as he told me, trying not to grin. It worked!

We made our way back to my cell. As we neared the familiar metal bars, I swallowed anxiously. She was all right. She had to be. Finally, I stood outside of the cell where my mother sat on the bed, crying into the palms of her hands.

"Mother." My eyes filled with tears as I saw the state she was in. Her head snapped up at the sound of my voice. Immediately, she rushed to the doors, gripping the bars from the opposite side of me. I looked around the cell to see if James was still there. He was gone.

"Emilia," she sniffled, reaching out and stroking my cheek. "You're here."

"I managed to convince him to let me see you." I pointed backwards with my thumb where I assumed my guard was standing. I heard him grunt in annoyance. My mother looked back at him, then toward me.

"Don't worry about me. I will be alright," she said. Her gaze quickly flickered toward the guard again. She whispered her next words, fear evident in her eyes. Fear for me, I realized. "Emilia, whatever you do, be careful.

Don't trust anyone, except for Rose. Keep your head down. Do not attract any attention to yourself from the king. Do not let him see you up-close. Please, just —"

"There you bloody are." I turned my head at my guard's interruption. He threw his keys to James, who appeared by the cell, carrying a tray of food. James skillfully balanced the tray on one hand, while he caught the heavy set of keys with another. Some of the steaming soup splashed out onto the skin of his arm, causing no reaction from him. "Find me the key for the dungeon door."

James flipped through each key quickly and singled out one of them, holding it between his thumb and index finger. He offered it to my brute guard.

"Let's go." The brute pulled me back toward him, and pushed me in the direction where we came from. Once again, I was being taken away from my mother and my cell.

I heard her protests, but I could no longer see my mother. I wanted to get back to her. Back to our safe space. After living so many years underground, we got used to those stone walls and metal bars. The dim light of our lone oil lamp on the table that barely illuminated our room. The cold floors and the thin mattress on the bed. It was home. The only home I knew.

I felt my adrenalin slowly dissipate and tears started to prickle my eyes. I was scared to leave these dungeons. The knowledge I gained from all the books I've read and stories from my mother about the outside world were just that. Knowledge. I had no real experience. It was all in my head.

We approached the same big metal door, and this time it clicked open when he stuck in the right key. My breathing escalated. This was it. I was about to enter a new world against my will. Sweat began to bead on my forehead. My heart started beating faster, thudding rapidly in my chest.

He pushed me forward, and I stumbled out into another hallway, immediately blinded by the bright light. I covered my eyes, as it hurt to look anywhere with this impossible brightness. How many lamps did they put in here?

I kept my eyes shut as I was pushed down this hallway. I felt people pass by us, and I was curious to see them, but I valued my eyesight and refused to be blinded. My eyes stayed shut until he suddenly halted and cursed, which caused me to be pulled back and bump into his chest. I opened my eyes in surprise and blinked a few times to adjust to the light, finally being able to take in my surroundings.

Sunlight. There were no lamps lit in this hallway. Sunlight was shining brightly through the floor-length windows. It was more beautiful than I have ever imagined.

I could see tall green trees outside. And the sky! It was so blue. Multiple white clouds were floating above with the wind. They looked so soft, I wanted to touch them. Happy tears welled up in my eyes. It was all so beautiful. I closed my eyes, this time to enjoy the warmth of the sun rays on my skin.

"Get off my chest."

The happy trance was broken when the brute's harsh voice reached my ears. I snapped back to reality, and that is when I realized that I have been leaning on the guard while admiring the outside view. I blinked away my tears and tried to stop a blush that tried to peek through on my cheeks. Embarrassed, I quickly leaned away from his chest.

"We're making a detour. You need better clothes. He will be unhappy if I bring you in like this."

He was taking me to the king then, I thought to myself. Mother's warning circled in my mind. I will do as she told me. She was the one who grew up in the outside world, and I have only ever seen our dungeon cell. I trusted her judgment more than my own in this matter.

He turned us in the opposite direction and we made our way to another wide hallway. Then he turned left toward a wooden door and barged in without knocking.

"S-sir! How can I help you?" A servant girl who looked close to my age blinked up at my guard.

"Where is Ella?"

"She - uh - she left to go to the market." She bowed. The girl looked completely lost, shakily looking at me and the big man behind me.

"You're new, aren't you?" the brute asked. She nodded. He sighed and pushed me toward her, letting go of my wrists. I rubbed them to ease the pain from his grip as I came face-to-face with the girl. Her eyes widened in surprise. "Wash her and put her in new clothes. Servant clothes are fine. I will wait outside."

He walked out without another word and slammed the door behind him. The girl's shoulders immediately sagged in relief when he left.

"Scary man, I know," I said, understanding her fear. She gave me a hesitant smile, nodding.

"I'm Yvette," she introduced herself timidly.

"Hello, Yvette. My name is Emilia." I smiled in response. "You don't have to do anything. Just show me to the wash basin and I can wash myself."

Immediately, she perked up. She shook her head. "No, no! Those are the only things I could actually do. Please, allow me."

She led me to another room where a wash basin with a short metal hose was situated in the middle of the floor. She turned one of the two big screws on each side of the metal hose, and water started to rush out of it, straight into the basin. I was fascinated by it. I have only read about it in books, but seeing it in real life...

"Is this... a bathtub?" I bit my lip, unsure of the name. It matched the description of what I've read perfectly, but I could be wrong.

"It is." She smiled, feeling the temperature of the water with her hand and turning the other large screw. When she looked over at me, she frowned in confusion. "You haven't seen one?"

I shook my head no. I haven't seen many things. Yvette studied me for a moment, curiosity in her brown eyes.

"You can take off your clothes and put them over there." She pointed at a bench in the corner, finally breaking our eye contact. "The water is almost ready."

I did as she asked and got into the tub, sighing at how good warm water felt against my skin. Yvette lifted one of my arms and started scrubbing it with a soapy cloth. It had a pleasant smell to it. The ones that I used smelled like nothing. "What is in this soap?"

"Do you like it?" she asked. I smiled and nodded. It smelled divine. "I make my own soaps, mixing them with different scents. This one is apple and white tea. My newest creation."

"It smells wonderful," I said honestly, inhaling the delicious fragrance.

"Thank you." She grinned.

Yvette scrubbed my entire body and then moved on to my hair, washing it gently underneath a stream of water that came from the metal hose. She had to unbraid my hair to wash it, and I felt a prickle of sadness when she did that, remembering my mother's skillful hands working on them this very morning.

I dried myself off with the soft towels that she handed me when I got out of the tub. Yvette left to get me some clothes while I dried my hair. I let it cascade down my back in loose waves. She returned in a few minutes, handing me a thick cotton dress and some undergarments. I put them on, the dress clinging to my body. She saw how small it looked on me and apologized profusely.

"It was the only servant dress I could find." She bit her lip nervously. "It must be Tanya's. She's the smallest girl here. Only fourteen. The rest of them must be in the wash."

I looked down at myself and felt slightly uneasy. I was used to wearing spacious clothes, since Rose usually supplied us with men's clothing. Large shirts and pants. She said that men did not notice when a pair of their pants was gone for a few days. They were large, but very comfortable. Sometimes she brought her own clothes, but she had very few of those.

The cotton dress I wore now reached right below my knees, exposing my legs, which I was not used to. Looking at Yvette's identical dress, it was meant to cover much more. Mine clung tightly to my figure.

"What is taking so long?" The guard who separated me from my mother barged in unannounced. The wooden door nearly flew off its hinges due to his force. Yvette jumped in surprise at the sudden intrusion, holding a hand over her heart. I glared at him. "I don't have all day —"

He closed his mouth as soon as he looked at me. His eyes travelled down my figure and back to rest on my face, jaw clenching. Then he glared at Yvette, making her take a step back in fear.

"What is this?" He pointed in my direction, while maintaining his mean glare on the poor girl beside me. She was too scared to answer. "Get her something to cover up with. Go."

She scurried away to another room. The guard had his hands in tight fists, jaw still clenched. He refused to look in my direction. We stood in silence while we waited for Yvette. I had nothing to say to him. He would likely ignore me even if I did.

I started to play with the hem of my dress when Yvette rushed back in, handing me a blue robe. I've seen Rose wear the same one before. It was identical to hers actually. Must be part of servants' attire.

I put it on over the dress, tying the strings at the front and adjusting the hood at the back of my neck. It reached all the way to the floor and was loose enough to hide my shape.

"Good," the guard grunted once he saw the cape on me. "Let's go."

He tried to grab my wrists to restrain me, but I dodged his hand. "Don't touch me. I am capable of walking without your help."

The tall man glared at me, but did not attempt to reach my wrists again. "Then walk."

I shot him a glare of my own, thanked Yvette for her help, and began walking toward the door. I stepped out of the room and turned left.

"The other way."

I huffed and turned around, heading right down the hallway. The guard walked behind me, continuously poking me in the back as a way to make me walk faster. I sped up. He matched my pace and started to poke me forward again. I gritted my teeth and sped up again.

"My Gods!" I exclaimed, throwing my arms up and turning around when he poked me again. "Could you please stop doing that?"

I bumped into his chest when I fully turned to face him. I took a step back and rubbed the tip of my nose in pain. Then I looked up at him, craning my neck. He was already looking down at me with his dark blue eyes. He raised one eyebrow and then responded. "You need to walk faster. I don't have all d — "

"Yes, yes, I know. You don't have all day. I got that," I snapped and turned back around, nearly jogging this time. My frustration with him distracted me completely from the fact that I was currently on my way to meet the king. The man who imprisoned my mother and I all those years ago.

He did not know that she was pregnant at the time, but when he discovered that she was, he didn't release her and left her to birth and raise her child in the dungeons instead. My mother never told me the reason she was sent down there. What could she have possibly done to deserve such a cruel punishment?

I was suddenly pulled back by the hood of my robe. "We're here."

I stumbled backwards, seething at his actions. There was no need for doing what he did. I would have stopped had he told me to. Taking deep breaths to calm myself, I pointedly ignored the brute. When I finally looked around us, I saw that we were standing in front of large double doors. They were decorated with intricate metal work that looked like one big painting of the sea and the castle of Kingdom Poseidon. There was so much detail put into it. My mouth hung open at the beauty of it.

The brute opened the doors without knocking, revealing a giant ballroom with white marble floors. As we stepped inside, I could see more of its interior. I gasped, unable to hold in my fascination. It looked very much like the ballrooms illustrated in books. Crystal chandeliers, curved staircases, and even a throne area at the end of the big room.

As soon as I saw a man sitting on the throne, my excitement vanished. The guard and I walked all the way toward the king. I kept my face down, eyes looking at the floor. It may have looked like submission to the king, but I was simply keeping the promise I've made to my mother. Finally, we stopped by the foot of the pedestal.

"My, my, how much you've grown, little one." I heard a raspy voice say.

Chapter 3: King Theon

"How is your mother? Still alive?" The king chuckled. I clenched my jaw in anger, keeping my face down, but did not respond to him. "What, are you mute or something? Answer your king!"

You are not my king, I wanted to say. I couldn't. I didn't want to get my mother in trouble. Instead, I took a deep breath to keep myself from snapping at the king and responded. "I am not mute, Your Majesty. My mother is well, thank you."

I bowed for added effect. Let him think that I was a submissive little girl. Inside, I was raging. I hated King Theon with all my heart. I realized just how deeply my hatred ran as soon as he spoke. Even the sound of his voice made my blood boil. I wanted very badly to look him in the eye and to see the man responsible for my mother's misery but then reminded myself of my promise to her.

"That's a shame. Can't believe she survived this long," he said, sounding impressed. My anger flared up. "Maybe I should stop feeding her. See what happens."

I wanted to lunge at him. I thanked the Gods for my self-control at that moment. Bastard.

"No matter," he continued. "That's not what I wanted to discuss with you. As much as I enjoy seeing you squirm, I will get to the point." He cleared his throat. "Your mother may have committed treason, but you are innocent...for the most part."

Treason? I almost looked up at that. Almost. What did my mother do?

"I'm clearing out the dungeons. Most of the prisoners have died already. The rest of them can be hung" — my breath hitched at that — "except for your mother, of course. I will not make it that easy for her. As for you," he paused, "I need more servants. You will do anything that is required around the castle. I am hosting a ball next week and everything has to be prepared for it. I've been feeding you for too long. It is time that you earned your meals."

Then I heard him laugh loudly, making me shiver in disgust. "As stupid as she is, my daughter has good ideas from time to time. Here I was, sharing my people's food with prisoners who have done nothing to earn it. When I told Athena about you -- the dungeon child -- she suggested that I make you work in my castle. Very clever, no?"

I didn't answer, and I didn't have to, because at that moment I heard another set of double doors open.

"Ah, Athena! I was just talking about you," King Theon cooed. "Come here, dearest."

I heard Princess Athena's footsteps approach us. "Is this her?" I felt a finger poke the side of my head.

"Yes, this is the dungeon girl."

"Oh my!" I saw her feet in front of me, walking around me. "Can you speak?"

"Yes, I can speak," I gritted my teeth. Did she think I was an imbecile?

"I see that you haven't been taught proper etiquette," I heard the princess say.

"Your Highness," I added begrudgingly. She gasped and clapped in excitement.

"Amazing!"

"That's enough, Athena. You can play with her later," King Theon said in his raspy voice. "Alexios." From the corner of my vision, I saw the guard beside me bow lowly. It was a little too exaggerated, almost mocking. I found that odd considering he was in the presence of his own king. "Take her to the kitchens. Let someone train her. You may leave."

"Yes, Alexios, do as your king tells you." Princess Athena giggled. Alexios grunted in response. We exited the throne room after I quickly bowed to the king and the princess. I couldn't wait to leave the room.

Once the double doors closed behind us, I exhaled in relief and leaned against one of the walls in the hallway. "That bastard," I muttered.

Alexios stood beside me, waiting for me to finish cursing out his king. Then he tapped my shoulder, surprisingly gently. "I have to take you to the kitchens."

"Lead the way," I said, ready to go there. Rose had told mother and I that she was on kitchen duty for most days. If I was lucky enough, she would be there today and I could ask her about my mother. I feared that King Theon was serious when he considered starving her. I could not let that happen.

After a long walk down a series of brightly lit hallways, we stepped into a kitchen. Immediately, the delicious smell of apple cakes hit my nose. I wondered how many they had made today. Perhaps there was a celebration that I didn't know of? I inhaled deeply once I stood in the middle of the room. Alexios looked around us, trying to locate someone.

"Rose," he called out. I snapped my head in the direction he was looking at. At the sound of her name, Rose looked in our direction. Her eyes widened when they landed on my face and she rushed to my side, wiping her hands on an apron and abandoning the food she was stirring by the fire. She threw her arms around me. I returned the embrace, feeling a single tear run down my cheek. I quickly wiped it away before anyone could see.

"Emilia." Rose kissed the top of my head. "You are all right."

Alexios stood to the side, watching our interaction. He had his arms crossed, which caused his muscles to protrude even more. He didn't interrupt us, but his foot was tapping lightly on the floor, giving away his impatience.

I nodded. "I'm all right. Have you visited my mother yet? How is she?"

She hesitated, glancing in the direction of my personal guard. Her eyes widened when she saw him, possibly because he was such a big man. She must have been distracted by the sight of me to even notice him before. I looked in his direction just in time to see him shake his head. Rose nodded and turned back to me. This time she looked directly into my eyes.

"My Gods!" she gasped and covered her mouth with one hand. I frowned. She didn't answer my question.

"Rose?" I said, confused. Her eyes were wide. I took a step closer to her and grabbed her face gently in my hands. "What's wrong? Did something happen to my mother?"

"No, she is perfectly fine. A guard brought her lunch today without me, but I visited her after," she whispered and continued to stare into my eyes.

"I will be bringing her dinner. I need to... speak with her." I exhaled in relief. She was all right. She was eating.

"Is something wrong with...me?" I asked. Mother had the same look of shock this noon when she looked at my face.

"There is absolutely nothing wrong with you," she said and shook her head. Her surprise must have worn off, because now she looked at me with seriousness. "Nothing."

"Then why did you have that look on your face?"

She swallowed. "I...I can't say. Let me speak to your mother first, yes?"

I hesitated. So there was something wrong with me. If she was unwilling to tell me anything, then I would have to wait. I nodded.

"Good," she sighed. "Now, why were you brought here — ?"

"She needs training," Alexios finally cut in, uncrossing his arms. "Servant duties. You have the most experience here, so you will train her. Teach her everything she needs to know."

Rose nodded. "Yes, y - sir. I will be happy to do so."

Alexios grunted, satisfied. "She's all yours." He walked out of the kitchen without another word.

"My Gods, finally." I rolled my eyes. "The brute is gone."

Rose gasped at my language, but then she started laughing. She shook her head, smiling. "Oh, child. You have a lot to learn."

~~~

I huffed in frustration as I dragged a large sack of flour across the floor. It was beyond heavy. I had to bring it to Tanya, a young girl whose dress I
~~~

currently wore underneath my blue robe. For someone so young, she sure knew how to do a lot of things. She was definitely more skillful than I was.

Princess Athena requested another batch of apple cakes to be made, and Tanya was the servant assigned to this task. She was an exceptional baker and I couldn't protest to that. She made those apple cakes that Rose brought for my mother and I earlier today. They were divine.

Rose trained me for four long hours before she introduced me to Tanya, who was to show me how to work the oven and make dough. We only took a break to eat some lunch since I missed it today.

I now knew my way around the kitchen and some parts of the castle. My training was mostly focused on cooking today, but Rose also showed me around the east wing of the big castle of Poseidon. My sleeping quarters were located in this area and so were other servants' rooms. They were conveniently close to the kitchens.

I asked Rose multiple times if we could sneak into the dungeons during my training, but she refused. She said it was too dangerous and that the king put more guards by the dungeon door. I would be in trouble if I was caught by them. It would put my mother in danger as well. I'd have to rely on Rose to check up on my mother before I came up with a plan to visit her by myself.

"Here," I said, out of breath. I put the flour sack by a table where Tanya was preparing an apple mixture to be put in the dough she would soon make.

I flopped down on a bench beside the table, swiping sweat off of my forehead. Tanya giggled. "You are just like Yvette. She can barely carry anything without exhausting herself."

I perked up when I heard a familiar name. "Where is Yvette?" I haven't seen her since she bathed me in her wonderful soaps this afternoon.

"She's helping the princess pick out a dress for the ball." Tanya rolled her eyes. "Princess Athena has hundreds of unworn dresses, but she wasn't satisfied with any of them. From what I've heard, she wanted to see more options." Then she lowered her voice to a whisper. "I also heard that she is making the seamstress work on ten more new gowns."

My eyes widened in awe. I had often wondered what it would be like to be a real princess and attend lavish balls dressed in beautiful gowns. Just like the princess in my favourite books. I couldn't imagine how much room a hundred dresses would occupy.

Tanya prepared the dough and started kneading it into a ball. Then she rolled it out with a large rolling pin and stepped away from it. She looked at me expectantly. My forehead creased in confusion and I raised one eyebrow.

Tanya giggled in response. "You have to help me spread the apple mixture."

"Oh, that's right!" Distracted with thoughts of the ball, I had completely forgotten about my task. I jumped up from the bench and grabbed a bowl full of apples mixed with sugar, cinnamon, and other spices. I followed Tanya's instructions and spread it over the open dough. Then I stepped away to let her roll it up and divide it into smaller pieces.

"Now we can shape them," she said, demonstrating how to do it. I followed suit and soon enough, we had apple cakes lined up on a square baking sheet.

"They're looking very good, girls!" Rose peeked her head in to look at our progress. We grinned in response. She patted my head and walked away to continue preparing tonight's dinner.

I salivated as the smell of cinnamon, sugar, and apples started to escape from the oven. Tanya and I put the cakes in once we were done shaping each one of them. I admired the oven while we waited for them to bake through, peeking in through the small glass opening that allowed me to see the sweets rise and bubble in the high heat. A real oven! Right in front of my eyes! Once the smell became very strong and potent, the apple cakes were taken out.

"Taste one." Tanya grabbed a hot cake quickly with her hands and put it on a table cloth. She broke it in half, then shook her fingers from the heat. Hot steam was coming out of both halves of it. Brown and syrupy sugar dripped down the sides of them, making me even more eager to eat them. I tentatively grabbed one half and bit into it.

"Mmm," I groaned. It was delicious. Tanya took the other half and took a bite as well.

"Shame we can't have more." She pouted as she finished her half. Then she wiped her hands on an apron that was tied around her waist and got a goblet of water to wash down the sugar.

As soon as I ate the rest of my cake, a tray of food was shoved into my hands. "Dinner time for the royals," Tanya said. She walked away from me and then came back with another tray in her hands. "My favourite part. I cannot wait to see Princess Athena."

I chuckled at her lack of enthusiasm. "Is this all for her?" I asked, raising my tray and motioning at the one in her hands with my eyes.

"Gods no. She may eat a lot of apple cakes, but she does not eat this much food," Tanya said. She looked at my tray. "That is for the prince."

"The prince?" I looked down at the food in my hands.

"Yes," she confirmed. "And trust me, I am doing you a favour. You do not want to be near Princess Athena this week. She is winded as it is with the upcoming ball and the numerous decisions she has to make about her appearance on that day." She rolled her eyes. "She will be even nastier toward you because you are new."

Tanya started to walk toward the kitchen exit, motioning for me to follow her. "Just follow me. Their chambers are close to each other. I will lead you to the prince's door."

I nodded, following behind her as we walked toward the west wing of the castle. I was nervous to meet the prince. If Princess Athena and King Theon were anything to go by, the prince was likely to be as bad as them.

"That is his door." Tanya pointed to a door to my left. "Knock three times and wait for an answer. If you don't hear anything, then you can walk in, put the tray on his table, and walk out quietly. He prefers not to be disturbed too much."

I took in a deep breath to calm myself. When I nodded, Tanya smiled and walked away toward the princess's chambers. I was left alone in a dark hallway.

I took another deep breath and knocked on the door three times as Tanya instructed. I waited for a response from the prince, but none came. Should I knock again or walk in? I decided to knock again and still heard no response.

I grabbed the door handle while carefully balancing the tray of food in my arms. Opening the door slightly, I peaked in. It was empty. I sighed in relief and walked into the prince's chambers. Noticing a small table by the foot of the bed, I made my way toward it and put down the tray.

"Oh no," I mumbled when I saw that one edge of the tray was protruding out. It would be very unfortunate if the prince's entire dinner fell on the ground. And it would be my fault if it did. I straightened everything out and ensured the tray was properly balanced on the table.

Satisfied, I let the tray go and turned around to quickly walk out. I slammed my face into a hard wall instead. Stumbling backwards, I tripped on the edge of a carpet and braced myself for the fall as I lost my balance, squeezing my eyes shut.

An arm snaked itself around my waist and caught me before I fell. I opened my eyes and gasped when I saw dark blue eyes staring back into mine. The blue seas were framed by dark long eyelashes, creating a contrasting frame around them.

"Y-you — "

"Bloody hell." He let go of me and reached for a towel that fell off of his hips. I squealed and slapped one hand over my eyes. I saw more of him than I wanted to. Heat crept up my cheeks as I felt the image burn itself into my mind.

I peeped through my fingers to make sure he got the towel back on himself before I fully removed my hand. He had tied it back around his hips, but his torso was still exposed.

"What are you doing here?" I asked when I got a hold of myself, snapping my eyes back to his face in a glare.

"This is my room," Alexios responded with a raised eyebrow.

"No." I shook my head. "This is the prince's room. You're a guard. These cannot be your chambers."

He snorted. "These are definitely my chambers."

My eyebrows creased together in a frown. Did Tanya mistakenly point me to the wrong door? No, I thought. She must have enough experience as a servant to know where the prince resided. Then that meant...

"You're the prince," I whispered, staring at him. "But why did you —?"

"I was on guard duty. Punishment by my father." Alexios crossed his arms across his chest, regarding me with an unreadable expression on his face. I looked away.

"Could you please cover yourself?" I said, crossing my arms as well.

He grunted. I heard some shuffling and then it stopped. "Satisfied?"

I looked back in his direction again. He now had bedcovers wrapped around him like a cape. I nodded. At least he was completely covered now.

"Knock on the door next time," he bit out and glared at me.

I glared back. He may be a prince, but to me, he would always be the brute who dragged me away from my mother against my will and infuriated me to no end. "I did knock!"

"You must have been only tapping on the door."

"Or you must simply be deaf," I retorted.

"Leave." He clenched his jaw and pointed at the door.

"Gladly," I huffed and walked to his door and opened it. I slammed it behind me. At least I thought I did. My strengths were limited.

Out in the hallway, I looked around my surroundings. I didn't memorize the path Tanya and I took to get to the west wing. I thought I would see her after we delivered our trays and we would walk back together. But she was nowhere in sight.

"Tanya?" I called out. Nothing. Every door in the hallway looked the same. My chances of finding the right door that lead to the princess's chambers were very slim. I was too scared to go wander around a big castle on my own. The sun has set and stopped illuminating the stone hallways, leaving only lamps that let many areas remain in complete darkness. I wished that Rose familiarized me with the west wing as well, because now I was stranded in unfamiliar territory.

I turned around to face the door I slammed shut a few minutes ago. There was only one option left...

I swallowed my pride and pounded my fist against the thick wooden door as hard as I could. This could definitely not be mistaken for tapping. I also wanted to see if he heard these knocks.

"Yes?" The door opened and revealed Alexios. He was dressed this time, but not in a guard uniform like I've seen him in before. He now wore proper attire that was fit for a prince.

"Bloody hell," he cursed when he saw me. "It's you again. What do you want?"

I gritted my teeth. I hated asking him for help, but I had no other option. "I need you to walk me back to the east wing."

He opened the door wider and stepped out, towering over me. "And why would I do that? My punishment is over. I don't need to look after you."

"Because I don't know my way around here, and it is dark, and the girl I came with is gone, and I don't know where the princess's chambers are to find her, and your door is the only —"

Alexios put his big hand over my mouth. "I will walk you back if you stop talking."

I nodded and moved his hand off of my face. He turned me around by the shoulders and pushed me forward harshly. "It's this way. Walk in front of me."

"Stop pushing me!"

He pushed me again. I clenched my jaw, breathing forcefully through my nose. "I said —"

Another push sent me stumbling forward. I cursed underneath my breath. How many times did I have to endure this? I stopped in my tracks and turned around, glaring. Alexios looked down at me with his infuriatingly beautiful sea-blue eyes. He arched his eyebrows, waiting for me to do something. My punches didn't had any effect on his strong body, but I tried anyway.

"You brute!" I punched his chest. His face remained impassive. I was more than aware that my behaviour was inappropriate, but for some unknown reason, Alexios brought out the violence in me that completely blinded my reasoning. I went in for another punch.

"What is happening here?" a familiar voice demanded and I froze with one fist in the air.

Chapter 4: Athena

"Dungeon girl?" Princess Athena gasped when I turned around and dropped my fist. "What are you doing to Alexios?"

I remained quiet. How could I possibly justify my behaviour toward the prince? It must have looked even worse when observed from an outside perspective. A servant being violent to a royal? Unacceptable. I was so blinded by my irritation with Alexios that I forgot about proper etiquette. He infuriated me to the depths of my soul and I've only met him today.

"I..." I bit my lip and turned to Alexios for help. His face was impassive and he didn't offer any explanation to the princess who was currently looking back and forth between us. I sighed. What was I thinking? The brute would never willingly help me.

I looked back at the princess, seeing her curious expression. She was still waiting for an explanation. Then she suddenly giggled, covering her mouth. "Don't worry, I saw everything. You're quite interesting, dungeon girl. No other servant would ever try that."

She cocked her head to the side, observing me. "Come to think of it, I've never seen anyone dare to raise their hand on my brother." I shifted my weight from one foot to another, suddenly feeling embarrassed.

"Are you occupied at the moment?" Princess Athena smiled. "I wish to get to know you. You could help me with my dresses?"

I was taken aback by her invitation, unsure of her true intentions. She may have worded it as a question, but I knew that I could not refuse a princess's wishes. I nodded. "I can help you, Your Highness."

Her grin widened.

Alexios grunted behind me. "Good. I won't be needed then. I assume you can show her to the east wing yourself?" he addressed his sister.

Princess Athena nodded, hooking her arm around mine and leading me away from the prince. I heard his door open and close behind us. He must have been very relieved to get rid of me. Our feelings were mutual.

I looked at the princess, an uneasy feeling settling in my stomach. She's known to treat servants poorly, and I wondered why she was being kind to me. There must be some ulterior motive. My mother's warning not to trust anyone in this castle except for Rose came to mind. I had to be cautious around Princess Athena.

The princess grinned at me when she noticed my stare. I smiled back, not wishing to show my distrust. In a few short minutes, we stood outside another wooden door identical to the one outside of the prince's chambers. Athena pushed open the door and we walked in, our arms still hooked together.

I looked around the room. Piles and piles of dresses in different colours and styles littered the carpeted space. There was a large pile on the floor, on a big bed in the middle of the room, and even on top of a tall dresser cabinet. There must have been hundreds of dresses in these chambers. My mouth hung open at the sight before me.

Princess Athena stepped over a red dress that lay on the floor by the entrance and pulled me with her. I was careful not to step on any of the beautiful gowns as I followed the princess to the middle of the room.

Even if her chambers were currently in a messy state, I could still see how beautiful and spacious they were. I didn't get a chance to observe the prince's chambers because of that unfortunate incident with his towel. I blushed in embarrassment as the image of Alexios resurfaced in my mind.

"What are you blushing about?" Athena inquired in a teasing tone. I cleared my throat, shaking my head and willing my mind to forget about the prince.

"Nothing, Your Highness," I replied.

"Am I making you uncomfortable?" the princess asked me, releasing my arm.

"No, Your Highness," I said. She did make me feel uneasy, but she didn't have to know that. "Your Highness?" Princess Athena raised her eyebrows when I addressed her. "Why did you want to get to know me?"

"I told you, you're interesting. And I'm fascinated by your life in the dungeons. Do tell me, is it true that you were born there?" I nodded my head. "You were raised in a cell?" I nodded again. "My Gods, I've never heard anything like it! I can't believe that my father kept you secret all these years. I only learned about you this morning!"

Her eyes were wide with wonder. I simply shrugged. It was normal to me, but I could understand how shocking it might be to others who lived their entire lives under the brightness of the sun. I lived my entire life in one dark room.

"You don't seem dull either," Princess Athena mused. I pursed my lips. It shouldn't be surprising why people would think that I was not educated, but it still felt unpleasant to be branded as an imbecile based on my living arrangements. I felt very grateful for my mother and Rose for providing me with so much knowledge about the world. If it wasn't for them, I would be exactly the person others imagined me to be. Dungeon girl. Uneducated and savage. "Can you read and write?"

I nodded once again, not trusting my voice to come out as anything but irritated. She doesn't know, Emilia. She's simply curious, I told myself.

Princess Athena gasped in surprise. "How did you learn?"

I hesitated. If I told her about the numerous books and papers Rose snuck into the dungeons for me, she could get in trouble and be punished for her acts of kindness toward an insignificant prisoner. For all I knew, the princess could be getting information out of me for the king. I had to tread carefully.

"My mother taught me." Thankfully, she didn't ask me to elaborate.

"That's right." Princess Athena nodded, pursing her lips in disapproval. "Your mother was locked in with you."

Yes, and now she's all alone because of your father who put us there in the first place, I wanted to say. Instead, I simply smiled at the princess to confirm her words.

"Work for me," she suddenly said after a long stretch of silence. I furrowed my brows, confused. I was already a servant who worked for her and her family.

Her sea-blue eyes looked serious when she looked directly into mine. "Work for me," she repeated. "I want you to be my personal servant. A lady-in-waiting...of sorts. You would have to be a noblewoman to earn the lady-in-waiting title, but no matter. It is my decision."

"I - personal servant? What would be required of me?"

"Your Highness," I added, remembering who I was addressing.

The princess waved her hand dismissively. "You may call me Athena when we are alone. Use the title in front of others. Especially my father." I nodded. "I want you to bring my meals, get me ready in the mornings, and do anything else that I ask of you. You will accompany me wherever I go."

"Yes, Your Highness," I said. I couldn't refuse her, although I really wished to. Tanya and every other servant I had met today were reluctant to interact with the princess because of her behaviour and outrageous requests. I could only imagine what I would have to endure as a lady-in-waiting. At her pointed stare, I corrected myself. "Yes, Athena."

"Good. That's settled then." She slapped her palms together and looked around her messy rooms. "Now, help me find a dress for the ball."

~~~

I ran through the dark woods, pressing down on my wound. Blood seeped through the cotton fabric of my ripped tunic, creating a large crimson stain by my abdomen. Everything hurt. It hurt terribly.

Moonlight weakly illuminated an old trail covered in ash. The trail I have been following for what seemed like hours in this never-ending forest. My feet kicked up ashy debris as they hit the ground, mixing in with the fumes from the fire. I covered my mouth and nose to keep myself from breathing it in. Tall dark trees cast long shadows on the trail as I ran for my life.

I tripped over a thick root of one of the trees and fell on my stomach, crying out in pain when the knife in my abdomen dug deeper into my flesh. I was losing the little strength I still had in me to keep my legs moving. To keep myself alive. This is the end, I thought. This is the day that I die.
~~~

I looked up when I heard a loud snap of a tree branch and was immediately horrified at the sight before me, forgetting about my pain for a short moment. A deer stood a few steps away from me, shaking on wobbly legs. Its one side was completely scorched by the fire, its flesh exposed, skin burned off. It looked terrified and lost. I understood the feeling. The deer stared behind me as if completely bewitched by something.

Then I smelled it. The fire. It was getting much closer. I tried to push myself up from the ground to continue running. My weak arms pushed away from the rough earth, lifting the upper half of my body before giving up and falling back down. The knife twisted even deeper into my stomach. I cried out in agony. This pain was worse than anything I have ever endured.

My legs and feet started to feel very hot. I smelled burning flesh before I realized that it was my own. The fire caught up to me, climbing up my body, burning away everything in its path, licking at my skin with its scorching heat. A loud, blood curdling scream escaped my sore throat as I burned alive, seeing my reflection in the wide eyes of the deer staring down at me.

I screamed and shot up in my bed, skin covered in sweat. I threw off my covers and looked down at myself. No wounds. It was just a nightmare. A horrible dream. Just a dream.

I've read about nightmares a lot in books and always wondered what they would feel like. Putting one hand over my racing heart, I realized that I have finally experienced firsthand what a bad dream could do to both mind and body.

My limbs wouldn't stop shaking and the image of that poor deer kept resurfacing in my mind. With a shaking hand, I swiped sweat over my forehead and took deep breaths to calm my racing heartbeat.

"Did you see it?"

I screamed and jumped out of bed, backing away into the corner of my room.

"You can hear me. That's good." A man stepped out of the shadows. He was wearing a crown on his head and a black royal mantle. His black eyes regarded me with authority and possession. I stepped backwards, pressing my back firmly into a wall, wishing that I could run out of my room, but the stranger was blocking access to the door. "Just as I predicted."

"Who are you? H-how did you get in here?" I asked in a shaky voice. I had closed the latch on my door before I went to sleep. Did he break it? I glanced at the door, but it was still there. Just as I left it.

The man's lips curled in a slow smile. "You are mine."

I shivered at his words, suddenly feeling very cold. I seemed to have lost all control of my body and couldn't move a single limb. Fear paralyzed me as I regarded the intruder. "I don't know you..."

"Oh, but you do," he said and took another step forward. My breath hitched at his movement toward me and I wrapped my arms around my-self, having nowhere to go. I was trapped in my own room. "Tell me, did you see it? The Dark Forest?"

"I...who are you?" I whispered. He couldn't have been asking me about my dream. It was impossible. The Dark Forest...was that what I saw?

"Just answer my question, child." He sighed when I didn't say a word. "Did you see the fire? Did you feel the pain?"

My heart picked up its pace once again, thudding forcefully against my ribcage almost as if it wanted to escape. "How do you know what I saw?"

"Ah, you did then. Excellent. Excellent."

"What do you want from me?" I asked. It was frightening enough to wake up after a nightmare and see a stranger in my room. It was even more frightening how he knew what my nightmare was about.

"Emilia." My breath hitched at the sound of my name come out of a stranger's mouth. Fear now completely overtook me. This was too much. "Allow me to introduce myself." He bowed slightly, holding up his mantle. "I am Cerius — or as my people called me, King Cerius of Typhon."

"Typhon?" I said, horrified. My mother told me about the fate of my father when he visited the kingdom of Typhon. She had told me that he died in a fire along with everyone else who was there on that dreadful day, including the king. The entire kingdom was left in ashes. There were no survivors.

"You survived," I whispered. The books were wrong and so was my mother. I looked up at King Cerius who was currently gazing down at me, black eyes shining with an unrecognizable emotion. He was clearly alive and well. I suddenly felt very lightheaded.

He shook his head. "What you saw in your nightmare was my memory. I did not survive."

"Wha —"

His hand suddenly shot out and reached for my cheek, but strangely, I did not feel anything upon contact. I saw his hand pass through my face as if it was made of thin air. I froze, telling myself that I imagined it. I had to have imagined it.

King Cerius gauged my reaction and raised one eyebrow expectantly. He sighed when I simply stared back at him, refusing to accept what my eyes just witnessed. I shook my head. It was a simple trick of the mind. Yes, that's all it was.

He repeated the same action, trying to touch my arm instead, but his hand completely passed through me again. This time I could not deny what happened, no matter how hard I tried to talk myself out of the impossible. Black spots formed in my vision and I collapsed onto the cold floors of my chambers, losing my consciousness. Last thing I remembered was the alarmed look on King Cerius's face as I hit the ground.

~~~

"Emilia?" a distant voice called my name, bringing me out of my unconscious state. I slowly opened both eyes, disoriented and confused. I groaned, suddenly feeling pain shoot up the side of my head.

"You hit your head when you fell. I tried to catch you but..." I looked up and saw King Cerius hovering over me and looking at his hands. He attempted to help me up, but they simply passed through me.

"You are a — a gho —" I couldn't say it. This was not real. It couldn't be. I shook my head vigorously. Wake up. Wake up, Emilia! I closed my eyes and opened them again to see if this was all just another bad dream.

"Why is this happening to me?" I croaked and let the tears that welled up in my eyes fall down each cheek. Deep down, I knew that this was real. I could feel an unfamiliar tug inside of me that compelled me to believe what I saw.

"Forgive me, child. I have not interacted with the living in a very long time." King Cerius tried to wipe off my tears, but I jerked away. He sighed. "I know this must be scary for you, Emilia, but I cannot waste time finding better ways to contact you. I've waited eighteen years for your Sight."

My sight? I furrowed my brows and wiped away a stray tear that escaped my eye.
~~~

"I've watched Lily raise you and tried many times to speak with you, but it was useless. You couldn't see or hear me then."

"How do you know my mother?" I demanded.

"How can I not know my own sister?" He raised one eyebrow.

I inhaled sharply. "Sister? Then that would make you --"

"Your uncle, Emilia. You are mine. My blood. My family."

"My mother never mentioned a brother," I said as my frown deepened. This ghost could be lying. Ghost... Oh Gods, what was I doing speaking with a ghost? What frightened me more was the sense of calm that I felt around him after my initial shock of finding out his true nature.

Something was wrong with me, I thought to myself. Any other sane person would have run out of their rooms by now. I could run...through him. As I considered my escape, the same unfamiliar tug that compelled me to trust my eyes urged me to stay and listen.

"Your mother kept many things from you, child. I'm assuming it was to protect you," King Cerius explained. "I would take us to her now, but those guards are still watching the door. I could easily get past them, but you..." He pressed his lips into a thin line. "Can you find a key to the dungeon door?" he asked me, black eyes boring into mine.

"I think I can," I said. There was no chance that I would trust him without speaking with my mother first. Why would she keep this from me? I thought we had no other family left in this world. I thought we only had each other. "Rose has a key, but I don't know where she keeps it."

"Ah, the servant. Yes. Leave that to me. I will find out," King Cerius said. I nodded.

"You said something about my sight before..." I hesitated, unsure whether or not I should ask him. I reminded myself again that he could be lying. But what would a ghost earn by deceiving me? "What did you mean?"

"Lily should have been more careful," I heard him murmur underneath his breath, gazing at the stone walls. Then his stare returned to me. "The Sight allows you to see me and other souls that wish to contact you. I suspected that you might develop it when you got older -- and I was right." He sighed. "I wish I had known that it would take so long."

My eyes widened. It seemed impossible and yet I could not deny it. I could clearly see and hear King Cerius. My head began to spin as I thought about the possibility of running into more ghosts. I shuddered.

"The Sight only manifests in pure-blooded descendants of the Sun people," King Cerius continued while I processed this new information. "Which is why it is very surprising that it passed on to you who also has Typhon blood running through your veins."

That made me look up at him in horror. "I have Typhon blood?" Then I shook my head. "No, do not say anything. I want to hear it from my mother herself."

"As you wish." He nodded. "But I should inform you that it would likely take a few days' time for you to get into the dungeons. I have been patrolling the entrance door all day and there were guards positioned at all times." Then his forehead creased in a deep frown. "I do not understand how that servant was able to get past them before."

"It was easier then. The king positioned more guards today to keep me away," I explained what Rose had told me.

King Cerius gave me a sideways glance. "He did no such thing. Those guards were always there. I keep watch on that entrance as much as I watch you and your mother, trying to find a way to get you both out, but there is only so much I can do without --" he paused and looked down at his hands with a sad look in his eyes. "But it's different now. You can see me."

He looked at me and in that moment. Moonlight peeked through my window and illuminated his face, allowing me to see that his eyes were not black like I had first assumed -- but dark brown like my mother's. Even the shape of them were like my mother's. The arch of their brows were similar as well. I could see the resemblance now.

I frowned and shook my head. "Rose wouldn't lie to me."

"Wouldn't she?" He arched one eyebrow. "How well do you really know her?"

How well did I know her? As far as I remember, she had visited my mother and I almost every day and yet she rarely talked about herself. All I knew about Rose was that she was a kind servant who went through the trouble of helping a woman raise her child in the dungeons. She was like a second mother to me.

"No. I trust her," I finally said. "If she lied, then there must be a good reason for it."

"Very well," King Cerius said. "I will find out where she keeps that key." He rubbed his chin thoughtfully. "You should rest now." He got up from his crouched position beside me. "The living need sleep to function. I will check on your mother."

"How is she?" I bit my lip anxiously, pushing off the ground and dusting off my nightdress. I had to find a way to get her out of the dungeons. I couldn't bear the thought of knowing that she was all alone in a small cell while I was here.

"She is well," he assured me. "Do not worry child. Nothing can happen to her in there. King Theon is too preoccupied planning his next invasion to be toying with Lily." His face was full of hatred at the mention of the king of Poseidon. "Sleep well, Emilia."

He walked right through my door before I could say anything else to him.

Chapter 5: Eyes

The next morning I felt very tired. I could not fall asleep after King Cerius left my room. My mind was filled with endless questions about my identity and the frightening newfound ability to see ghosts. There was also the mystery of my mother. How well did I know her past? If King Cerius was my real uncle, did I have other family as well?

"You must pull it tighter, Emilia," Princess Athena said as I tied her corset.

"I'm sorry, Your Hi — Athena." I corrected myself. I pulled at the strings of the white corset with more strength.

"Much better." She nodded in satisfaction and I tied the strings together. The princess walked away from me to select a dress from a pile on the floor of her chambers. She walked around the mountain of colourful fabric with one finger pressed to her chin. "Ah! This will do for today." Athena picked up a blue dress and pulled it out from underneath several other gowns, causing them to topple and make an even bigger mess on the floor.

Then she proceeded to walk toward a pile of dresses on the opposite side of her bed while carrying the blue gown on one arm. "Not this one... no... perhaps?...no." She continued to dig through the pile, throwing the undesirable ones behind her, which created yet another mountain of gowns. I watched in slight amusement as Princess Athena continued to look for a dress.

"This!" She finally plucked one out and grinned. Then she glanced toward me and titled her head to the side, squinting her eyes while holding up the dress. "Yes, this will do just fine."

Athena came up to me and handed me the second dress she'd selected. "Put this on. It will match your eyes perfectly."

I frowned. My eyes were brown like my mothers. I didn't see how this dress could ever match their colour.

"Well? Go on," she urged me. "Your are my lady-in-waiting now, and I cannot have you wear that servant dress around the castle. Put it on." She smiled, then held up her blue gown. "I can dress myself."

After a moment of hesitation, I changed into the dress she gave me. I folded up Tanya's servant dress and tucked it inside my arm. I planned to have it washed and returned to her.

"Just like I said," Athena gasped and walked toward me, now dressed in the blue floor-length gown. She looked beautiful. "Perfect match."

I frowned again. "Take a look," the princess said and pointed to a tall mirror in one corner of the room.

I walked over to the mirror and looked at myself, immediately covering my mouth with one hand to muffle a startled scream that escaped me when I saw my eyes. They were no longer brown. Wide and gold like the sun, my eyes stared back at me through the mirror. Princess Athena was right -- the dress matched perfectly.

Thousands of questions circled in my mind. Is that why mother and Rose reacted the way they did yesterday? What did this mean? Why did I have to hide them from King Theon? Why --?

"Beautiful, no?" Athena said cheerily. "Come do my hair now."

I tore my gaze away from my own reflection and made my way toward the princess who was already seated in front of her vanity table. She held up a hairbrush for me to take when I reached her. I took it and started to carefully brush her silky locks, trying to avoid the small mirror in front of us. I couldn't resist taking another look at my eyes, so I glanced up at myself as I continued to handle Athena's hair. It felt surreal. How could eyes change colour in one day?

"What's wrong?" Princess Athena asked, and I realized that I've been frowning at myself. My gaze shifted toward her curious eyes staring at me in the reflection.

"Nothing," I said, looking away from the mirror. I put down the brush and started to braid her hair. I was not as good as my mother and could not fully master the intricate style she always did on my hair, but I knew a few others. They were simple enough for me to be able to perfect over the years using my mother's long hair. With trained fingers, I created a beautiful crown on Athena's head, letting the rest of her locks flow freely down her back.

When I finished, the princess gasped. Her eyes widened in the mirror as she admired her hair. She turned around in her chair and looked up at me.

"I've had many servants do my hair over the years," Athena said. She looked back at her reflection in the mirror. "They are trained for their job and yet..." She smoothed one hand gently down one side of her braided crown. "You styled my hair better than any one of them."

I smiled at her praise. "Thank you, Athena. I am pleased that you like it."

"Did your mother teach you?" she probed.

"Yes," I replied simply.

Athena nodded. Then she clapped her hands, getting up from her chair. It was so sudden and loud that I jumped up in surprise and clutched my chest. "We should get going for breakfast. Father requested my presence and you are coming with me. As my lady-in-waiting, you are expected to attend."

My heart started racing. "Will I be seated beside you?"

She chuckled and shook her head. "No, Emilia. You must only be present in the room to attend to my needs, if I should have any." Athena paused when she reached the door, glancing over her shoulder at me. "And please remember to address me by my title in front of the king."

"I will remember, Your Highness." I released a breath of relief. It would be easier to hide from the king's gaze if I wasn't in his direct line of sight. I still did not understand why it was important for me to not show my eyes to King Theon, and I desperately wanted to get answers from my mother. I hoped that King Cerius would find a way for me to see her.

"Good," the princess said and opened the door of her chambers. We stepped into the sunlit hallway just as Alexios opened his door. His eyes landed on mine as he shut it, and then he proceeded to walk toward the direction of the grand dining hall, passing right by us without a single word.

"Well someone is cheery this morning," Athena commented. She proceeded to walk in the same direction as Alexios, with me trailing behind her. "Walk beside me." I did as she told, falling into step beside the princess.

As we rounded a corner, we almost collided with two royal guards in dark blue uniforms. I held Athena back by her arm as soon as I saw their shadows.

"Y-your Highness, I apologize. I didn't see you," one of them stuttered. He looked very familiar and I soon realized that it was James - the guard that accompanied Alexios when I was dragged away from the dungeons.

The other guard did not say anything. He simply stared at me in a way that made me very uncomfortable. I looked away from him and focused my attention on James, who looked flustered as Athena glared at him.

"Be careful next time," she threatened. "You are lucky that Emilia has such good reflexes or else this could have ended very differently."

"Emilia." The guard beside James smiled. There was a glint in his eyes that I did not like. He looked like a hunter that found his new prey. "What a beautiful name." He reached out and grabbed a lock of my hair, tucking it behind my ear. "What a beautiful lady."

"Do take your hands off of her, Sir Edgar," Athena snapped.

Sir Edgar withdrew his hand, but kept his eyes on mine as he addressed the princess. "My apologies, Your Highness."

"Don't apologize to me," she said impatiently.

"Ah, Emilia. Darling." He took my hand in his and kissed it while maintaining our eye contact. I shuddered in disgust and felt like I was going to vomit at any moment. "My most sincere apologies," he said, his voice laced with anything but sincerity.

Athena tugged at my arm and drew me closer to her, away from the old man. My hand was released from Sir Edgar's hold and I put it behind my back to wipe off the slimy residue left over from that awful kiss.

"Sir, we must not be late to the gathering," James interrupted, shifting his weight from one foot to another uncomfortably.

"Yes, of course!" Sir Edgar exclaimed. "Forgive me, ladies, I must depart. Duty calls." He laughed. With one last smile in my direction, he left along with James.

Athena glanced back at their retreating figures with a disgusted look on her face. She turned to me and hooked one arm around mine, leading us to the dining hall. "Stay away from Sir Edgar," she warned me. "He's a terrible man. Unfortunately, my father trusts him and we have to tolerate his presence in the castle." She rolled her eyes.

As soon as we made it into the dining space, her entire demeanour changed. She let go of my arm and grinned, skipping over to the table. "I smell apple cakes!" she giggled. "Father, did you request them for me?" Now seated to the left side of King Theon, Athena rested her chin on her hands and smiled up at him like an excited child.

"Sure dearest," King Theon said distractedly without even gracing the princess with a single glance.

I felt lost as I stood at the door by myself and looked around the room in hopes of finding other servants to join. Athena failed to mention where I should be standing during their mealtime. My eyes landed on a group of servants by a small table. Amongst those people, Yvette stood a few feet away from the rest. She had her hands interlaced in front of her and was looking at the ground. I quietly made my way toward her and thanked the Gods that King Theon had his back to the servants. He hadn't noticed me yet.

"Hello, Yvette," I whispered when I was by her side. Her wide eyes met mine and then she slowly smiled, recognizing me.

"Good morning, Emilia," she whispered. Someone from the group of servants to our left cleared their throat to get our attention. A tall and willowy woman raised her hand up towards her lips and pressed one finger against them, wordlessly telling us to be silent. Yvette looked back down toward the ground.

"Father, have you read my --" I heard Athena say at the table.

"Alexios," King Theon interrupted in his raspy voice, directing his gaze to his son. He coughed. "Have you learned anything from your punishment?"

Alexios grunted. "Yes, father."

"And what was it that you learned?" The king coughed again. He grabbed a golden goblet and brought it to his mouth, sipping on its contents.

The prince sighed and placed down his spoon. "Not to authorize anything without your approval."

"You'll do well to remember that in the future," King Theon said sternly.

"Father --"

"Had I been blessed with another son," he interrupted Athena again. "I would have thrown you in the dungeons for what you've done. But, alas, you are my only heir."

A long stretch of silence followed the king's words, and the only sounds that were heard in the room were the clinking of spoons and forks against ceramics as the royals ate their breakfast. Alexios was angrily stabbing at his fruit. Athena sat quietly and took small bites of her apple cake. King Theon sipped on his wine, taking no notice of the atmosphere in the room. Or perhaps he did not care.

"Athena has something to say, father," Alexios finally broke the silence. He was still abusing his fruit with a fork, eyes on his bowl.

"What is it, dearest?" King Theon sighed and looked at his daughter. "Do you need more dresses? You can have as many as you would like, but please do not pester me with your stupid problems. Go on and spend time with those gossiping court ladies. As a king, I have bigger issues to attend to."

After a slight pause, Athena giggled loudly. "Of course, father. I did want to ask for more dresses. You always know everything."

He chuckled, rubbing his big belly. "Men tend to have brains, dearest." Then he pushed back his chair and stood up. "Now if you'll excuse me, important people are waiting for me at the gathering. Eat up, children." With those last words, King Theon left the dining room, followed by two personal guards in blue and gold uniforms. I felt immense relief at his departure.

A few minutes after the doors closed behind the king, Alexios barked out an order. "Everyone, out!"

All the servants and guards rushed out of the room. Assuming that the order also applied to me, I followed Yvette to the door. "Emilia, stay." Athena said and I halted. Yvette frowned up at me, but then left the room when I stopped following her.

"I said everyone, Athena." Alexios looked at his sister and then directed his gaze at me.

"We can trust her," Athena said. "I think she could help us."

"You can't be sure of that."

"Has my intuition ever let us down, Alexios?" the princess asked with one eyebrow raised.

Alexios paused to consider her question. He grunted. "I don't like this."

"You never like anything, dear brother." Athena rolled her eyes and then motioned for me to come to the table, pulling out a chair right beside her. She noticed my hesitation. "Don't worry, father won't be back for hours and we have people guarding the door. Come, sit."

I slowly approached the table and sat down beside the princess. I could feel Alexios's eyes on me, so I looked up at him with arched eyebrows. He scoffed and looked away, crossing his arms. Immediately irritated, I crossed my arms as well.

"Well," he said, addressing Athena. "You better start. I don't have all day."

"Have an apple cake," Athena said to me and pushed a plate full of delicious apple treats toward me. She scrunched up her nose. "I cannot bear to be near them. I hate apples."

That caused me to frown. Was she not the one who always requested them to be brought to her chambers? Tanya must have made about a hundred of them yesterday. I didn't question the princess and instead took one apple cake and bit into it. It was delicious as always. Definitely Tanya's creations.

Athena chuckled. "I must be the only girl not fond of apple cakes."

"Athena," Alexios said sternly.

"Right. I will start." The princess cleared her throat. She turned to me. "Are you able to see ghosts?"

I coughed, a chunk of apple cake getting stuck in my throat. After a long fit of coughing, I was able to swallow the persistent ball of food. I looked at the princess with wide eyes.

"You are from Soleil, are you not?" Athena tilted her head to one side. "You eyes give you away."

"I..." Kingdom of Soleil? My mother never told me where she came from. Was I -

"You must be. Only the Sun people have those eyes, Emilia," she said. "And they possess the Sight."

I gasped. The Sight. King Cerius told me about it only yesterday. I saw my eyes this morning. I tried to piece it all together in my mind, but one fact prevented me from creating a full picture. I had Typhon blood. King Cerius said that only pure-blooded descendants could have the Sight. He must have been speaking of pure-blooded Sun people, I now realized.

Mother's warning not to trust anyone suddenly came to mind. I didn't know what to do. Follow my mother's warning or believe the words of strangers? It would have been a much easier decision had the words of strangers not have had some truth in them.

"Well? Can you see them?" Athena asked.

My eyes snapped up in the direction of Alexios, but it wasn't him that caught my eye. It was the movement of a shadow that appeared behind him. When a dark figure approached the table, I saw that it had a crown and wore a dark mantle.

"King Cerius," I whispered and leaned against the back of my chair, feeling relieved that it wasn't someone else.

"King Cerius?" Alexios questioned. "The late king of Typhon?"

"Be quiet Alexios." Athena waved her hand to silence him. She followed my gaze and looked back at me, watching carefully.

King Cerius walked through Alexios and stopped in the middle of the table, right in front of me. Only half of him was visible now, as if his torso sprouted out of the table itself. I looked up at him.

"Emilia." He smiled. "I found a way."

I couldn't help but let a smile of my own escape at his words. He found it much sooner than I've anticipated. "Where is it?"

"The servant - Rose - she uses an old underground tunnel to get to the dungeons," King Cerius said. Then he paused. "I do not have a sense of smell, but... I believe that the tunnel does not agree with the human nose." He scratched at his beard. "Rose did not seem particularly pleased with the smell."

"Therefore," he continued. "I should warn you to wear something to cover your nose. We must go tonight. The sooner Lily sees you, the better."

"King Cerius?" Athena said. My uncle raised one eyebrow and turned to the princess. She was looking in his general direction. Her eyes were on his shoulder as she spoke. "Could you help us?"

King Cerius's eyebrow shot up even higher. Athena continued. "We need to know what father is planning. Please. Help us. We are on the same side."

"Athena," Alexios said in a warning tone. She held up her hand once again to silence him. Alexios grunted, displeased, but didn't say another word.

I watched King Cerius as he regarded Athena. He glanced at me and nodded. "Tell her that I will help. I've seen what Theon has done to these children. They despise their father as much as I, possibly more."

"He..." I looked between the siblings. I wondered what King Theon had done to his own children to turn them against him. "He said that he is willing to help."

Athena let out a breath of relief. "Thank you," she whispered in a shaky voice.

"I still don't like this," Alexios chimed in.

"Brother, this will help immensely. Everything we had worked for all these years almost got destroyed by your slip up. Father almost threw you in the dungeons! He said so not too long ago." The princess pointed to the empty seat where King Theon sat for breakfast only moments ago. "Think about our students. Our people's future. We cannot afford another mistake."

The prince pursed his lips then nodded, agreeing with his sister.

"I trust Emilia." Athena looked at me then back at Alexios. "My instincts have never let me down."

"You're right," Alexios said, locking eyes with me. "We need her."

Chapter 6: Cassia

I walked down dimly lit hallways of the castle, careful not to make any noise that could bring attention of the guards patrolling tonight.

"Turn left here," King Cerius instructed.

I turned left and kept walking. Every now and then, I would look around my surroundings to ensure that I wasn't being followed.

"Do not worry, child. I will warn you of any trouble. Keep walking. We're almost at the passage."

It was much darker and colder in this part of the castle and I was glad for the thick robe that I wore. It kept me warm. My eyes quickly adjusted to the dark, years of experience in the dungeons coming to my aid. We reached the end of the hallway where there was nothing but a stone wall. A dead end.

King Cerius hovered his hand over each stone. "This." He stopped at one of them. "Press on this." I pressed on it and heard a distant sound of clicking. He repeated the same action, hovering his hand over another part of the wall. "She pressed...this one. Emilia -" I pressed on the second stone, hearing another distant click and grinding of stones. After pushing on a few more of them, a loud whirling noise started.

"Step back!" King Cerius yelled out. I jumped back just before the ground below me dropped. Large blocks of stone came out of one side of the giant hole, one after another, creating a stairwell.

When the whirling sound stopped, I looked up at King Cerius for further instructions. He motioned for me to descend. I lifted up the skirts of my dress and robe before putting one foot down on the first step. As I reached the bottom, I could see that a few oil lamps hung on the walls of the dusty place. They illuminated a low and narrow pathway in a pale yellow glow.

An unpleasant smell suddenly assaulted my senses and I immediately covered my nose with the fabric of my robes. I couldn't place it. It wasn't something I had smelled before, but it was surely nauseating. It was an odd mix of sweat and...mud? There were a few other scents that I could not recognize that interlaced into one horrid combination.

"My Gods, what is this smell?" I asked King Cerius in a low whisper.

I almost screamed when I saw him walking beside me -- headless. He ducked down and his head appeared. "This ceiling is too low to fit my height," he explained. "As for the smell...I cannot help with that." He pointed at his nose. "I do not have senses."

"Right. I forgot."

The tunnel seemed endless and it felt like we have been walking for hours, although I was sure that it hasn't been that long. King Cerius seemed to remember what route Rose had taken when she visited my mother last night. He kept instructing me where to turn as we walked.

"Are you certain that you remember where Rose had --"

I heard a loud gurgling noise and laboured breathing, followed by heavy footsteps. It sounded like someone big was running in our direction, feet slamming against the ground. A loud roar shook the walls and I panicked. The sound did not seem to be that of a human.

A quick flash of blue appeared in front of me and pushed me behind them. "You shouldn't be here, Emilia."

"Rose!"

"Stay behind me," she commanded as the heavy footsteps got louder. Whoever it was -- they were getting closer.

A large shape came out from an opening in the distance. It looked like a big human, but with one long horn protruding from its forehead. With every thud of its bare feet hitting the ground, it got closer and closer. That's when I saw that it only had one eye. I gasped. The horrible smell got stronger as the creature approached.

"Rose, we have to get out of its way!" I said, panicked.

Rose stood her ground. "Stay behind me, Emilia."

The creature roared and halted in front of her, breathing heavily. The awful smell of him was unbearably horrid. I fought the urge to cough, lest it anger the beast. From behind her shoulder, I could see the one-eyed being extend one hand and patiently wait for something.

Rose reached inside the pocket of her blue robe and took out a golden spoon. I've seen similar ones this morning at breakfast. They were only used by the royals. She proceeded to place this spoon into the palm of the creature's hand and then stepped away. I could see that she struggled to breathe as well because of its powerful stench.

The creature huffed in satisfaction and turned around before running off toward the passage where it came from. Rose exhaled forcefully and then turned around to face me and give me a stern glare.

"How did you get here? It is a dangerous place, Emilia. Especially if you are by yourself and have nothing to offer to the cyclopes."

A cyclops! That's what the creature was. I suddenly remembered reading about cyclopes in one of many books about the origin of Asterin. The book was old and many of its pages had been torn off as if someone had wanted to keep those parts of history to themselves. I'd read that cyclopses were the native inhabitants of this island before Asterin came to be and humans took over. All the cyclopses were shunned to the outskirts of the island and were forced to go into hiding. Most of them hid underground.

Rose put her hands on her hips like a scolding mother. "Did anyone see you?" I shook my head no.

I shot my uncle a displeased look for not warning me about the cyclopes in these tunnels. He put up his hands in front of him. "I...failed to mention this detail."

"An important detail, uncle." I huffed.

"Uncle?" Rose looked at me with wide eyes and dropped her hands from her hips. "Of course," she said as I opened my mouth to explain. She put one hand on my chin and tilted my face upwards. "Your Sight...Incredi ble," she breathed, observing my eyes. "Your...uncle is here?" Rose looked around in bewilderment.

"Yes, he..." I pointed to my right, where King Cerius stood watching us. "He is right here. He is the one that found this passage. By following you." I returned my gaze to Rose. "Why didn't you tell me that there was another way?" I asked. "You made me believe that I couldn't see my mother unless the guards by the dungeon door were no longer there. You said that the king put more guards to keep me away. It wasn't true, was it?"

She shook her head. "I was trying to protect you," she sighed. "It's true that there are guards by the dungeon door, but they have always been there and there is no way for us to get past them. I couldn't tell you about these tunnels because I made an oath to keep this a secret from others. It would have been too great of a risk to bring you here. Even with me by your side. The cyclopes are not very...fond of humans."

I frowned at Rose. "Humans?" I paused. "Are you not human?"

"No. Not entirely." At my questioning look, she elaborated. "My mother was a human. She fell in love with a cyclops. When she got pregnant with me, her family disowned her and threw her out of their house for loving an undesirable." She looked away, but not before I saw the hurt in her eyes. "They didn't want to have a half-monster for a granddaughter."

Rose reached behind her head and untied the blue scarf that she always wore around her forehead. When the thick material fell away, I could see a long thin scar right above the middle of her eyebrows. "I was born with three eyes. Two human and one cyclops. My third eye was underdeveloped, so it was cut out and sewn shut by the midwives."

I covered my mouth in horror and felt tears fill up my eyes. Rose continued. "My mother died shortly after giving me my name. Her human body couldn't handle childbirth. And my father...he was shunned from his circle and was killed by humans before he could see me be born." One tear rolled down my cheek. Poor Rose. "The cyclopes can smell human blood, but they can also smell the blood of their own kind, which is why they don't attack me when I'm in their territory. They let me pass through these tunnels if I bring something valuable with me."

"This poor woman." King Cerius looked saddened by her story. "It is difficult even for an adult to experience rejection solely based on their appearance. I cannot imagine how a mere child could bear such pain. And to be rejected by her own family? Grow up without parents?" He shook his head.

"Oh please don't cry for me Emilia," Rose said when she faced me once again. "It's all in the past." I let out a sniffle and threw my arms around her in a tight embrace. She returned it, embracing me just as tightly.

A quiet sound of crumbling rock reached our ears, but it was loud enough to get our attention. Rose and I looked in the direction of that sound, behind us.

"Bloody hell," someone swore and came out of hiding from behind one of the pillars in the tunnel.

"What are you doing here?" I demanded, stepping away from Rose. "Did you follow me?"

Alexios brushed off some dust from his tunic. "Of course I followed you."

"Why?" I glared at him.

"It seemed very suspicious that you were walking around the castle late at night and talking to air." He glared back. "Hello Rose," he added, glancing in her direction and nodding in acknowledgement.

"Hello Alexios." She smiled warmly. I couldn't believe her.

"How can you like him?" I asked in bewilderment. "He's a brute."

Alexios rolled his eyes. Rose laughed, covering her mouth. Even my uncle chuckled.

"He is!" I exclaimed, looking at all of them. "And I wasn't talking to air!" I said to Alexios. "My uncle was with me."

"King Cerius is your uncle?" Alexios raised one eyebrow.

"He...Well he...He said he is! And I believe him now," I said. As those words left my mouth, I realized that it was true. I did believe that King Cerius was my uncle. Perhaps it was the uncanny resemblance between him and my mother or the feeling in my soul that cleared all traces of doubt I had away from my mind. "I would still need to ask my mother of course," I whispered. I had to confirm.

"I see," the prince said.

"Now if you'll excuse me, I need to get to my mother." I turned around and started walking. I heard his footsteps behind me. I whirled around and saw that Alexios was still following me, falling into step beside Rose. "Why won't you leave? Stop following me."

He glared at my face. "I have to ensure that you do not stir up any trouble."

I walked up to Alexios, cursing his height that forced me to look up at him. "The only person that has been causing trouble in my life lately is you. How dare you drag me around like a lifeless object? Do you know how much you bruised my wrists with your giant hand?" I poked at his chest with one finger with every sentence that came out of my mouth.

His blue eyes looked down at the finger poking his chest before they locked with mine. We simply glared at each other for a moment, never breaking eye contact, never blinking. Then he took one of my hands in his and slowly pushed back the sleeve of my dress. His rough fingers traced along the inside of my wrist, where there was a visible dark purple bruise. An involuntary shiver ran down my spine.

Alexios gently dropped my hand and frowned, meeting my eyes. "I apologize for causing these bruises. It was not my intention." He ran one hand through his hair and sighed. "Does it hurt?"

I shook my head, unable to trust my voice. I was surprised at his reaction. I thought he would only continue to argue with me and find an excuse for the way he handled me that day.

I cleared my throat. "Well. If you must follow, then I cannot stop you." I turned back around and continued to walk. I tugged down at the sleeve of my dress that Alexios pushed up, instantly reminded of the tingling sensation I felt from our skin to skin contact.

"He's a good boy, Emilia." King Cerius appeared beside me. "You shouldn't judge him so harshly. His experiences should have turned him into a cold-hearted man like his father, but they didn't. Quite the opposite really. He's is following in his mother's footsteps." He smiled at the ground ahead. I glanced back at Alexios before quickly turning my eyes away when he caught me looking.

"What happened to his mother?" I whispered quietly. I knew that the queen of Kingdom Poseidon died a long time ago, but I didn't know anything else about her or how she had died.

"Cassia," King Cerius said. A sad smile appeared on his face. "She was an incredible woman. Very intelligent and kindhearted. She was forced into marriage with King Theon and had to abandon her studies at a school in Typhon -- where I'd met her. But that didn't stop her from learning." He paused. "A few years after her youngest child was born, she opened a small school for girls and women. The Kingdom of Poseidon has a long history of neglecting women's education, and it became worse when Theon inherited the throne. His first order as king was to restrict all girls from attending school. When he discovered that Cassia has been teaching them at the castle..."

"What did he do?" I asked, afraid of the answer.

He released a heavy breath. "He hung her in front of their own children and the people of Poseidon." I gasped. "He called it treason. She had violated his trust and broke the law that he'd enforced upon his people. Cassia refused to reveal the identities of the ones she had taught, which saved their lives. But hers... Her life could not be saved."

My heart squeezed in my chest. Poor Cassia. Oh Gods, Athena and Alexios! They've watched their mother die right in front of their eyes. Ordered by their own father! I didn't know how they were able to live in the same castle as that monster without showing their hatred toward him. How could they bear it?

"Alexios tried to save his mother," my uncle continued, throwing a glance behind us at the prince. "He managed to fight off the guards that held him in place and run up to the gallows, but...it was too late." I wiped off fresh tears from my cheeks. I felt my eyes and nose slowly swell up from crying. "The boy was only five years old," he murmured and shook his head in disbelief.

"Couldn't you help at all?" I asked in a whisper.

"I watched it all unfold without any ability to help. In my current form."

I drew in a sharp breath. "You were already -- "

He nodded, wordlessly answering my question. I looked down. My heart felt heavy from hearing so many terrible life stories of the people around me. I wanted to help them somehow. Help ease their pain.

"We are almost at the dungeons," Rose announced.

"Is that where you are going?" Alexios asked. He sighed. "I should have known."

"I already said that I was going to see my mother. Where else would she be?" I turned my head and raised one eyebrow. My Gods, why couldn't I be kinder to him? It came so easy with other people.

He clenched his jaw. "I didn't hear you say that."

"I'm not surprised. You are not a very good listener." I rolled my eyes.

My uncle sighed and squeezed the bridge of his nose with his thumb and index finger. "Emilia."

"I am a good listener! Tell her, Rose." Alexios turned his head toward Rose while pointing at me.

"Alexios is a very attentive listener indeed," she confirmed with a nod. She tried to suppress a smile but failed miserably when her lips tugged up in the corners.

"Then why didn't you hear what I said?" I challenged Alexios.

"Because I was --" He stopped himself and ground his teeth together. "No matter. Let's just get to your destination."

I shrugged and turned my head to face the tunnel in front of me. We had to pass several smaller passages before we emerged through a secret door in the walls. Familiar large stone walls greeted me when we all stepped out into the dungeons. I ran my hands across the surface of several stones of the hidden door, fascinated by it. "Incredible," I murmured. Just how many secrets did this castle have?

Before I took a step in the direction of my old home, my uncle held up his hand. I stopped. "Did you hear that?"

"What?"

"Stay here. I better go and check. Wait until I come back," my uncle said before disappearing through the wall to my left.

"Is something wrong?" Rose asked. Her face was filled with worry.

My expression mirrored hers as I considered all the awful possibilities. "I don't know," I whispered. "My uncle said he heard something and went to check on it."

"I heard it too," Alexios said with a frown. "It sounded like someone's voice. No...it sounded like more than one."

"Mother could be in trouble!" I exclaimed and Alexios instantly slapped one hand over my mouth.

"Do you want to bring attention to yourself?" he hissed. "It could be guards."

I removed his hand from my face. "You're a prince!" I whispered. "They answer to you. They have to. Can't you order them to leave?"

"You are so naive." Alexios shook his head. "Even if I order them to leave, my father will hear of this. Most of the guards are his spies. And how would I explain my late night visit to the dungeons without raising any suspicion?" My shoulders deflated. He was right. "You said that King Cerius went to see what was happening. We should wait for him."

"You wench!" I heard someone's loud voice and a sound of metal hitting metal. "Answer me! Where did he hide it? I swear to Poseidon, I will find it!"

"I don't know! And even if I did -- I would never tell you!"

"That's my mother!" I said. "I don't care what happens to me. I am going." I ran, following the sound of my mother's voice. Please, Gods, don't let them hurt her.

"Emilia!" Alexios yelled after me, but I kept running.

Chapter 7: Escape

A lexios caught up to me and held me back by my arm.

"Let go!" I complained, trying to get out of his strong hold.

"He can't hurt her. Look." He motioned forward with his eyes. We were standing behind a large pillar, hidden away in the shadows. I willed my eyes to look in the direction he was pointing to and instantly relaxed. One tall man in an official guard uniform stood outside of my mother's cell. She was at a safe distance away from him behind thick metal bars, and the door was locked.

"He doesn't have a key," Alexios whispered beside me. I nodded and squinted my eyes toward the guard, recognizing him from this morning. Sir Edgar.

"How did you find me?" my mother demanded.

"I had the pleasure of running into a certain golden-eyed beauty this very morning. And I must say -- she resembles her mother very much." Sir Edgar chuckled lowly and shook his head. "Imagine my surprise when I was informed that the very person I have been looking for all these years has been locked up right below my feet!"

He started pacing back and forth in front of the cell, muttering words underneath his breath. "The damn king and his secrets! I could have had that power in my hands much sooner had I known."

My mother remained quiet. She had assumed a seated position at the far end of a bed — a good distance away from the crazed old man.

"Now." Sir Edgar gripped two metal bars with his hands. He tried to fit his head through the space between them, but it was too narrow for his large skull. "Tell me, dear Lily. Where. Is. The trident?"

"I gave you my answer, Edgar. You are wasting your time with me. I do not know where it is."

A strangled sound of frustration came out of the old man's throat. He slammed on the bars with both firsts and stepped back, breathing heavy. "Liar!" He screamed. "You do know! And I will get that information out of you, so help me Poseidon!"

Sir Edgar tried to break the heavy lock on the door of my mother's cell with no avail. He cried out and unsheathed his sword, ready to swing it down on the lock. I tensed. Would it break?

Alexios gripped my arm tighter to get my attention. When I glanced at him, he shook his head, signalling me to stay where I was.

A loud clank of metal hitting metal echoed throughout the dungeons. Sir Edgar failed — the lock remained unbroken. He screamed in frustration and dropped to his knees, heaving. His sword fell out of his hands, hitting the ground.

Alexios and I frowned at each other, both of us questioning the man's sanity.

"I will be back tomorrow, dear Lily." Sir Edgar finally rose to standing position. He picked up and sheathed his sword. "With a key. I would advise you to rethink your answer by then to avoid... unnecessary pain."

As soon as I heard his retreating footsteps followed by the familiar sound of the swinging dungeon door, I pulled my arm out of Alexios's hold. He released me and let me run to my mother.

"Mother!"

She gasped and immediately jumped off the bed to stand in front of me. She reached out with her hands and I took them in mine, squeezing in reassurance. "Emilia, my darling!" Mother sniffled. Her eyes were shiny with tears. "I've missed you so." She reached up to tuck a stray strand of hair behind my ear and caressed my cheek. Then she suddenly frowned, looking behind me.

Glancing back, I saw that Alexios stood there, leaning against the stone walls of the dungeon. I looked back at my mother and squeezed her hand. "He's with me. I - uh... I trust him."

Mother's eyes snapped to mine. She opened her mouth to speak, but was interrupted by Rose who walked up beside me and nodded at my mother, causing her mouth to close.

Finally, my last companion made his appearance, walking out of a wall. "I told you to wait for me," my uncle said.

"Well, I couldn't! Where did you even go? I didn't see you on my way here," I asked.

"I heard a sound and followed it, but..." King Cerius scratched the back of his head and looked away. "It turned out to be rats fighting for bread crumbs. When I came back, you were already gone."

I groaned and slapped a hand over my face. "Uncle."

He cleared his throat and motioned to my mother with a tilt of his head. "You might want to explain who you are talking to."

My eyes were met with the sight of my mother's shocked face. She kept opening and closing her mouth like a fish — no words came out. "Ce-Cerius?" she whispered and looked at me, waiting for a confirmation. I nodded. "Cerius?!" She now said angrily. Her hands balled into fists by her side, breathing heavily through her nose.

"Where exactly is he standing right now?" she asked me. I pointed to my right and her angry eyes followed. She glared at my uncle's head. "You have a lot of explaining to do, brother."

"Now I see where you get that temper from," Alexios muttered quietly, but my ears were able to catch it.

"I do not have a temper," I snapped at him. He raised one eyebrow in doubt. I crossed my arms like a child. "You bring it out in me."

I looked back at my mother and grabbed her hand through a gap between two bars, instantly bringing her attention toward me. "Mother, you have a lot of explaining to do as well." Her expression softened and she nodded, agreeing with my words. "But not now. I need to get you out of these dungeons before—"

"If you plan on freeing your mother, it must be done tonight," Alexios stepped in. "That bastard could be back in the morning for all we know, and —" He clenched his jaw. "You do not want to know what he is capable of."

"I agree," Rose said. She glanced worriedly at my mother. "He is a very bad man. I-I don't wish for him to harm you, Lily. We must get you out of this place."

"But how?" I wondered out loud. "We need a key and an --"

"Don't worry about the key. I can get it. I know where they are all kept," Alexios assured me. I bit my lip, debating on whether or not I should trust him with finding the right one. Judging by how he handled that set of keys last time...we could lose a lot of time. Seeming to have read my thoughts, Alexios rolled his eyes. "I will get the right key. I promise."

"I can take us through the cyclopes tunnels. There is a pathway that leads to a waterfall behind the castle," Rose offered. "But it is dark and slippery, and we must be careful not to fall into the rock pit." She gave us all a grave look. "No one comes out of that pit alive. The bottom is lined with sharp spears."

I swallowed. "Is there another pathway that leads outside?"

Rose shook her head. "I'm afraid not. And if there is, I do not know of it. This is the only way that does not lead inside the castle where guards could catch us."

"This all sound great, but what about after Lily escapes? Where would she go? Live under the waterfall?" my uncle questioned. I voiced his concerns to others.

"For that," Alexios said. "We will need Athena's help."

~~~

Alexios kept his promise and brought the right key for the door of my mother's cell. As soon as he unlocked it, my mother stepped out, but one of her feet remained planted on the floor of her cell. She hesitated to take another step forward.

"Mother?" I frowned. "What's wrong?"
~~~

She smiled nervously. "I- This-" She sighed. "After nineteen years... I'm afraid to see how much the world has changed." With a shake of her head, she walked out of her cell. "But I will not dwell on that. This is not the time."

"I don't wish to rush you, but we must hurry. Athena is waiting with Pegasus by the waterfall and the sun would soon rise. The cloak of darkness is our only chance to get you away from the castle unseen," Alexios said.

My mother nodded and closed the door. Throwing her cell one last glance, she looked at Rose. "Lead the way, my dearest friend."

We were soon walking on slippery stones of a dark and narrow tunnel. It was too narrow to fit two people through it, so we walked in one person at a time. Rose lead the way while my mother followed after her with me and Alexios close behind. My uncle went in ahead of everyone else to check for any danger. He came back and reported that there were no cyclopes ahead.

"This tunnel smells worse than the one we came in from." Alexios coughed.

I held in a cough of my own. "My Gods, it sure does." It was the absolute truth. The presence of water had turned the horrible smell of cyclopes into an impossibly unbearable stench.

"Not too long now," Rose announced ahead, which caused Alexios and I to simultaneously sigh in relief.

Impatient to get out of this tunnel and away from its smell, I picked up my pace. Wrong decision. My foot slipped right under me and I lost my balance. I tried to catch myself by holding onto a wall but it was no longer there. Instead of the hard surface of a stone wall, my hand was met with empty air. I yelped and shut my eyes, but the fall never came.

"This is the second time I catch you, Emilia," Alexios grunted, pulling me back against him by my waist. "You should really pay attention to where you step with your feet."

My heart thudded forcefully against my chest. First time was in his chambers, right before -- I shook my head and ignored the heat that crept up my cheeks. Gods, this was not the time for this.

"Yes. I will. Thank you," I said and pulled away from him. I hoped to Gods that my voice came out even.

"Emilia!" Mother turned around. "Are you all right?"

"I am, mother," I assured her. "Don't worry. I just slipped."

"Be careful, darling."

The sound of falling water became much louder as we neared the opening at the end of this tunnel. When we finally made it out, a breathtaking sight filled my vision. A beautiful waterfall. It dropped from high above the ground I stood on, and the water was illuminated by the light of the moon, making it glisten. It looked magical.

I gasped when I saw a pair of large white wings come out from behind the waterfall. The beautiful wings were attached to a big white horse, and a woman sat on its saddle. It was the princess. Athena leaned forward toward the horse's ear and said something. As soon as she sat back, the horse spread its wings and started to fly toward us.

"Is that...Pegasus?" I asked Alexios, keeping my eyes on the magical winged creature.

He nodded. "Athena rescued him when we were children. He only listens to her, which is why I asked for her help."

I had so many questions, but no time to ask them. Athena and Pegasus gracefully descended to the ground in front of us. The princess climbed off and reached into a sack that hung by the saddle, retrieving two apple cakes. She brought those to Pegasus's mouth and he happily devoured them. Patting his head, Athena turned around to face everyone standing by the tunnel.

"Hello," she greeted my mother with a smile. Then she turned her attention to me. "I suppose you would like to ride along to ensure that your mother is in a safe place?"

"I do," I answered without any hesitation. I wanted to see it with my own eyes.

"Well then, climb on you two." Athena motioned to Pegasus.

I looked at my mother and found her gaze already on me. She reached out and took my hand. "If you trust her, I trust her too," she whispered. "Your Sight can see a rotten soul better than anyone. What do you see, Emilia?" When I frowned in confusion, she squeezed my hand and smiled encouragingly. "Concentrate. Relax your body and let your eyes take over. Look at the princess and tell me what you see."

I did as she asked and concentrated, feeling a slight headache coming on. At first Athena looked like she always did in my eyes, but little by little that image started to change. I saw a ripple and then — I gasped.

"She's...glowing," I whispered. "There is a faint golden glow around her. I — what does this mean?" I turned to my mother.

Her smile widened. "It means she has a pure soul, my darling." She patted my cheek. "You did well."

Curious, I tried to do the same with Alexios. I looked at him and concentrated, feeling that headache come back. My vision changed and I saw the same golden glow around him as I did with his sister. A pure soul.

"What are you doing?" Alexios's voice broke my concentration and I was now staring at his puzzled expression.

"Nothing." I quickly turned back around and faced forward. My mother raised one brow, looking between us.

"We must go now. It takes an hour to get to the school and the sun would soon rise. I loaded Pegasus up with apple cakes so he might take us there much faster, but we mustn't be careless," Athena said.

My mother and I both nodded and walked up to Pegasus. He turned his head toward us as we approached. I tentatively reached out with one hand and brought it to his mane, then stopped before I touched it. His deep-blue eyes followed my movement but I didn't see any signs of protest so I gently ran my hand through his mane.

"Hello Pegasus," I said. "I'm Emilia."

Pegasus whinnied and rubbed his head against my hand in a greeting of his own.

I heard Athena giggle beside me. "He likes you." I grinned.

The princess demonstrated how to get on Pegasus's large saddle. It was big enough to fit four people. My mother and I climbed up behind Athena and settled in.

"Hold on tight!" the princess called out. I wrapped my arms around her waist and my mother did the same with mine. Athena looked back to check on us and then leaned forward on Pegasus. "To the school, Pegasus."

Immediately, he spread his wings. I only had a few seconds to admire their beauty before we were flying. I looked down and instantly regretted that decision, snapping my eyes back up to the back of Athena's head. When I started to feel dizzy, I closed my eyes shut.

I heard my mother whistle and let out an excited laugh. "I've forgotten how good this felt!" she exclaimed. "Emilia, are you seeing this? Look at these clouds. They're all within reach. Feel the breeze on your skin." I shook my head. "Go on, darling. It's incredible." She laughed again. "I've missed this feeling!" She howled.

Her excitement was contagious and I cracked open one eye to peek at my surroundings. We were flying much higher now. The castle was barely visible anymore and clouds surrounded us. I opened both of my eyes and stared at the moon that seemed so much closer — I felt like I could reach out and touch it.

I carefully unwrapped one arm from around Athena's waist and lifted it up to touch the clouds. I giggled when I saw them separate where my hand passed through. I'd imagined them to feel soft to the touch — like cotton — but they didn't feel like anything. Just air.

"Isn't this amazing?" Athena exclaimed.

"It's incredible!" I said. I closed my eyes, this time to feel the breeze against my face. My lips tugged up into a happy smile. I felt like nothing could get us here. Nothing bad could happen when we were amongst the clouds — away from land and cruel people.

We flew like this for a while longer. All of us were enjoying the ride. Even Pegasus seemed happy to be able to spread his wings and fly in the vast sky.

"Hold on tight! We are about to descend," the princess announced. I wrapped my free arm around her waist once again, feeling my mother tighten her hold on me as well. "Hold on with your legs too!" Athena instructed. I squeezed my legs closer to Pegasus's torso. He adjusted his wings and started to slowly descend.

A cliff came into view and the sound of ocean waves filled my ears. I soon saw the large body of water as we came down close to the ground. Pegasus's hooves landed on the surface of the green cliff.

"Pegasus! My son!" A woman with a thick scarf wrapped around her hair ran up toward us as soon as Pegasus landed. He folded his wings and waited for the woman to approach him. "Are you eating well?" The woman asked him and ruffled the mane on his neck.

Pegasus whinnied and nodded his head, motioning to the sack by the saddle.

"I see Athena has been feeding you apple cakes again. She spoils you a little too much, don't you think?"

Pegasus made a sound of protest and straightened up.

The woman laughed and then looked up at the people on his saddle. "Ah, Athena brought some friends?" She eyed my mother and I curiously.

Athena jumped off Pegasus and helped us climb down. "Hello Medusa. This is Emilia and her mother --" She glanced at my mother.

"Lily," mother introduced herself with a smile.

"Lily needs somewhere safe to stay and I thought this would be a perfect place for her," Athena said. "She could help with the girls. She taught Emilia a lot by herself."

Medusa studied my mother for a moment and I used that time to look into her soul. Concentrating, I willed my eyes to see beyond her exterior and was satisfied with what I saw. She had the same glow as Athena and Alexios. I sighed in relief.

"Any person in need of help is welcome to stay here," Medusa said. Her hair suddenly started to move inside her scarf. I sucked in a breath and stepped back. Medusa groaned. "They're awake. Haven't I told you that you must sleep until sunrise?" she muttered while untying the scarf around her hair.

I stared with wide eyes as multiple snakes rose up on her head where hair should have been. Medusa saw my surprised expression and chuckled. "Don't worry, they don't bite," she said. "Unless you're Poseidon, of course." All the snakes on her head hissed at the mention of the sea God's name.

"Shhh," she cooed at them. "There is no need to worry about him anymore. He's long dead. The only good thing he ever brought into my life is our son." She gave Pegasus a loving gaze and smiled. He whinnied in response.

Medusa turned and started to walk away -- in the opposite direction of the ocean. She lifted her hand and waved us over. "Follow me. I will show you around."

Athena hooked one arm around mine and another around my mother's, then pulled us forward with her. "I have a strong feeling that you are both going to love this place."

Chapter 8: Portal

Medusa led us to a thick forest full of colourful wild flowers and tall green trees. Fireflies were flying above and disappearing into their homes as the sun slowly came up, casting its golden glow around us.

"It's breathtaking," mother gasped, voicing my own thoughts. She turned her head from left to right and admired the lively greenery.

Athena, whose arms were still hooked around mine and mother's elbows, nodded in agreement. She took in a deep breath and sighed contently. "Mmm. The air here is so much better too. You won't find this in Poseidon."

Medusa scoffed ahead. "You definitely won't find this in Poseidon. Not anywhere near the castle at least. That selfish bastard. To this day I cannot believe that he named his own kingdom after himself. Someone needs to change it."

"He named the island after his lover." Athena shrugged. "I wouldn't say he was entirely selfish."

Without turning around, Medusa laughed and continued walking ahead. "He only named it after her to appease her father who wouldn't let his daughter run away with a stranger that claimed to be the God of the sea." She snorted. "He raised this island and named it Asterin to impress that old man and show off his own powers. Nothing more."

"But the books say Poseidon raised this island to gift it to his one true love," Athena argued.

"Rumours that mortals wrote down and published." Medusa dismissed it with a few flicks of her hand. "Poseidon had many lovers. Asterin was one of them -- although at her time she truly did have all of his attention. He always did confuse love for lust." She shook her head. "I thought he had loved me too. Once. But all it did was destroy my life. Look where it got me." She stopped and turned to face us with a flat look on her face. "Snakes for hair and a horse for a son."

I let out an involuntary laugh then immediately slapped one hand over my mouth. My eyes went wide. Dropping my hand from my mouth, I stammered. "I - I - I am so sorry. I did not mean to laugh at --"

Medusa interrupted me with a loud cackle. She put her hand up. "No need to apologize. I laugh at my own past-self all the time. Pegasus and I are quite a mother-child pair."

Heat crept up my cheeks. I felt terrible for laughing. It could have been my fatigue and hunger that elicited such an inappropriate response to her words, but nevertheless, it was wrong. I opened my mouth to apologize again, but she held up her hand to silence me and shook her head with a smile. At that exact moment, my stomach growled loudly.

"Someone is hungry," Athena said with raised eyebrows and a pointed stare at my midsection. "Oh! Wait here."

The princess released my mother and I from her hold and ran over to a tree to my left. Underneath that tree, a thick ring of bright red flowers surrounded its woody trunk. They were shaped like tulips -- flowers that

I've seen in an illustration in a book before, but they were much larger than how I'd imagined they would be. Athena bend down and plucked one flower off of its stem and returned.

"This," she said, opening up its closed petals and revealing round berries as red as the flower itself inside, "is a tulipberry." She tipped over the tulip onto her palm and its red berries spilled out into a small pile in her hand. Taking one of them, Athena held it up for me to see. Then she threw it up and caught it with her mouth, swallowing and grinning in satisfaction.

"Try one," she offered.

I curiously peeked down at the berries in her hand and reached out to take one for myself. The tulipberry was as big as the pad of my thumb and was smooth to the touch. I held it up to examine it further. Lightly squishing the berry in between my thumb and index finger, I tested its firmness.

"Just eat it already," Athena laughed.

"I was trying to compare it to other berries that I know of. I've never heard of flowers that hold fruit inside their petals," I explained with a small smile. Then I finally put the tulipberry in my mouth and tasted it. It was sweet and savoury all at once, which surprised me. As soon as I swallowed it, I felt as if I'd just finished eating an entire meal instead of one small berry.

I was speechless. How could a small thing like that satisfy my hunger in mere seconds? Hundreds of questions started to rise up in my head. I must have been completely lost in thought, because everyone was looking at me worriedly when I looked up from the red tulips where my eyes had apparently wandered off to.

"Well?" Athena asked excitedly. "What do you think?"

"How is this possible?" I asked. "I feel full already."

"It isn't nature's gift, if that's what you're wondering," Medusa answered. "Tulipberries were created by the Goddess Hecate when the people of Asterin were starving after the Great Civil War. One red tulip could feed an entire family for days. These flowers used to grow everywhere, at the time."

"Great Civil War?" I wondered out-loud with a frown.

"Back when people fought over which God they would follow. You see, once Poseidon established his kingdom and got bored of human company, he had invited other Gods and Goddesses for a grand celebration which ended with disputes over the beautiful island. People were divided, and new kingdoms were created on Asterin's land -- much to Poseidon's dismay. It was his own fault. Should not have brought them all here." She shrugged, then turned around and continued walking. We all followed, but not before I plucked out one red tulip.

"Here mother. You must also be hungry," I said and offered the flower to her. She smiled and took it.

"Thank you, my darling." With expert hands, she quickly unwrapped it by pulling down each petal one at a time and proceeded to eat one plump berry. She seemed to have experience with tulipberries and I wondered why she never told me about them. I would have loved to know that such fascinating flowers existed in the outside world.

Before I could ask her about it, I heard a familiar voice in the distance. Then several other voices followed. It sounded like a chant of some kind, but I couldn't make it out. When we followed Medusa out of the forest and into a large clearing, I couldn't believe what I saw.

Girls of all ages stood around a low rectangular fence, chanting a name over and over. Inside the enclosed battleground, Alexios was sparring with a little girl who was half his height. With a real sword! She couldn't have been more than six years old!

I would have ran up to stop him if it wasn't for the little girl's next move. She handled her own sword expertly and swung it at Alexios who barely dodged the blow. As soon as their swords collided, the girl twisted her body and managed to disarm Alexios. His sword flew out of his hand and landed straight into the ground.

"Surrender!" the little girl yelled out, pointing the edge of her long sword to his throat.

Alexios lifted his arms up in surrender then started to clap. "Well done."

A loud cheer erupted and the chanting got louder. "Nora! Nora! Nora!"

Nora gave Alexios a toothy grin and sheathed her sword, turning around and bowing to the girls who clapped and cheered in turn.

"Nora! Nora!"

"Athena!" Noticing our group, Nora jumped over the fence and ran over to the princess. Athena crouched down and opened her arms to embrace her. "Did you see me? I finally beat him! Did you see me? Am I as good as you? I made his sword fly away!"

"From what I just saw, you might even be better than me," she replied thoughtfully.

Nora blushed and looked down, suddenly shy. "You think so?" she mumbled with a smile.

"Definitely." Athena nodded confidently. "I could barely hold a real sword at your age, let alone use it like that. Very well done. Truly."

"Thank you." Nora hid her face in the crook of Athena's neck. After a moment, she pulled away and grinned brightly. "Alexios taught me well."

Athena pretended to gasp. "What about me? Have I not trained you as well? Fine. I will pretend that all those hours we spent training didn't happen. You can give Alexios all the glory." She pouted and turned her face away, giving Nora a side glance.

The little girl giggled and put two small hands on each side of Athena's face to make turn her head forward. She squished her cheeks. "I was only joking. You taught me very very very well."

"You hear that Alexios?" Athena called out. "I taught her very very very well." She stuck her tongue out at her brother, which made all the girls laugh.

Alexios rolled his eyes at her and bent over to take his sword out of the ground. He sheathed it and jumped over the fence to head toward us. "I wonder who taught you." He raised one eyebrow. Athena scoffed. "That's right. I did."

"How was flying?"

It took me a moment to realize that his question was directed toward me. I pointed at myself and raised my eyebrows in question. He nodded. "Yes, you."

"It was ... good," I said.

"She loved it. Lily loved it too. Come to think of it, have you flown before, Lily?" Athena suddenly frowned. "I think I remember you saying that you've missed the feeling. Of flying?"

My mother laughed nervously. "No, no. I meant that I missed the feeling of freedom and fresh air."

"Oh! I was confused. As far as I know, Pegasus is the only one that can fly humans. I was curious if you've perhaps known him before -- before..."

"Before father locked her in the dungeons," Alexios finished.

"Yes." Athena looked down.

Mother shook her head. "Last night was the first time I've flown on Pegasus," she said sincerely. "Thank you," she added after a few seconds of silence. Looking between Alexios and Athena, she gave them both a warm smile. "For helping me. I don't know what would have happened if he had returned." She omitted details in front of Medusa and the girls, but the four of us knew who she meant. Sir Edgar.

"You'll be safe here," Alexios said. "From both of them."

Athena nodded and smiled at my mother.

Nora, who's been quietly watching our interaction, stared at my mother and I. When I caught her gaze, she smiled and waved. The corners of my lips tugged up and I gave her a little wave in return. That seemed to be enough for her to feel comfortable enough to run up to me and openly stare at my face. "Wow, you're tall. Like Athena."

I chuckled. "Am I?" I crouched down to her level. "What about now?"

She giggled and shook her head. "Not tall at all." I grinned.

Nora took my face in her hands and squished my cheeks just like she did with Athena not too long ago. I felt like a fish with my lips puckered up. She stared into my eyes. "You're pretty. I like your eyes. They look like the sun! Don't they?"

She turned around and that's when I noticed all the other girls surrounding me. They came up to me one by one and looked into my eyes, before agreeing with Nora and stepping back. One girl that looked to be close to thirteen did not seem very impressed. She took one look at my face and rolled her eyes, then walked over to stand beside Alexios, crossing her arms and giving me a pointed glare.

When Nora finally had enough of me, she moved on to my mother and everyone else followed suit. I watched as she pulled at my mother's sleeve to get her attention, then proceeded to introduce herself. Soon after, the girls convinced my mother to tell them a story, which is how I found myself sitting on grass behind a group of young girls and listening to my mother recite my favourite tale about an abducted princess.

Athena sat beside me and was listening intently to the story along with the rest of the girls. Medusa joined as well. What surprised me even more was Alexios. He seemed to hang onto every word that came out of my mother's mouth. He even asked questions.

"But you said the king was away. How did he know?"

My mother smiled kindly at him. "He had very loyal messengers. They informed him of the abduction."

When the story reached its end, Nora was the first one to speak. "Is there a book with this story?"

"I'm afraid there isn't," mother answered.

"Then I will write it!" Nora grinned. "So I can read it again and again."

We all laughed. "Before you complete your book, I can tell it to you again if you wish," my mother offered.

"Yes!"

"Can you tell me too?" another girl spoke up.

"Me too!" an excited voice of another girl exclaimed.

"Lily will be staying here starting today. She will be your new teacher. Please behave, girls," Medusa said. "Have you each introduced yourselves?"

"I did!" Nora grinned proudly. Everyone else shook their heads.

While they were introducing themselves, I turned to Athena and whispered. "How did Alexios get here? He was in the castle when we left and Pegasus was with us."

"He used the portal," she whispered back.

"A what?"

"Right. I should explain." She cleared her throat and moved closer to me. "There is a portal in the castle that can bring you here through Hecate's gate. We couldn't bring you and Lily through the portal because it would not have let you through without Hecate's approval. That's why I had to bring you on Pegasus. But do not worry." Athena patted my knee. "Now that you're here, we can ask Hecate for her approval and you can use it too. Flying on Pegasus is risky, especially in daylight. Hecate's portals are a God-sent. Truly."

I looked around us. "Did they all come through...a portal as well?"

Athena glanced at the girls and nodded. "There are many secret portals all over town. The girls come through the ones that are closest to them. Their parents think that they are attending schools for ladies where they teach them etiquette and how to be a proper lady -- which I do teach them so their parents can see that they are learning what they want them to learn, but this place is much more than that."

"Have their parents seen the school?"

"They've seen the decoys." She grinned.

"From what I understand," I started. "Their parents think that their girls are going to the decoy schools every day, but they use Hecate's portals to come here instead? What if a parent decides to visit one of those schools and doesn't see their child there?"

"That's right. As for your last question, we hold special days when parents can come in and sit in a class to watch their daughters be taught if they wish. A parents' assessment day of our work. On those days, the teachers stay in those buildings for show. The girls wear their uniforms and act like proper ladies all day. Parents leave satisfied and don't complain when they are denied access on other days -- if they visit at all. Most of them have to work."

She shrugged. "This system has worked for years. But if there is a persistent parent asking to see their daughter, we get notified. The portal can transport us in seconds."

I nodded. "You have a system then."

"Of course. Can't have my father know about this. Gods know what he would do," Athena said quietly. "His laws are unfair, and although I do not have as much power as him, or even Alexios -- I want to make a change. I always hated how he looked down on me and dismissed my opinions, but his disinterest in me turned out to be a blessing. I can do a lot of things right under his nose and act like an imbecile to ward off any suspicion."

She suddenly sprang up and offered me her hand. "Let's go. I want to show you the portal." I hesitated and looked at my mother. She was sitting with Medusa and answering endless questions from the girls. "Don't worry. She's in good hands."

I took her hand and she helped me get up from the ground. She pulled me toward a building that looked like a large temple with a statue of a woman in the middle.

"Where are you going?" Alexios asked and we turned around.

"To the portal. And before you ask, no. You cannot come with us," Athena said.

Alexios scowled. "I wasn't going to ask."

The thirteen-year-old girl who seemed to dislike me sat beside Alexios and openly glared at me. I frowned in confusion. What have I done to displease her? When Athena and I were a good distance away from everyone, I asked her that question.

"Oh, do you mean Agatha? The one who seems to gravitate toward my brother all the time?"

I nodded.

"Don't worry, she acted that way with me too not too long ago. Well... until she discovered that I was his sister. Now she is... warmer? At least her glaring had stopped." She shrugged. "Give it time. She might warm up to you."

"I very much doubt that," I whispered. That was one icy glare she gave me.

"We're here." Athena stopped and pointed to a large stone statue of a woman. She held a torch in one hand and had a sword in another. She was covered in a long robe, but her crown peeked thought the hood atop head. It was a statue and yet...she looked alive. Her piercing eyes seemed to be staring into my very soul.

There was writing underneath the beautiful woman's statue. "Goddess Hecate. Only the pure of heart. Only the worthy." I read out loud and furrowed my brows. "This is her gate?" I asked Athena.

She stared at me with wide eyes. "You can read that?"

My frown deepened. "Yes? Can't everyone? It's in simple writing." I pointed to it.

Athena shook her head and continued staring at me. "It's written in the language of the Gods. No one can read it without the ancient scrolls."

"Are you certain? It looks like simple writing to me." I came closer to see the letters better and concentrated, trying to see if I was wrong, but nothing changed.

"Welcome, Emilia. I've been waiting." A woman suddenly came out of the statue and looked down at me with a smile.

I screamed.

Chapter 9: Prophesy

"Emilia. Emilia, darling. Wake up."

"What happened?"

"I don't know. She just screamed and fainted."

"She must have seen something. Did she say anything before she lost consciousness?"

"No, Alexios. I already told you. She just screamed and then fell. Now she won't wake up. Lily, try again. Maybe your voice can bring her out of it."

"Emilia? Please wake up, darling. Come back to me."

"How is this going to help exactly?"

"Would you please be quiet, Alexios? Let her mother help."

"I just don't understand how asking her to wake up would --"

"Oh! Did you see that? No. I'm sorry, I thought I saw her move."

"Seriously Athena?"

"What? I thought I saw her hand twitch."

"Mother?" I tried, but my lips refused to move. My eyes refused to open and my body stayed frozen. After a while I couldn't even hear anymore.

Suddenly, my mind became foggy and I stopped feeling anything until I saw a faint light in the distance. Moonlight. And within that light stood a woman in a robe, holding a burning torch in one hand which did nothing to illuminate her covered face.

"Emilia." Her misty voice reached my ears. "I am Hecate. The Goddess of magic and sorcery; keeper of celestial gates and protector of souls. At last, you are in my sanctuary. I have been waiting for your arrival." She bowed.

I tried to speak, but my voice was silenced yet again. The Goddess continued. "A child of light, born in the darkness. He knew he couldn't disturb the prophesy. He did not wish to abandon you. It was merely his duty. Forgive him. For these sacrifices have great purpose. The prophesy must not be disturbed. Sacrifices must be made." She started to disappear into thin air, her figure becoming one with the mist around her. "Remember my words to you."

"Sacrifices must be made."

"What did she say?"

"She's moving!"

"The prophesy... must not - must not -" I felt my body shake. My head jerked from left to right as I squeezed my eyes in pain.

"My Gods, take her to the infirmary. Now!" I heard Medusa order.

Strong arms lifted me off the ground and carried me away. With each footstep that distanced me from Hecate's statue, I felt my headache lessen and the pain became more bearable. I slowly opened my eyelids and was met with breathtakingly blue eyes that regarded me with worry.

"She's waking up," Alexios said without taking his eyes off of mine. His forehead was creased in a frown.

I was brought into a large room with several identical white beds perched up against opposite walls. Alexios carefully laid me down on the first one and stepped back to allow my mother to come to my side. She sat down on the edge of my bed and put her hand on my forehead.

"How are you feeling, darling?" she asked. Taking her hand off my forehead, she checked my eyes and then pressed two fingers against the side of my neck. Her hand came back to rest on my forehead again.

"Tired," I croaked. I was trying my best to stay awake, but sleep was pulling me in.

"Your fever has gotten worse," mother said worriedly. She turned to Medusa. "Do you have any elderflowers here?"

I didn't hear Medusa's response. Instead I let sleep completely consume me.

Voices. Too many voices speaking all at once. Arguing. I was sitting on a throne similar to the ones around me that were positioned in a circular shape, facing each other. It looked like a meeting room.

"I will not accept it! How can you ask this of me?" A tall man with golden hair spoke with outraged bewilderment.

"I know this puts you in a very difficult position, but the Fates do not make mistakes. It must be done. It is in the prophesy, and you've lived long enough to see what happens when we interfere," a man with hair and a thick beard as white as clouds reasoned.

The golden-haired man scoffed. "Difficult position? Difficult? It's impossible. You are asking me to sit back and do nothing? I refuse. What if you were in my position, Zeus? Wouldn't you do everything in your power to prevent it?"

"I wouldn't," Zeus said firmly and shook his head.

"Then you are a heartless bastard."

"That is enough!" Thunder boomed outside. Zeus rose from his throne and pointed one finger to the man with gold hair. "You seem to have forgotten our ways after all this time away from Olympus and that is the only reason I will forgive this behaviour. You are not to interfere. Do you want death on your hands? Is that it?"

The golden-haired man slumped his shoulders and dropped his head. A moment later his head lifted and he looked directly at me. "Hecate. You can do something, can't you? You are a Goddess of sorcery after all. You can do anything. Tell me you can fix it." There was so much desperation in his eyes, it was impossible to miss.

I shook my head, sadness overtaking my feelings. "I'm afraid I cannot. The string of destiny is much too fragile to be tempered with. If it snaps... it takes the soul along with it to the underworld. You must leave it alone. As much as it pains you, you know very well that it is your duty to let the prophesy happen."

Those words only fuelled the suffering man's rage. He fisted his hands, knuckles turning white with the force. "Where are the Fates?!" He rose and stormed out of the room.

"He will come to his senses. Eventually." Zeus sighed and sat down.

The scene around me changed and I found myself standing on a balcony with an empty golden goblet in my hand. I turned and walked inside open chambers, placing the goblet down on a table. There was an empty jug of wine, and the remains of someone's dinner were left half-eaten.

I sighed and looked down at the ground where an unconscious man laid on his back. His chest rose and fell with every shallow breath he took. He looked almost unrecognizable from before. His hair was long and unkept, and a long beard now covered his lower face, stained with red wine.

"You've served your duty well," I said and lowered myself down to the white marble floor. Seeing dried tears on his cheeks, I patted his face. "Not too long now. You will be reunited soon. Sleep well, Helios."

I woke up with a yelp. It felt as if my head was about to split itself in half. I cradled it in my hands and turned to my side with a whimper. The unbearable pain lasted a few more seconds before it dissipated. I could finally breathe.

"Emilia!" My mother rushed to my side. She put the back of her hand on my forehead. "What's wrong? Is it a headache?" She frowned and replaced her hand with another, feeling my temperature. "The fever is gone."

"I brought what you asked." Medusa came in with a small cart. "I couldn't find any elderflowers. We must have run out of those. I've sent someone to gather them in the forest."

"Thank you, but I don't think I would be needing them now. Her fever has gone down." Mother turned to Medusa.

"Already?" Medusa arched her brows in surprise. The snakes on her head turned their heads in my direction.

"I found them!" Nora ran in, holding a dozen elderflowers in her hands. She offered them to Medusa.

"Thank you, darling. Now run along. Your geography lesson should begin soon."

Nora nodded and waved at me before sprinting out of the infirmary.

"I feel much better now," I said as I lifted myself up into a sitting position on the bed. The headache was completely gone and I felt a surge of energy enter my body. It was odd how quickly I've recovered from that unbelievable pain.

Helios. That was the name of the golden-haired man from my dream. No. It was not a dream. I was experiencing someone else's memory again -- just as I did a few days ago when my uncle showed me the fire in the Dark Forest.

"Can the Gods enter your dreams?" I asked.

My mother stared at me with wide eyes.

Medusa looked surprised as well. Her snakes rose up and focused their curious eyes on me with interest. "It is possible, but very uncommon. The Gods do not like to meddle with the minds of mortals and not many of them are even capable of doing so. It requires a lot of power." She sat down on a bed beside mine, putting the elderflowers in her hand on the cart she'd brought in, then tilted her head to the side. "Has a God tried to communicate with you?"

I nodded.

"Hecate," my mother whispered. "Of course."

I frowned. "How did you know?"

She hesitated and then lifted her eyes to meet mine. "This is her sanctuary. I... I recognized it when we came out of that forest. If a God visited you in your dream, it has to be her. What did -- what did she say to you?"

"She said something about a prophesy and sacrifices --"

"No." Mother shook her head with force. "It cannot be true. You must have misremembered."

"She truly said that." I squeezed her hand. "What does it mean?"

"I don't know the full prophesy," she started. "I've only heard stories twenty years ago. A saviour who rises from darkness and defeats all evil -- but at the cost of their own life." She looked down on the floor. "That day... when your eyes changed colour, I had a strange feeling. I cannot explain it, but it was very strong. It was -- it was almost as if something was telling me to protect you. To keep you from danger. They were taking you away from me and I wasn't strong enough to stop them. I couldn't warn you. I didn't know what I was warning you from. Or who. I thought perhaps only King Theon was a threat to my daughter, but now..."

Mother turned and took my hands in hers. "If Hecate herself told you about the prophesy, I have a feeling that you are connected to it. That same strange feeling is eating away at me now and I don't know what to do. I'm terrified for you," her voice trembled. "I hope to Gods that I'm wrong and you will take no part in any of it. Not you. Gods, please not you." She fell into my arms. I wrapped mine around her and gently caressed her hair to soothe her.

Medusa looked deep in thought as she watched us with a slight crease between her eyebrows. Her snakes were still regarding me with much interest. She rose from the bed she's been sitting on and offered one hand to my mother and one to me. "Follow me."

Mother looked down at Medusa's outstretched hand in front of her and took it after a moment of hesitation. I took her other hand. We followed Medusa out of the infirmary. As we walked down quiet hallways and past teaching rooms where many voices of girls could be heard from a distance, we stopped in front of tall wooden doors.

Medusa pushed them open and motioned for us to come inside before closing them behind us. I stopped and stared at the sight before me. It was a library. Much larger than I'd imagined one to be. The bookshelves were taller than the door we'd walked in from, stretching high up and touching the ceiling of the grand room. Beautiful ladders were propped against each shelf to make their books accessible.

"I want to show you something. I think it might help you," Medusa said as she weaved through bookshelves with mother and I following close behind.

We approached a statue in the corner of the room. It was another statue of Goddess Hecate, but smaller than the one outside. Medusa pulled at the torch in the statue's hand and a bookshelf beside it started to move, revealing a locked door. She pulled out a silver key and unlocked it.

Inside, there was a small room with a single bookstand in the middle. The silver stand held a thick book bound by black leather. It had many thin intertwined silver lines running all across the leather's front and an eye was drawn in the middle with a clear crystal as its iris, which seemed to be staring at us as we approached it.

"This belonged to the Fates. They recorded their visions in this journal many years ago. Perhaps the prophesy you speak of would be here as well," Medusa said.

"How did you get it?" I asked.

She shrugged. "I stole it." When my mouth hung open in surprise, she continued. "I wanted to see Pegasus's fate, but there was nothing in there about him." She sighed. "Let us see if they've recorded what you need."

Medusa opened the book and placed one palm of her hand flat on the surface of its worn out paper inside. "Show me the prophesy of Asterin's saviour."

As soon as she pulled her hand away, the book started to flip its own pages until it slowly stopped to rest on a page which contained one word: 'No.'

Medusa huffed and tried again. She put one hand on top of that word and asked the book to show her the prophesy. This time it rested on the same page and the 'no' slowly disappeared into the paper until it was completely empty. Then nothing happened. The page stayed blank.

"I will feed you to the snakes." As if on cue, her snakes hissed at the book, their slithering tongues coming out of their mouths.

The book closed with a thud.

"Oh for the love of Olympus," Medusa groaned. "I will come here everyday and clean this room. No speck of dust will be left to touch you." The book opened halfway and stopped. Medusa sighed. "And I will clean your crystal until it sparkles."

Satisfied with that answer, it sprung open and started to flip through its pages until it stopped. Black ink appeared on the paper and started to draw an image.

"A sun?" I arched my brows.

"I see a sun as well," my mother said.

The book flipped to the next page and started to draw again. It started to draw wings.

"Pegasus!" Medusa leaned in close to the page and refused to blink as the ink continued to create more lines.

The wings started to resemble those of a bat as more detail was added to them.

Medusa gasped. "What happened to his beautiful wings?"

Then the rest of the creature appeared and it looked nothing like Pegasus. It was not a bat either.

Mother sucked in a breath. "Could it be --?"

"A dragon? What does a dragon have to do with anything?" Medusa said, sounding disappointed. She leaned away from the book.

The next page was flipped and showed a third illustration. It was a trident. The use of black ink on browning paper made it look like a simple spear with three prongs. Was this perhaps Poseidon's trident? I leaned in to examine it, but the book slammed shut before I could trace the lines of ink with my fingers.

"This is all we will get from it. The book only shows what it wants to show and nothing more. It is very unpredictable," Medusa explained. "We should let it rest now. It is is already angry with me and I do not wish to anger it any further."

We came out of the room and Medusa locked the door behind us, putting the silver key in her pocket. "I do hope it offered some answers for you."

Athena ran in and stopped in front of us, catching her breath. "Emilia," she panted. "I thought you were in the infirmary. Gods, I feel like I've been running around for hours trying to find you. We must go. Now." She grabbed my arm and pulled me behind her as she ran toward the doors. I didn't even get a chance to say goodbye to anyone, let alone ask her what was happening.

"I'll explain everything later, but right now we need to transport to the castle," she said.

Hecate's outdoor statue came into view and we kept running toward it at full speed.

"A-Athena, we are going straight toward the sword," I said worriedly.

"Close your eyes. It will make it easier." I closed my eyes and braced myself as the princess and I neared the tip of the sword, and then -- I felt weightless. It felt as if we were floating in water that felt airy and light and warm. I felt safe. I opened my eyes and got a small glimpse of the glistening beauty around me before I suddenly found myself in Athena's chambers at the castle. It looked exactly the same as the last time I saw it. Dresses scattered everywhere in tall piles.

"How was that?" Athena asked.

"Scary, at first. How could you run into the sword like that?" I said with wide eyes. If I wasn't being pulled by Athena, I would have never been able to do it on my own.

She waved her hand dismissively. "It's not real. Just an illusion. I think... That's what Alexios told me a long time ago. Now, let's get dressed into proper attire." She walked away from me and started toward a pile of gowns by the window.

"Proper attire?" I frowned and followed her.

"Yes." Athena picked up one beautiful gown from the tip of the pile and examined it with squinted eyes. "Have I worn this already?" She put one finger on her chin and then shook her head. "No. This will do. Now for your dress." She walked around the mountain of colourful silk until I could no longer see her behind it. "Aha!" She came out with a second gown in her arms. "This will do. Here, put this on." She handed me a dress made of green silk.

I looked at it and my frown deepened, then I lifted my eyes to meet Athena's. "Why did we come back to the castle?"

"We have an urgent matter to attend to and it couldn't wait. I've completely forgotten about it until I got reminded by Alexios. I am required to make an appearance -- especially at today's meeting before the ball. My lady in waiting is all the talk amongst the noble ladies at the moment, which is why I brought you with me. You must be by my side," she explained. "I have never missed a single one. It is an excellent opportunity to gather information on my father and his council. Keep your ears open." She pointed to her ears.

I nodded. "Athena?"

"Yes?" She raised her brows in attention.

"What exactly will we be attending today?" I asked.

"We, my dear Emilia, will be having tea with the ladies of the court."

Chapter 10: King's Concubines

Tea time with noble ladies of the court began a little over an hour ago. Aside from initial curious glances and probing questions that I've received when I walked into the room with Athena, they paid me no mind and continued to chatter on about the latest news in the castle.

I learned that each one of them came from very powerful families of Kingdom Poseidon. They had enough power to question the king's decisions without getting charged with treason.

Loud chatter and laughter suddenly died down and all heads turned toward the entrance where two women accompanied by their servants walked in with their heads held high. I heard gasps and hushed whispers all around me as they slowly approached the table.

They bowed to the princess and one of them spoke. "Your Highness, I'm afraid we missed your invitation to this delightful little gathering. The servants likely made a mistake delivering the message on time. My deepest apologies." She bowed once more.

"You were never invited," Athena hissed beneath her breath, quietly enough that even I - who sat to her right - could hardly catch it. Her initial surprise at the intrusion was skillfully replaced by a delighted smile in a matter of seconds. "Lovely to see you, Lady Ursula. Please, join us." She gestured for the servants to place new chairs by the table. "Lady Maria, please."

Lady Ursula and Lady Maria situated themselves on the left side of Athena, throwing me curious glances as they did so.

"This must be your lady in waiting, is she not, Your Highness? Em - Emora?" Lady Ursula asked, picking up a puff pastry from a platter and dusting off its powdered sugar coating.

"Emilia," I corrected and gave a small bow of my head.

Lady Ursula flicked her hand. "Yes yes, that's what I said. What I want to know is how you got this title so fast. Were you not merely a prisoner not too long ago? You should have gone through proper promotions like everyone else, and yet here you are."

"Lady Ursula, I believe that I get to decide who deserves to be my lady in waiting," Athena said. "Don't you agree?"

"Of course. I was merely curious, Your Highness." She smiled broadly and started to play with diamond jewels on her necklace. Her smile did not reach her eyes.

I tried to pay it no mind, but Lady Maria's staring started to get very uncomfortable. I shifted in my seat and met her gaze. She did not look away and simply continued to stare at me, narrowing her eyes. I cleared my throat and broke our eye contact, picking up my teacup and taking a sip.

"You allow her to eat with you, Your Highness?" Lady Ursula raised her eyebrows in surprise, only now noticing the half eaten pastry on my plate.

"I don't see anything wrong with that. Do you, Lady Ursula?" Athena asked with a smile.

She shook her head in response. "Not at all, Your Highness. Simply curious, that's all. You've not made it a habit of letting any servant close to you in the past. I am a bit surprised to see it."

"She is different," Athena said, offering no further explanation. "Please, are there any more questions on your mind? I would be delighted to answer them while we are here."

"You are so kind, Your Highness. I do have some more questions. If you don't mind, can Emora answer them for me?" Lady Ursula forced a smile in my direction. I could still feel Lady Maria's intense stare, but this time I chose to ignore it. With a nod of approval from Athena, Lady Ursula proceeded with her request. "Tell me, Emora, where are you from? Poseidon? Soleil? Perhaps even Pesok? You eyes tell me Soleil, but... there is something different about you."

She leaned in closer toward me and that's when I noticed the colour of her own eyes. They looked like mine -- golden -- and yet, they didn't at the same time. The tone was different somehow.

"I... I don't... know," I said. "My mother never told me."

"So it is true then?" She leaned back. "You were born in the dungeons?"

I nodded.

"What a pitiful life you must have had so far. His Majesty was very kind to release you. Poor thing. Must be scared to be separated from your prisoner mother. As wretched as that scheming little wench is, she is your only family after all." I fisted my hand, but refrained from using it when Athena gently put her hand over it. "But do not worry, Lady Maria and I will take good care of you here. Isn't that right, Lady Maria?"

Lady Maria nodded. "We will take very good care of you."

I evened out my breathing and forced a smile. "That is very kind of you, my ladies. But I believe Her Highness has already taken me under her wing."

"So I've noticed... but it wouldn't hurt to have His Majesty's concubines on your side, my dear Emora," Lady Ursula said.

I widened my eyes. That explains their expensive attire and a group of servants that followed them in when they entered. They're King Theon's concubines. Of course.

"I appreciate your heartfelt concern for Emilia, but I assure you, there will be no need for that," Athena answered for me. She clapped her hands once. "Now. I believe that's enough questioning for today. Let us start discussing the upcoming ball. There is much to be done. Father has invited everyone in Poseidon and even the kings and their families from other kingdoms. Although I do not expect every kingdom to attend, we must be ready for them."

"This could be my only chance to get the attention of Prince Leo," one of the court ladies squealed.

"Annabelle, isn't Prince Leo already married?" another one asked her.

"Yes, but Princess Liana is on her death bed now. It is only a matter of time before she is gone from this world -- and out of my way. He can make me his second wife," she responded. "And I'll be damned if anyone else gets that spot." She pointed around with her finger threateningly. "Do not get any ideas. He is mine."

"Prince Leo? The crown prince of Gora?" I asked. I've read about him recently in a book about Kingdom Gora. It was the last one that Rose had brought for me before I was released from the dungeons. He had done a lot for his people at a very young age, taking over the responsibilities of his father that was gravely sick at the time when their people needed a ruler the most. It was very admirable.

"Yes." Annabelle crossed her arms and sniffed, casting her suspicious eyes on me. "Why do you care?"

"Oh, I was only curious to know if I remembered it right," I said. With a final squint of her eyes, she looked away.

King Theon's two concubines rose from their seats and bowed. Athena raised her brows. "Leaving so soon, Lady Ursula? Lady Maria?"

"We were only visiting, Your Highness. Do excuse us. We have an urgent matter to attend to," Lady Ursula said.

"Very well. If it is urgent, I won't keep you. It's been a pleasure to have you here," Athena said with a bright smile. As soon as they left the room along with all of their servants, she rolled her eyes and slumped back in her seat. "Not."

"Are they really your father's concubines?" I asked.

"Yes." She grimaced. "More like spawns of evil. The only good thing they've ever done is failing to produce any heirs for my father. That's the only reason they show me any respect. They think I can help them get in my father's good graces. Help them become his wives," she scoffed. "As if he ever listens to me. Even if he did, he would never take a wife."

"Your Highness, what about the theme. Have we decided on that yet?" Annabelle asked. "Can I suggest a black and white ball? Everyone will only wear black and white. No colour. I don't think we've hosted one like that before."

Athena tapped her chin thoughtfully. "That's not a bad idea. I will consider it."

"Ooh! Even food can be black and white!" someone exclaimed.

Annabelle gave her a look of distaste. "Are you stupid? We can't make the food black and white only. Are you going to colour all the fruit yourself?"

A court lady in a blue gown suddenly gasped and demanded everyone's attention. "I almost forgot! My father told me that King Theon caught a ghost during a council meeting! Can you believe it?"

Athena and I exchanged a look. I widened my eyes. "A ghost? How?"

The lady in blue motioned for everyone to gather around her, as if she was about to tell us a very important secret.

"Annabelle's father saw a ghost listening in at the meeting. He wore all black and even had a crown on his head," she said in a hushed whisper. Athena and I exchanged another look. Uncle Cerius. "King Theon used a special device to catch him and keep him from escaping. A ghost! I bet that device is laced by magic."

"He is not my father, Gemma," Annabelle corrected. "He's just married to my mother. That does not make him my family."

"All right. Annabelle's mother's husband saw the ghost. Is that better? You know, if he really was your father, you could have inherited his Sight. What a shame," Gemma said. She shook her head. "But that's not the point. Our king caught a ghost! No one has ever done that before."

"He's not my king," I whispered to myself.

"Did your father say where they're keeping that ghost?" Athena asked.

Gemma shrugged. "He didn't. I don't think anyone but His Majesty knows."

"Are you certain? Not even a single clue as to where he is?" I asked. If that device was truly laced with magic and it could capture free spirits, how did King Theon know to bring it to his meeting? Was he expecting my uncle there?

"Why are you so curious about it?" Annabelle raised one brow. "Do you want to see it for yourself, is that it?"

"Yes," I said. "I do." And I want to free him if I can.

"I have an idea!" Gemma exclaimed. "Why don't we all spy on our fathers and try to find clues as to where the ghost is being kept? All these preparations for the ball are causing me too much distress. I need a distraction. This seems like a perfect one. Who's with me?"

The court ladies remained quiet. I held my breath, waiting for them to agree. It would be much easier for me to find my uncle with their help.

"Please," Gemma whined. "I am sure you are all growing tired of all the fittings and pestering from our mothers and servants." She pushed out her bottom lip.

"We are," Annabelle said, "but what's the point in finding this ghost? We can't see him without the Sight." The other court ladies voiced their agreements and nodded their heads.

Gemma smiled wickedly. "I saved the best for last. King Theon's device doesn't only trap ghosts -- but make them visible to everyone. My father nearly fainted when he saw that ghost slowly appear in front of his eyes. Or so I heard from my mother. She tells me these things."

I sucked in a breath. "Can they hear him too?"

Gemma nodded. Chatter in the room picked up and excitement filled everyone's eyes. Those who were doubtful about Gemma's plan before, now seemed to reconsider their decisions. I crossed my fingers behind my back and prayed that they would.

"All right," a girl with pale blue eyes said after the chatter died down. "Let's find this ghost."

~~~

"I will try to get some clues from my father as well," Athena said as we walked back to her chambers. "He is very good at keeping secrets from everyone, but I will try my best to get some information out of him. If we put everyone's clues together, I am sure we'll find your uncle."

"Thank you," I said. "I hope we find him soon. Do you think your father can do anything to him?" I bit my lip in concern.

"What, as in torture? I doubt it." She shook her head. "He's already dead. He shouldn't feel any pain."

"But he got caught by that device. It even made him visible. What if your father has other devices that could cause pain to a spirit?" I asked.

"Fair point." Athena frowned.

We rounded a corner and came face to face with James. He bowed in a greeting. "Your Highness. Lady Emilia."

"Hello James," Athena said. "I was just about to look for you --"

A group of servants walked by us in the hallway, bowing their heads and eyeing us curiously.

"Let's talk in my chambers," Athena whispered. "Too many eyes and ears out here."

I closed the door of Athena's room behind us and stifled an amused smile when I saw James's shocked face at the sight of all the dresses here. He tried
~~~

to school his features into a neutral expression, but he didn't succeed. With
wide eyes and an open mouth, he gaped at the tall mountains on the floor.

Athena crossed her arms and blew out a piece of hair that fell on her face.
"Yes, I know. A lot of dresses. There's a perfectly good reason for that, but
I will not reveal it yet. Now. Any news on Sir Edgar?"

James cleared his throat and focused his attention on the princess. "I
brought him the letter as you've instructed. He left for Pesok with a group
of guards the same night."

"Good. It will take him at least a week to get there. A few days to realize that
it was all a ruse, and another week to return to Poseidon." Athena grinned,
satisfied.

I tilted my head to the side. "What letter?"

"Oh, you know. A little backup plan I've created the night we got your
mother out of the dungeons. I had to get Sir Edgar out of the castle
in case something went wrong. Besides, if he went looking for her the
next morning and discovered that she went missing -- my father would be
informed immediately."

"So you wrote him a letter?" I asked.

"A Pesok guard wrote that letter." Athena winked. "It just so happens that
their king found a clue as to where Poseidon's trident was hidden and is on
the verge of acquiring its power for himself. And James here," she put one
hand on his shoulder, "happened to intercept it and give it to Sir Edgar."

I looked at her in awe. "He wants the trident's power for himself, and a
letter like that would ensure his departure from Poseidon."

"Exactly," she said with a firm nod.

"You are..." I stared at her.

"Always two steps ahead? Very clever? Should have a seat in the royal council?" She batted her eyelashes in an exaggerated way.

"Incredible," I finished with a laugh.

She smiled. Then she shook James's shoulder. "Do you think that I'm incredible too, James?"

"I...yes, You Highness," he responded. A slight rouge tint coloured his cheeks. He cleared his throat. "I must go now. It is almost time for lunch. Rose will be waiting for me to accompany her to the dungeons."

"Ah yes, Lily's meal schedule must go on. Who do you give the food to? There are no more prisoners left to feed," Athena said.

James shrugged. "Rose gives it to someone there. I don't know who -- she tells me to wait by the door. Though there is always a strong and...unple asant smell around her when she returns."

Athena wrinkled her nose and waved her hand. "All right, that's enough information. You may go."

He bowed his head and left. Two minutes after he closed the door behind him, we heard a knock.

"Your Highness, I've brought your lunch," a familiar voice said, muffled by the thick wood of the door.

"Come in."

Tanya walked in with a tray of food, bowing her head. She gave me a small smile and then carried the tray to a little dining table by the window -- one of the only places in this room not covered by dresses.

Having delivered princess's food, she swiftly walked back to the door, but lingered beside it, her back facing Athena and I. "Emilia," she said quietly, turning around and meeting my eyes. "I thought you should know this. His Majesty ordered some servants, including myself, to arrange a new room for you."

"Why?" I asked, knitting my brows together.

She shrugged. "I don't know. I only know that it is in the west wing -- not too far from here."

"Take us there," Athena ordered.

"Yes, Your Highness." Tanya bowed. We followed her to my new chambers. "This is it." She pointed to the door in front of us.

Athena looked around and frowned. "This hallway... It's where Lady Ursula's and Lady Maria's chambers are." She turned to Tanya. "Are you certain that my father ordered it? It wasn't one of his concubines?"

"Yes, Your Highness. He called us to the throne room and gave us his order. To give Emilia this room in the west wing," she responded.

"Thank you Tanya. You may go back to the east wing now," Athena said absently. The frown wouldn't leave her face. I chewed on my lip in distress. Something didn't feel right.

Tanya bowed and turned to leave, her silhouette getting smaller as she walked away. When it completely disappeared, Athena took my hand and pushed through the door of my new chambers. I stumbled in with her into a spacious bedroom.

"I don't understand," I said. "Why did your father give me this room? It looks too extravagant for a servant."

"What did he tell you the day you were freed from imprisonment? Did he say why he freed you?" Athena asked.

"He said that I should work at the castle. That you suggested the idea," I said.

Her frown deepened and she shook her head. "I didn't suggested anything. My father never listens to me even when I do. The first time I came to know of your existence was when the noble ladies let me know during one of our meetings. The morning before your release."

"But what..." I trailed off. What was the real reason? And why would he use his daughter as an excuse? I furrowed my brows and tried to think back to that day. I started pacing the room, one hand on my chin.

"It was my birthday that day. My eyes changed colour on that day as well... But how does it all connect? Why make me a servant? Why am I suddenly given a room beside his concubines? Is he--" I sucked in a breath. "Is he planning on making me his next concubine?" I cold shiver ran down my spine.

"Gods no," Athena said. "You are far too young for that. But I do find it all too strange... My father is possibly the hardest man to read in this castle. He has a way of throwing people off his scent until it's too late to catch it. He must have something brewing in that head of his. There must be something he wants from you."

"But I have nothing to offer! I've lived all my life locked up in a dark prison cell with my mother!" I exclaimed, still terrified of the idea that I could become a royal concubine. I would rather die than be close to that monster. "What does he want? My Sight? Is that it? Don't other people have that too?"

"I don't know," she sighed. Then she looked thoughtfully at the door. "What are you planning, father?"

Chapter 11: The Ball

It's been days, and there were still no clues as to where King Theon was hiding my uncle. None. It unsettled me more than it should.

I sat on a bed in my new chambers and stared out the window, watching as the leaves of a peach tree from a garden below swayed with the wind. If I stared at it long enough, would I feel as peaceful as I imagined that tree to be? Bathed in sunshine and caressed by a gentle wind? With nothing to worry about, but creating sweet fruit?

I doubted it. Yet I couldn't look away. Not until a knock on the door woke me from my trance.

"Emilia, it's me."

I stood and walked to the door. When I opened it, Rose's smiling face greeted me from the other side. I smiled back and stepped away to let her in. "Good morning, Rose."

"Good morning, darling," she said and pushed in a cart that contained my breakfast. "How are you feeling about your chambers today? Are they still not to your liking?"

I shrugged. "I do like the view of the garden."

"It is quite beautiful, isn't it?" She smiled and set my table by the window, with a vase of fresh flowers and delicate platters. I was still not used to having all of my meals served to me in this manner. But I was glad it was Rose. She was one of the only people that made me feel comfortable and safe in this castle.

"The ball is tonight," Rose reminded.

I nodded. "I know. I have been helping Princess Athena with the preparations. Is all of Poseidon really invited?"

"Yes. His Majesty extended his invitation to all of his people, nobles and commoners alike. It will be one of the grandest balls in the history of Kingdom Poseidon," she said. She then bent low to pull out a rectangular box from the bottom of the cart. "I have something for you."

"Oh?" I smiled and sat up straight, craning my neck to see what was inside it. Books? Paper? Perhaps some painting tools?

"This will be your first ball and I know how much you loved those books about princesses as a child. You would always talk about how much you wanted to attend balls and wear beautiful dresses, just like they did. You even made your mother and I teach you how to dance. Do you remember?" She chuckled and placed the box beside me on the bed.

"I want you to enjoy yourself tonight. Feel like a princess," she said, opening the lid and pulling out a beautiful light blue gown made of lace and tulle. It had a full skirt and reminded me of a cloud. When I touched the material, it felt soft and airy. It was beautiful beyond words.

"This...is for me?" I whispered in awe.

Rose smiled, her eyes crinkling at the corners. "This is for you, darling. Do you like it?"

"I love it," I breathed and reached out to touch it again. "It's beautiful."

"I'm glad," she said and caressed my hair. "I will leave it here with you. Eat your breakfast. I will be back to start preparing you for the ball."

I nodded and watched her walk out the door. When it closed behind her, I stood and ran up to a floor-length mirror with the dress, suppressing my squeal of excitement as I looked at my reflection with the ballgown pressed against my front. I twirled in one place with a childish smile on my face.

Today. Just today I will forget about everything and let myself enjoy these moments to the fullest. Just today I will allow myself to feel like my life is a fairytale.

Today I will feel like a princess.

~~~

Yvette bathed me in one of her fragrant soaps once again and I came out of the bathing room smelling peaches all over me. It made me smile from ear to ear.

"You are wonderful, Yvette," I told her. She giggled and thanked me, promising to make some more peach soaps as a gift.

Then it was time to get into my blue gown. Rose helped me get dressed and did my hair. She pinned it all up and left some wavy strands fall and frame my face.

"You look breathtaking," Rose said, meeting my eyes in the mirror in front of us and giving me a pleased smile. I returned it. "You are ready for the ball, my darling. Princess Athena is waiting for you in her chambers."

"Right. I promised to meet her before going to the ballroom." I stood and took one last look at my reflection. I looked like my mother. "Thank you, Rose. For everything."
~~~

"Enjoy tonight as much as you can," she said.

"I will," I responded and embraced her before leaving.

When I entered Athena's chambers, my jaw went slack. I stared at the state of her room. It was spotless. Gone were those tall and colourful mountains of dresses. I could finally see the carpet!

"What...happened here?" I looked at the princess. "Where did all the gowns go?"

Athena put down her bottle of perfume and wiggled her eyebrows. "You'll see very soon." She walked up to me. "You look beautiful! This isn't the dress I gave you, but this one suits you even better. Where did you get it?"

"Thank you. Rose gifted it to me," I said, giving a little twirl. "You look very beautiful as well, Your Highness." I bowed.

She laughed and twirled in her dress like I did. "Thank you very much, my lady. I believe it is just about time for us to go."

"Lead the way," I said enthusiastically and offered her my arm. She hooked hers around my elbow and we stepped out into the hallway together, skipping to the ballroom and receiving a few giggles from the servants around us.

We composed ourselves when we stood by the entrance doors, in front of two guards who bowed their heads to us and opened them to let us in. Loud music and laughter greeted Athena and I as we walked in. All heads turned in our direction.

"See anything...familiar?" Athena gave me a cheeky smile.

I raised my eyebrows and looked around the room. "What should I be seeing? Oh. Oh. The gowns!" I exclaimed, noticing very familiar fabrics worn by almost every woman here. So this is where those piles of dresses in Athena's room disappeared to. She gave them all away for the ball.

"My father paid for every commoner's gowns tonight and he doesn't even know it." She snickered. Then she grabbed my hand. "Let's go. I need to make a quick appearance in front of him and his council, but I will leave you with Gemma and the girls. Is that all right? It won't take long. I will be back before you know it."

I nodded and let her lead me to them.

Gemma gasped when she saw me and touched the skirt of my dress. "Stunning. Who made this?"

"I don't know. It was a gift from my second mother." I grinned.

Other noble ladies gathered around me to admire it. "I like the dress," Annabelle said. "Would have looked better on me though."

"No it wouldn't have," Gemma protested. "It looks like it was made for her." She leaned in close to me and whispered, "Don't mind her. She hates it when she isn't in the spotlight. You look great."

"Thank you," I whispered back. "You do as well."

"I am happy that Princess Athena dismissed the black and white idea for the ball in the end. It would have looked so...bland had she not," a blonde girl said.

"Hey! That was my sister's idea. It was good," someone protested and pushed through the skirt of the blonde girl to fix her with a glare. A glare that I was all too familiar with.

"Leave it, Agatha. Some people just don't have any taste," Annabelle muttered.

"I'll say." Agatha folded her arms. She met my gaze and her icy glare returned. "You again! Stay away from His Highness. He's mine."

I raised my eyebrows. "I'm sorry, but I don't know what you mean. What did I do?"

"I saw the way he looked at you and I don't like it." She continued to glare. "Leave him alone."

I was instantly struck with realization. Now I understood why she didn't seem too warm with me at Hecate's sanctuary, when all the other girls were more than welcoming. She thought I would take Alexios away from her. She didn't need to worry. I wasn't interested in him. Not in the slightest.

"Leave who alone?" Alexios suddenly appeared beside me and arched one eyebrow at Agatha. I nearly jumped out of my skin, startled at his closeness.

"Y-Your Highness," Agatha stuttered and bowed. Everyone else in the group followed suit. I did as well. Gods know who was watching. "Leave... The ghost! She should leave that ghost alone. Yes. She - she has the Sight, you see, and... she saw a ghost just now and wouldn't let them be, so I -"

Alexios chuckled and reached out to pat her on the head, like an older brother would a little sister. Agatha's cheeks became as red as her dress. "Don't worry. I'll make sure she doesn't bother any ghosts tonight. I have to have a talk with Emilia, if you ladies don't mind."

"Of course not, Your Highness. She's all yours," Gemma said. Agatha narrowed her eyes at me. I returned her gesture.

"Are you all right? I haven't seen you since I left you in the infirmary." Alexios led me to a long table filled with food.

"I am." I nodded. "Thank you." My eyes lingered on a beautiful rolled pastry covered with a chocolate glaze.

"Good." He put one of those pastries on a small plate and offered it to me.

"Thank you," I said and took it. Our fingers brushed against each other and I quickly retrieved my hand. "Don't you have better things to do than to tend to me? I think I can manage --"

The chocolate pastry slid and fell from my plate.

Alexios replaced it with another. "Try not to drop it this time. You think you can manage that?"

I scowled. "Yes."

"Good." A ghost of a smile played on his lips.

A short man with spectacles rushed over to Alexios. "Your Highness, His Majesty requests your presence."

That smile was gone instantly. "I am present, am I not, Albert?"

Albert started to sweat. "You Highness, please."

He sighed. "Fine. Tell him that I will be with him shortly."

"But he wants to see you now," Albert insisted.

Alexios glanced at me and sighed again. "Very well, let's go."

They both walked away, Alexios turning his head once to look at me before he disappeared into the crowd with Albert.

I now stood alone by the big table. If I wasn't feeling hungry, I would have been worried to be separated from familiar faces. The ballroom was filled with strangers; some dancing to the beautiful music being played by an orchestra; some socializing with each other; some drinking wine by themselves.

I bit into the chocolate pastry, which looked similar to the one that Rose once brought to my chambers with my breakfast. This one tasted even better. I reached for a second one as soon as I finished eating it.

"My wife adores those too." I looked up to see a tall man with shoulder-length hair pointing at the pastry in my hand. His grey eyes met mine and he offered me a kind smile. I wiped my mouth and gave a small bow, which made him burst into sudden laugher. "You have chocolate around your mouth."

I felt my cheeks heat up in embarrassment and looked around the table for a cloth to clean myself up.

"Here." The tall man offered me a grey handkerchief, embroidered with a triangular emblem. I thanked him and wiped each corner of my mouth and my chin. "It's gone now," he chuckled. "I must say, I was not expecting to be amused tonight. Thank you for making it a little more bearable. Even if it was unintentional."

I gave an embarrassed laugh. I didn't do anything other than make myself look like a pig. "I am very sorry for dirtying your handkerchief. I will have it washed and returned to you as soon as I can."

He put up his hand. "You may keep it. I will be returning back to my kingdom soon. I have no need for it."

"You're not from Poseidon?" I asked. If he was from another kingdom, then he must be a royal. Only kings and their families were invited from the rest of Asterin.

He shook his head. "I'm from Gora. To keep our allegiance with Poseidon strong, I had to attend tonight. His Majesty King Theon is an unforgiving man. Refusing to travel an entire week to Kingdom Poseidon and to leave my sick wife by herself for one ball could shatter our agreements. Put my people in danger. Which is why I am here. I had no choice."

"Prince Leo! You Highness!" Annabelle ran toward us, her skirts gathered into her fists and lifted off the floor to make it easier to move her legs. "I've been looking for you."

I widened my eyes. I was standing and talking with the crown prince of Gora! I made myself look like a fool in front of him. All my hopes of speaking with him about his accomplishments were ruined. I had so many questions.

Prince Leo frowned at Annabelle. "Good evening. I don't believe we have met before?"

She bowed. "My name is Annabelle and --"

"Liana's friend!" He snapped his fingers. "Yes, I remember you now."

"How is she? I heard that her illness got worse." Annabelle feigned concern, but I knew better. It was all an act. Just days ago, she announced to everyone about her plans of becoming his second wife as soon as Princess Liana passed away.

Prince Leo's face crumpled and he looked down on the ground. "She is doing her best to stay with us, but I'm afraid she is not getting better."

Annabelle sniffled and pretended to wipe a tear off her cheek. "That is devastating. Poor Liana. And you? Are you all right, Your Highness? Having a sick wife must be very difficult for you. My family can offer you support. I can offer you support. All you need to do is ask." She touched his arm.

He removed her hand. "Thank you for your concern. I will pass it on to Liana. She should know what kind of friends she has here." His grey eyes were cold.

"Of course. I only want the best for her, Your Highness," she said, completely unaware of Prince Leo's change in demeanour.

"I'm sure you do, Annabelle," I said knowingly. She shot me a glare which made her look exactly like her sister.

"There you are, darling!" Rose grabbed my elbow. "Enjoying the ball?"

I smiled. "Yes, Rose. Thank you for --"

"You are so welcome, dearest. Would you come with me for a moment?" she said.

"Oh, uh, yes of course. Is something wrong?" I frowned and let her lead me away from the table. She didn't respond and just kept pushing us through the crowd of people, toward the throne. "Rose? Where are we going? Rose?"

"Ah yes. I knew this dress would suit you well, little one." I froze when I heard his voice. "Is it to your liking? I had to choose one that represented my kingdom of course, and I must say -- blue is your colour," King Theon continued to speak. I kept my head down. "It complements your golden eyes very well."

I snapped my eyes up and met his icy blue gaze, seeing his face for the first time. It was as cold as I'd imagined it. Ruthless.

He laughed loudly. "Did you think I didn't know? I know everything, Emilia. Everything. My Rose here is my most loyal servant. She reports every little detail to me."

"Rose?" I looked at her. "What is happening? It isn't true, is it? You would never do that, would you? You aren't..." Rose let go of my elbow and moved to stand by King Theon.

"His Majesty's spy?" she said with an arch of her brow. Her voice. It wasn't her voice. It wasn't the voice that I grew up with. Her voice was always kind and gentle -- loving. Not cold and emotionless. "I am. Always was. Even before your birth. You think I took care of you because of my big heart?" She pushed her bottom lip out mockingly. "Of course you did." She chuckled. "That's what I made you believe all your life."

My eyes filled with tears. "Then why?" I croaked. This was all a dream. A nightmare. I needed to wake up. I was still asleep. I had to be. This wasn't Rose.

"To raise you into a proper woman while keeping you hidden from -- you don't need to know what. You see, your cell was very special. It was built for someone like you." Her lips curled up into a smile that lacked any warmth.

It is just a dream. A nightmare. I'm still asleep. I closed my eyes, feeling tears slide down my cheeks. A dream. A nightmare.

"Don't you feel special?" Rose continued. I opened my eyes. "I taught you everything you know."

"My mother taught me everything I know," I said weakly.

"Yes, but where would you be without everything His Majesty sent for you to learn? You should feel very special indeed. He allowed you to be educated. He even let your mother stay in the same cell with you, so she could teach you what she knew as well. You should be bowing at your knees in front of His Majesty. He did so much for you."

I felt sick to my stomach. It was all a lie. Every moment my mother and I have shared with Rose wasn't real. Every gesture of kindness, every smile and every word -- was a lie.

"But I loved you," I whispered. "You were like family to me."

Rose held my gaze and said, "You mean nothing to me."

My heart shattered into small pieces. It hurt to breathe. I suddenly felt numb, standing as still as a statue. I could hear everything around me, but every word sounded foreign to my ears.

"Emilia! I've been looking all over for you! I thought you would stay with Gem -- Emilia? What's wrong?" Athena's voice said something. "Father, what is happening here?"

"I will be making an announcement now, dearest. All will be explained. A little patience please."

Then I heard Alexios's voice. "Father? Why is she here?"

"Good. Both of my children are by my side. Albert, get everyone's attention. I will announce it now."

"Certainly, Your Majesty. Ahem... His Majesty King Theon The First of Poseidon will be making an announcement! Attention! His Majesty has an important announcement!"

It was suddenly very quiet. I could no longer hear the buzzing sound of many voices that were there before.

"My people! My allies! I am happy to see you all here for this important event. There is a reason why everyone was invited tonight. There is a reason why I made this ball most special. Most extravagant. There is something to celebrate... As you are all well aware, my latest wife Cassia was taken from me many years ago. It had been difficult to rule Poseidon without a queen by my side.

"I have finally found one. I'm announcing my wedding! My bride is an heiress to three kingdoms -- by blood. This ball is in her honour! Our marriage will strengthen Poseidon's allegiances. Asterin will be united! There will be long lasting peace, at last!"

Cheering. Cheering I could recognize. Why was everyone cheering? What did King Theon say? All I could do was stare at Rose.

"Take my bride to her chambers, Albert. And take some guards with you."

"Yes, Your Majesty."

"Bride? Emilia? Father this is absurd!" Athena's voice again. Foreign words. I wished I could understand them. "You can't be serious!"

Albert took one of my arms and started leading me away from the throne.

Last thing I remembered was seeing black smoke around Rose -- where I'd always thought a golden glow would be.

Chapter 12: White Dragon

When my initial shock of Rose's betrayal wore off and the numbness I felt subsided a little, I remembered everything that happened at the ball. I sat on the floor of my chambers, hugging my knees and leaning my back against the foot of my bed, replaying King Theon's announcement in my mind.

He planned to marry me.

I was raised underneath this castle for that purpose. To become the wife of that old tyrant who locked my pregnant mother in a small prison cell and spied on us all these years through Rose; who had his wife killed in front of his own children for educating those who lacked education; who seemed to know much more about me than I did about myself.

My Gods, he knew about my mother's escape. Sending Sir Edgar away from Poseidon didn't matter now. If only Rose hadn't --

I felt tears prickle my eyes once again. How could she? I sniffled and wiped off a single tear that ran down my cheek. I've been crying ever since the guards left me alone in my chambers. The quiet shuffling of feet by my door told me that they were standing outside -- keeping me in here.

I wished I could fight them off. Escape this castle and never step foot in it again. I wished I had the strength to do it. But I barely had any strength to even stand on my own two feet right now. My legs were too weak. I was too weak. I hated it.

I angrily wiped my eyes on the skirt of my ball gown. I didn't care if it got ruined. It could get ripped and soiled by mud for all I cared.

Pushing off the floor with two hands, I tried to stand up, but a commotion outside my door made me lose my balance, and I dropped back down on the carpet. I heard a loud yelp and clashing of metal, and then -- silence. Something was wrong.

I quietly crawled behind my bed. The moment I laid myself flat on the floor and rolled underneath it to hide, someone kicked open the door and I heard heavy footsteps. Several of them.

"Where is she?" a deep voice asked.

"I don't see anyone. Lady Ursula, are you certain she was brought here?" another unfamiliar voice said.

"I saw her being thrown inside this very room with my own two eyes. I'm certain. Search the room. She must be hiding somewhere," Lady Ursula ordered.

I tried to make myself small and hoped to Gods that they wouldn't look under the bed. Please don't look under the bed.

First they opened a door that lead to the bathing room. The familiar creaking sound couldn't be mistaken for anything else. "Not here."

Then I heard every closet door open and close. "Not here either."

After that, I heard the transparent glass door of my balcony being opened.

A loud sigh. "You imbeciles. Can't you see through the glass? There's no one there. You still haven't even searched the most obvious place."

"Apologies m --"

"Forget it. We're not paying you for your brains after all."

My eyes locked with Lady Maria's when she bent down to look under the bed. The satisfied curl of her lips made my skin crawl. They found me. "Here you are! Why don't you come out now, hm?" I shook my head no and crawled away from her, to the opposite side. "Have it your way then."

I screamed when two large hands got a hold of my arms and dragged me out from the other side. A large man in clothing as dark as the night outside put one of his hands over my mouth to muffle my screams of protest. I bit it but it was of no use. His hands were covered by thick gloves.

"Though understandable, your resistance is useless, child." Lady Ursula approached me. "You are only wasting your energy."

I glared at her.

"My, my. Look at the way she's looking at you, Ursula. Is that how you will behave when you become queen? Are you this ill-mannered? That won't do. We must protect our kingdom from the likes of you." Lady Maria came around the bed to stand beside Lady Ursula. "Which is why we are getting rid of you tonight."

"I believe it is the right thing to do. For the people of Poseidon, of course." Lady Ursula said.

I wanted to say something, but a gloved hand over my mouth prevented me from doing so. If they thought I was ill-mannered from a simple glare, they've just been spared from hearing some very ill-mannered words.

"Of course," Lady Maria echoed. She stepped closer toward me. "I have much to say to you, though I'm afraid we are very short on time. But I will say this. We will have mercy on you. You'll do well to remember our kindness when you wake up."

Lady Ursula smiled. "Sweet dreams, child."

A foul smelling cotton cloth was put over my nose and mouth. And then my body went limp.

~~~

Water was splashed on my face and I awoke with a gasp, coughing. Three things were for certain. I was inside an old metal carriage. Two men that dragged me out of my chambers were in here with me. And my hands and feet were tied together by thick ropes.

"Drink." A flask was brought to my lips. I turned my head away. "Die of thirst then."

The man who had pulled me from under my bed took the flask away and drank from it. He had a deep scar on the right side of his face, from his eyebrow down to his chin where his beard was split in two. The second man in the carriage with burn marks on his bald head slept leaning against one of the walls. His loud snoring filled the otherwise silent space.

I cleared my dry throat and looked at the scarred man in front of me. "Where are you taking me?"

"Far away from Poseidon were my instructions," he said.

I closed my eyes and leaned my head against the cold metal behind me. Small, closed spaces did not scare me. What I feared was not knowing what else King Theon's concubines instructed these men to do with me. With my eyes still closed, I asked, "Were you also instructed to kill me?"
~~~

"No. But if you are to die, it will not be done by us. We are not murderers."

"Then what are you?" I opened my eyes, meeting his black ones.

"People. People who are trying to make a living and survive."

"Are there no better ways to make a living than...this?" I asked.

He sighed. "Not for people like us. We have no homes anymore; everything is in ashes. No one hires the undocumented, but Poseidon's nobles pay a hefty sum for us to do their dirty work in secret. And I have to feed my family."

Black eyes... Everything in ashes... Were they from Typhon?

"That's enough talking. We have a long road ahead of us and I would like to spend the rest of it in silence. Drink this. It's water. You've been asleep for two days. You must be thirsty." He extended an opened flask toward me again, this time putting it in my tied hands.

I hesitated at first, but then remembered that he drank from it earlier and nothing bad happened. It wasn't poisoned. I lifted it to my lips and drank it all with hungry gulps, relieving my dry throat.

I didn't try to speak with the scarred man anymore. We spent the rest of the ride in silence, listening to the snoring of the bald man beside me.

For the next few days, we travelled farther and farther away from Kingdom Poseidon, taking many stops to let the horses rest and eat. They fed me bread and water, the same food as they ate themselves. I spent every moment inside the metal carriage, looking at the sun through the only small window it had. At least the sun rays could reach me here.

On the seventh day, I was freed from the ropes around my wrists and ankles and the doors of the carriage opened wide to let me out.

"We're here," the scarred man said, holding the door open and waiting for me to come out.

I took one step forward and stumbled, hissing at the pain around my ankles. The skin where those ropes were tightly tied stung and was rubbed raw. I took a deep breath and tried to ignore the pain, stepping out of the carriage and into an open landscape with nothing else in sight but grass and tall grey mountains.

"I think the northern side of Asterin is far enough from Poseidon. Our work here is done. Try not to die." The scarred man gave me a flask of water and some bread wrapped in cloth before climbing back inside the carriage and closing the door.

"Wait!" I exclaimed. But it was of no use. They were already turning back around, leaving me behind in the middle of the mountains. Gods know where.

I tried to even out my breathing before panic completely swallowed me whole. Think, Emilia. Where are you?

He said this was the northern side of Asterin. I imagined the map of Asterin in my mind. Poseidon was on the southern side. Soleil was above. Typhon to the west of Poseidon and Soleil. Gora and Pesok were on the northern side. I was surrounded by mountains, not sand.

Kingdom Gora. I was in Kingdom Gora.

But where exactly? There was no building in sight. No village or castle. I looked around and tried to find the highest mountain. If I climbed it, I would be able to see something and know where to go.

I ripped the bottom of my ball gown's skirt to have something to tie the flask and cloth covered bread to my waist and began to climb, thanking Gods that it wasn't too steep. Once at the top, I heaved and panted, then dropped to the ground to rest. The climb was a lot more challenging than I'd thought it would be. My ankles started to hurt even more.

Wiping sweat off my forehead, I took out the flask and drank some water, tying it back around my waist. There wasn't a lot left inside. I knew that I had to save it as much as I could.

I stood and looked at the ground below me, searching for the castle. I had no clear plan, but one thing was for certain: I had a higher chance of surviving amongst the Mountain People than alone in this wilderness with a limited supply of water and food.

There. The castle. I could see it below me, surrounded by many buildings. Relieved that I now knew where to go, I prepared to climb down when I suddenly heard a low growl that made my blood run cold.

I held my breath and turned around slowly, carefully. I gulped. A mountain lion stood a few yards away, with its teeth exposed. I took a step back when I heard another growl from my left. Whipping my head around, I saw another mountain lion approach. They were both as big as horses and they both had their hungry eyes locked on me -- their prey.

Frozen in one place, I watched as they began circling around me, licking their muzzles. If I ran, they would catch me in seconds. That wasn't an option. I had no means of protecting myself. I had no weapons nor any physical strength or abilities to wield them. I was no match for these large predators. There was no hope for me.

I would die in the middle of the mountains. Eaten by lions. I tried to accept my fate. If this was what the Gods planned for me, then I had to accept it. I just wished I would have had a more honourable death than this.

The cats lowered their head and limbs, ready to pounce on me, but just as they were about to attack, a large shadow loomed over the mountain, followed by a loud roar. Something impossibly big landed behind me and roared once again, scaring off the mountain lions who ran off in a hurry, leaving only dust behind them.

My body shook in terror and I was afraid to look up at the creature whose head casted a long shadow on the ground in front of me. Sweat beaded on my forehead. My heart beat frantically against my chest, as if trying to escape and save itself.

I closed my eyes and waited for the creature to eat me. At least I would be eaten in one bite, judging by its size. It was better than getting ripped apart by mountain lions. I kept my eyes closed and waited. But nothing happened.

Suddenly the creature dropped to the ground, causing the mountain to shake beneath my feet. I yelped as its body circled around me into a cocoon. It had white scales like a snake's and wings like a bat's. Then its head appeared in front of me, golden eyes that resembled my own staring back at me.

It simply laid on the mountain, keeping me captured inside a tall prison of scales, not moving a muscle -- just watching me with curiosity. It chirped and ran its long tongue over my entire face.

"Ahh!" I screamed and backed away only to feel warm scales on my back. When I ran one hand down my face, it came off with a slimy, clear substance. Saliva. "Did you just...lick my face?"

The dragon chirped and nodded. Then it tried to lick me again.

I quickly held up my hands in front of me. "No!"

It retracted its tongue and dropped its head to the ground, continuing to look at me with its golden eyes. A hot steam of air hit me when it exhaled through its nose.

I coughed, then widened my eyes. "You can understand me?"

A simple chirp was my response.

"I'll take that as a yes," I said. My voice was still uneven from fear. Why wasn't it attacking me?

The white dragon lifted its head in attention, as if it heard something, looking around the mountain. Then I heard it too. Human voices. They were getting closer and closer to us.

Another small chirp from the dragon and its scales began to change colour, one by one, like a mosaic. In seconds, its body blended in completely with the grey mountain beneath.

"You said this mountain wasn't too tall!"

"Uh - I don't remember it being this tall." A pause. "We've climbed so far already. Let's just get to the top! I promise, the view is worth it."

An exasperated whine. "No. I'm too tired and my legs hurt. And my dress is ruined! I'm going back to the city."

"Wait for me!"

Their voices slowly faded as they walked away. I couldn't see them over the dragon's body, but I knew that they must have been far enough from us because its scales changed back to their white colour.

"If you're not going to eat me, can you let me out please?" I said, pointing to its giant body. "I need to get to the city. You see, I only have this left to eat." I showed the small piece of bread. "If I stay here for too long, I could die of starvation. Or thirst." I pointed to my nearly empty flask.

The dragon tilted its head and chirped softly, but didn't move.

I crossed my arms. "How long do you plan on keeping me on this mountain? How am I going to get any food here?"

It moved its head to look around the mountain and then dipped it low to pick up something with its mouth. Throwing a small rabbit in front of me, it tilted its head, chirping again.

"I'm not killing this poor rabbit!" I threw my arms up.

The dragon pushed me aside with its muzzle and then blew fire onto the small animal.

"Ahh!" I screamed, looking at the now cooked rabbit beside me in horror. I looked up and pointed my finger at the giant. "Bad dragon!"

It made an offended sound in it throat and narrowed its eyes at me, releasing hot air from its nostrils. Then it dipped its head down and ate the cooked rabbit in one bite, spitting one small bone at me. It hit me in the forehead.

I sighed. "All right. I'm sorry. I just...was not expecting you to do that. I... Thank you. For trying to feed me. That was very, uh, kind of you."

The dragon chirped happily and then licked my face. Again. I had to wipe off its slimy saliva off my skin. Again. I held in my groan of frustration and used my ruined ball gown to clean myself.

Suddenly, the white dragon looked up at the sky. A short moment later, it unwrapped its body from around me and pushed me forward with its nose as if telling me to climb down.

I looked back at it. "Why the sudden change? Not that I'm complaining."

It gently pushed me forward again.

"All right. All right. I understand what you're trying to tell me. I'm going."

Climbing down was easier than up, especially with a dragon to hold on to while descending. I jumped a short distance down to flat ground and shielded my eyes from the sun as I tried to find the road to the city. I saw it when I was up on the peak of the mountain.

"There it is!" I said and began to march in that direction. I only took two steps forward when the dragon pulled me back by the skirt of my dress with its teeth. "But the road is over there. Do you wish for me to walk through the field?"

The white dragon shook its head and then dropped to lie flat on the ground, throwing up a storm of dust around us.

I coughed and covered my mouth and nose. The dragon looked at me expectantly, motioning with its eyes to the base of its giant neck. "Y-You want me to climb up there? I think I would rather walk." I heard a growl of a mountain lion somewhere in the distance. "I changed my mind. Up I go -- ah!"

It picked me up with one large paw and positioned me on the base of its neck, tilting its head and pointedly looking at the spikes in front of me. I held onto them. Satisfied, it turned to face forward and then spread its wings. They stretched from one side of the mountain to the other. I gaped at them.

"Do you have a name?" I wondered.

His name is Nephos.

I gasped and looked around me. No one was here. The voice was in my head. "Who's speaking to me?"

I waited, but there was no response. No more voices in my head. I must have imagined it. Didn't I?

"Nephos?" I tried. The dragon chirped in attention and turned to lock his golden eyes with mine. "That is your name." He chirped again with a nod. I took a deep breath. I didn't imagine that voice. It was real. And...I've heard it before, though I couldn't remember where or when. "Nephos, will you take me to the city?"

It made a low sound in its throat and then flapped its giant wings to lift off the ground. We ascended higher and higher into the pale blue sky obscured by soft white clouds. Nephos blended in with them completely as we flew over the mountains toward the city of Kingdom Gora.

Chapter 13: Poison

Nephos flew us over the city which must have looked beautiful from this height, but I was too afraid to look down. Unlike Pegasus, he didn't have a saddle and holding on to the spikes on his neck was challenging. I didn't want to fall off in the middle of the flight.

Instead I focused my eyes in front of me, where the castle of Kingdom Gora on top of a grey mountain appeared to grow in size as we neared it. A statue of Goddess Artemis stood strong by the entrance, drawing her bow and protecting the kingdom.

Nephos circled above and around the castle and dove down toward a large balcony wrapped in green vines. He hovered beside it, wings flapping softly, then picked me up with one paw and placed me on it.

I looked around me in confusion. "Is there a reason why you chose this balcony? There is an entrance, you know."

He chirped and motioned to the sky with his eyes.

I tilted my head to one side. "Up? You're leaving?"

He shook his head and motioned to the sky again, then to the balcony door, pushing me toward it with his nose.

"You want me to go in there."

Nephos nodded and looked at the sky again.

I sighed. "And now you are either telling me that you are leaving me here or...I don't understand what you are trying to tell me."

He released a sharp breath through his nostrils as if frustrated and rolled his eyes. Then he motioned to the sky again. Looked up and then at the balcony door, then at me. I shook my head. I still didn't know what he was trying to tell me.

He made a low sound in his throat that almost sounded like a groan and pushed me toward the balcony door one last time before flying away toward the sky. He didn't even look back. Bad dragon.

"Nephos!" I called him and waved my arms in the air. He turned his head and came back to hover beside the balcony. Pushing his head close to my face and locking our eyes, he tried again. He pointedly looked at me and then up at the sky where the sun was.

He's telling you that I gave him these orders.

I jumped and clutched my heart. That voice again. I looked up at the sky. "Who are you?"

That is of no importance now. Someone in there needs you. Time is running out.

I swallowed and looked at the balcony door. I heard wings flapping behind me, the sound getting farther and farther. Nephos left. I didn't know if I could trust that voice in my head, but there was no other way to get off of this balcony now other than using the door in front of me.

I slowly opened it and peeked in. They were someone's sleeping chambers. I saw a large bed in the centre of the room. Someone laid in it with thick covers over them and a white cloth over their forehead. No one else was in here.

Carefully slipping in through the door, I closed it behind me and approached the bed. A woman as pale as the cloth over her forehead breathed heavily beneath the covers. I could see the colour of her veins through the transparent skin of her neck. They were green.

I put two fingers to the side of her neck and checked her pulse. It was uneven. Her heart was beating at an abnormally slow pace, skipping beats.

Pale skin, green veins, difficulty breathing, abnormal heartbeat --

"She was poisoned," I whispered with wide eyes.

"She was," a shaky voice confirmed. I whipped my head around and saw a small girl, not older than seven or eight, sitting by the foot of the bed. She had her arms wrapped around her knees and was rocking back and worth in one place, sniffling.

"Hello," I said gently and approached her, crouching down. Mother once told me that it was good to get on the same height level with children to appear less intimidating. "Do you know what happened to her?"

She wiped her eyes with her small fists and nodded. Meeting my eyes she said, "You can see me?"

"Of course I can --" Oh no. I reached out and tried to take her hand in mine, but it went through her. She was a ghost.

"No one could see or hear me no matter how much I tried to tell them who p-poisoned..." She sniffled. "I saw who did it. I saw them."

"Could you show me? I know how to help her, but I need to see how she was poisoned," I said.

"How do I show you?" She looked at me.

I frowned. "I don't know." How did I see the other visions? They must be a way. "All right. Maybe you could tell me instead. What did you see? Do you remember?"

"I was playing hide-and-seek..." Suddenly, I felt lightheaded and had to sit down on the floor. My eyelids felt heavy. And then they closed.

I was hiding in an empty cupboard. The crack in between its two doors was wide enough for me to see through, so I watched as servants hurriedly ran around a busy kitchen. I giggled quietly when I saw a young girl run in and look around the kitchen before running out again.

"They'll never find me," I whispered.

Just then, a woman in a silver dress dragged one servant behind her and away from the others, closer toward the cupboard. The other servants were too busy to notice, focusing on their tasks as the woman in silver placed a dried flower in her hand.

"Put this in Princess Liana's tea when you serve it today. And don't forget to put in a pinch of salt this time. She would have started to slowly die already had you not forgotten that part. It's important. If you ruin my plan again...you and your child won't live to see tomorrow." She held a small knife by the servant's stomach.

A sharp gasp came out of me and I covered my mouth. But it was too late. She'd heard it.

"Go," she hissed to the scared servant and hid the knife away. Opening both cupboard doors, she smiled at me. "Who do we have here?"

I started to cry and shake my head. "I -" I hiccuped. "I didn't see anything. I won't tell anyone, I promise."

"Of course you won't," she cooed and grasped my small wrist in one hand, dragging me with her out of the kitchen, down a flight of stairs and into an old storage room where thick dust covered every surface. She closed the door behind us. "No one will ever know."

I saw a silver point of a knife and then --

I sucked in a gush of air and awoke from that horrible memory. The little girl was gone and I was alone in the room with Princess Liana.

I put my head in my hands and took a moment to breathe. What a despicable woman. That child did nothing wrong. She didn't deserve to die. I hoped that her soul would rest in peace in the afterlife, now that she showed her story.

A weak cough coming from the bed reminded me of my purpose here. She needed my help and now I knew exactly how she was poisoned.

Mountain chamomile is harmless on its own; goats graze on them in the mountains, but when that flower is dried, boiled and mixed with salt -- it creates a toxin. That toxin was now coursing through Princess Liana's blood, killing her slowly.

I approached the princess and checked her pulse again. I didn't have much time. I needed --

Someone opened the door to her chambers and walked in quietly, closing it behind them. I recognized that shoulder-length hair and grey eyes from the ball. Prince Leo did not notice me at first, but when he took his eyes away from the princess, he halted and put one hand on the hilt of his sword. "Who are you and what are you doing in my wife's chambers?"

I put my hands up in front of me. "Prince Leo, we met in Poseidon. At the ball." I waited for him to recognize me, but he frowned and didn't move his hand away from the sword. "I got chocolate all over my face and you gave me your handkerchief."

Recognition finally lit his eyes and he relaxed. "Right, I remember now." He glanced at the princess, then back at me, tensing up again. "Would you like to tell me why you are in Gora, and in my wife's chambers of all places?"

"There is a lot to explain, and I will. But first I need to help Princess Liana. She doesn't have a lot of time left. The poison is now in her lungs and if I don't give her the remedy soon, she... She will die, Your Highness." I looked at her pale face.

The princess coughed again and turned to her side, moaning in pain. The cloth that was on her forehead fell to the pillow.

Prince Leo immediately rushed to her side. "Liana!" He took her hand in his, then brushed her hair off her face gently. "My Liana." Squeezing her hand, he turned his head to lock his worried eyes with mine. "Save her. Please."

I nodded. I could do this. I could save her. My mother taught me how. "I need you to bring me dried mountain chamomile, hot water, and sugar. A large basin and a large towel." The same flower that poisoned her contained the remedy within it.

When Prince Leo brought me everything I needed, I prepared the mixture in a basin. He helped me hold the princesses's head over the steam of the mixture and I covered her with a large towel to keep it in. "She has to breathe it in," I explained.

The prince rubbed circles on Princess Liana's back in a soothing motion as she brought the antidote into her lungs and bloodstream with every breath she took. "How do you know that this will help her?" he asked me.

"I know what poisoned her. Saw it rather, through a vision..." I told him about the ghost of a young girl and the memory she shared with me.

His hands stopped moving on the princess's back and he locked his jaw. "What did you say that woman was wearing?"

"A silver dress," I said.

"A noble in the castle..." He fisted his hands. "Did you see her face? Would you recognize it if you saw her?"

I nodded. "I would."

When the remedy cooled down and stopped producing steam, I lifted the towel off of Princess Liana's head and put the basin away. Prince Leo laid her down on the pillow and moved to stand when a hand caught his hand.

"Leo," the princess croaked.

He widened his eyes and came closer to her, grasping her hand with both of his and giving it a light kiss. "Liana," he breathed. "I'm here. I'm here." He looked up at me. "Her skin is getting its colour back."

I checked her pulse. It was still skipping beats, but less now. "It's working. The remedy is working," I said with wide eyes. I knew that it should, but to witness it myself... "It's working," I whispered.

Prince Leo released a strangled sob and embraced his wife, burying his face in the crook of her neck. "Thank you," he cried. "Thank you. I thought I would lose her. I thought I was going to lose my Liana."

Well done, Emilia.

There it was again, in my head. I looked up at the sky through the window. I wanted to know who that voice belonged to.

It took more than an hour, but little by little, Princess Liana started to get better. Her breathing was normal. Her skin no longer pale. And her heartbeat no longer skipped.

Prince Leo was the first face she saw when she awoke from her sleep. She had fallen asleep soon after calling out her husband's name. She smiled and brought her hand to his cheek, wiping off a tear. "My prince." She turned her head and saw me, smiling still. "Hello." Her voice was gentle and sweet.

I smiled. "Hello, Your Highness --"

Someone barged into the room. "Liana! You're awake, my dear sister." The woman rushed to her side and started to cry. "You had everyone worried sick. How are you feeling? You look much better. Oh, my little sister, I believed you were dying." She sobbed and clutched her hand.

I stood frozen as I watched the scene in front of me. "Get away from her."

Princess Liana's sister turned her teary eyes to me. "What?"

"Get away from her!" I said and pulled her back from the princess.

She fell on her buttocks and gasped, looking up at me with angry eyes. "How dare you? Your Highness, who is this wretched wench?" She looked at my ragged ballgown.

Prince Leo stood and looked down at her, then he directed his gaze toward me. "Was it her?" he asked calmly. But his eyes were burning with rage.

"It was her. I'm certain," I said.

"Get up Tianna," he ordered the woman on the floor in that same calm voice.

"Could you help me, Your Highness?" Tianna sniffled. I glared at her.

"I said get up!" Prince Leo yelled at her. She flinched, but slowly started to stand.

"I don't understand why you are angry with me, Your Highness. You should be reprimanding this girl for her behaviour." She pointed at me. The face of that innocent child she killed appeared in my memory. I wanted to lunge at her.

"Guards!" the prince called out. Two guards walked in and stood straight, waiting for his orders. "Throw this woman in a cell."

Tianna gave me a satisfied smile. "Enjoy the dungeons, you wench. I hear they're dark and full of rats. You will love your new home."

I smiled back knowingly. "Oh yes you will."

The guards grabbed her from both sides and tied her wrists. She widened her eyes and thrashed, trying to free herself.

"Leo, why are you doing this?" Princess Liana's soft voice was filled with confusion.

"Your Highness, I don't understand!" Tianna stopped struggling and became teary eyed once again, looking between her sister and the prince.

"Then let me explain it to you." I stepped in front of her. "You poisoned your own sister and killed an innocent child for overhearing your plan. How dare you walk in here and pretend to be a loving sister after what you've done? You sicken me."

She snapped her eyes to meet mine. "How --"

"Is that true, Tianna?" the princess croaked. "Tell me it isn't true. You wouldn't do such horrible things. Not you."

"Of course I didn't do any of that! She's lying!" Tianna objected. "You believe the words of this stranger over mine?"

"I... I don't know," she responded. "But she isn't a stranger. She saved my life."

Tianna laughed. "She saved your life? How do you think she knew how to do that? For all we know she could have poisoned you herself and helped you to gain your trust."

"She couldn't have possibly done that all the way from Poseidon," Prince Leo said. "I know she was there. I saw her."

"She could have sent someone to do it!" she argued.

I raised my brow. "Sent someone? Why would I try to poison a princess from another kingdom?"

Tianna paused to think. "Your Highness, she must have done it to get close to you. You said it yourself that you saw her in Poseidon. She must have favoured you and wanted to get rid of Liana. And then this wench used mountain chamomile to poison my little sister! Look at her! She doesn't look trustworthy."

Everyone went quiet.

"What did you say I used?" I asked.

She rolled her eyes and sighed impatiently. "Mountain chamomile. You used its toxin to poison her. Are you deaf?"

"How did you know what poison she used, Tianna?" the princess asked in a shaky whisper.

Realizing her mistake, she widened her eyes. "I... I..." She sighed and locked eyes with her sister. "I know because I did it."

Princess Liana's eyes filled with tears. "Why would you do that?"

"Why? Why?" She laughed humourlessly. "Because you stole him from me! You stole the crown prince. Father had arranged our marriage. Everything was going well. I was to be crown princess! Me. And when that old, sick man died and cleared the throne, I would have become the queen of Kingdom Gora. But you and your - your innocent looks and sickeningly kind heart stole his affections before I even got the chance to choose my wedding dress!"

"But you told me that you were happy for me. For finding love. You said that I saved you from an unwanted marriage forced by our father. Was that all a lie?"

"Of course it was a lie!" Tianna screamed. "You were always so slow, I wondered how on Asterin you were my sister! Why can't you just die? You shouldn't have been born. And you!" She looked at me. "Why couldn't you just stay in Poseidon? You ruined everything." She clutched her own hair and pulled on it like a crazed woman.

The princess clutched onto Prince Leo and sobbed. He turned his head to the guards. "Take her away!" he ordered. "Throw her in the darkest cell!"

The guards started to drag her out of the room. They stopped when I ran up to her.

"What did you do to the servant that served the poisoned tea to Her Highness?" I asked Tianna, now remembering the pregnant woman that she'd threatened.

She smiled and leaned close to my face. "I killed her."

I squeezed my eyes shut. Another innocent life taken. When I opened them, Tianna was already gone, taken away to the dungeons.

I heard Princess Liana's pained sobs behind me and my heart broke for her. I understood her pain. It wasn't too long ago that I too experienced betrayal from someone very close to me. It was a deep scar that I would bear for the rest of my life.

I looked at the princess as she cried into the chest of her prince and thanked Gods that I was able to save her life today. I wished I could have saved the lives of the servants who crossed paths with that despicable woman. But she was locked away now. She wouldn't be able to harm anyone. Not anymore.

That voice reappeared again in my head.

You did well, Emilia. Well done, my daughter.

Chapter 14: Grandfather

"Kingdom Gora thanks you, Emilia. You saved our future queen and found the murderer among us. And I, as a father who is happy to see my son with his healthy wife again... You have my deepest gratitude." King Ira of Gora bowed down to me at the foot of his throne.

Prince Leo followed his father's lead and knelt beside his own throne on the right side. "As with I. Please accept my deepest gratitude. I am forever in your debt. If you ever need Kingdom Gora's help, know that you will receive it. As a future king, I make that promise to you."

After meeting the king and receiving a warm welcome to his kingdom, I was asked by Princess Liana to accompany her to the gardens. She was now fully recovered from the poison and looked healthy with her rosy cheeks and bright grey eyes.

As we walked slowly through the colourful and blooming maze of the garden, we learned more about each other. I've taken a liking to her very quickly. Her gentle and kind nature drew me in, and I could see a good friendship growing between us.

When we stopped by a clearing where a field of familiar red flowers covered the ground like a carpet, I gasped and pointed at them. "Tulipberries!"

Liana smiled. "Yes. We grow them to feed the poor, and I believe these were harvested not too long ago. See how the petals are open?" She pointed to a tulip below. "The flowers are empty now."

I crouched down to look inside one and saw three berries at the bottom. Taking them out, I showed the princess. "Are you hungry by any chance?"

"Ah! They missed some," she said. Her stomach growled and she laughed, extending her hand to take one berry. "Thank you. It appears I am."

A large shadow suddenly covered the field and we both looked up at the sky. Nephos flapped his large wings and landed hard on the tulip field, crushing the poor flowers beneath him. He lifted one paw and looked under it, shaking off a petal that got stuck in between his claws.

"Nephos, you destroyed them." I gasped and turned to Liana. "I am so sorry. Is--"

"Not to worry. They will grow back as good as new," she said, looking at Nephos in awe. He was now chasing his own tail and crushing more flowers with his weight.

I frowned. That wasn't my reaction at seeing this giant dragon for the first time. "You aren't...scared of him?"

She shook her head and tilted it to one side. "I wonder if they know each other."

She put her thumb and index finger between her lips and whistled twice. A short moment later a silvery grey dragon landed beside her gracefully. I wondered why Nephos couldn't do that. Perhaps it had to do with his size. The grey dragon was much smaller than him, nearly twice as small.

Nephos stopped chasing his tail and straightened his posture when he saw the creature. The two dragons stared at each other.

"What's its name?" I asked Liana.

"His name is Vunos," she responded. "Leo and I named him when we found him in the mountains many years ago. The poor thing was on the verge of death. He was even smaller than he is now, and he can barely emit fire. Only small fire balls."

"I see. It's a good thing you found him. You saved his life."

Liana nodded. "How did you find your dragon?"

"He was the one that found me." I shrugged. "He saved me from being eaten by mountain lions and brought me to you."

She smiled and looked at Nephos. "Then I have him to thank as well. I will give him one of Vunos's goats as gratitude. Will he like that? Oh! I think they do know each other." She laughed and pointed. "Look."

Nephos approached Vunos and pushed his head down with a giant paw. Vunos growled and slapped it off, lunging at Nephos. Soon they were rolling around on the field -- crushing more tulips while play fighting.

Then suddenly Nephos stopped and looked up at the sky, blocking Vunos's advances with ease. He must have been getting orders from someone there. Someone who I tried to speak to after the last time I heard their voice in my head, but failed to receive an answer.

The white dragon picked me up and placed me on the base of his neck, chirping once. Without any warning, he lifted off the ground, flying up and sending a gust of wind toward the ground where Liana stood, squinting her eyes from the force of it.

"I apologize for this!" I said loudly over the wing flapping. "I have no control over his actions!"

"That is all right! Thank you for everything, Emilia!" Liana called out from below. "I hope I see you soon! You are always welcome here at the castle!"

I tried to wave, but quickly put my hand back on Nephos when I lost my balance. We were soon too high up for Liana to see or hear me. I sighed, wishing that I could have said my goodbyes.

"Where are you taking me now?" I asked Nephos.

He chirped.

"Right. I don't know why I even asked. I don't understand you."

We flew among the clouds and this time I chanced a peak at the ground below us, then gasped. It was beautiful. The castle. The city. The mountains. They all looked breathtaking from up here, framed by white clouds.

I suddenly remembered the time when mother and I flew on Pegasus with Athena. She seemed to have known the feeling of flight. I wondered if she had flown on a dragon before.

Soon the landscape below started to transform from mountains to sand. For a moment I could only see desert, until buildings with spherical roofs started to appear. Then more and more of them. And then -- a palace. It was the largest building I could see, stretching wide across the sand.

Nephos chirped and started to descend toward it. When we came closer to the ground, the force of his wings caused a sand storm around us. I squinted and covered my nose and mouth with the sleeve of a dress that Liana gave me.

Nephos landed and shook off sand that got on his scales, which made me lose my grip on his spikes and fall off of him. I landed in soft sand, coughing up some of it.

"You knew that I would have a soft landing and that's why you dropped me, right?" I asked.

The dragon refused to look at me, only giving me a guilty side glance. Then he turned his head and nodded. Too quickly.

I scowled and got up, shaking out my dress. "Liar. You are lucky there was sand. I wonder what they would have to say about it." I pointed to the sky.

Nephos followed my finger with his eyes and then looked back at me. He approached me and licked my face before I could do anything to stop it.

I scrunched up my nose and wiped off his saliva with my hand, but granules of sand stuck to my skin instead. I took in a deep breath and forced a smile up at the giant. "I will take that as an apology."

He made a noise of content in his throat and nodded, resting his head on his front paws and watching me silently. His golden eyes shifted from me to the palace, then back to me again.

Sighing, I looked at the palace in front of me. "I believe that is where I have to go, is it not?"

He lifted his head and chirped, pushing me toward it with his nose.

"All right. To the palace I go." I marched toward the door in front of me. It was unguarded. From my mother's stories, I thought the palace of Pesok would be swarming with guards everywhere and yet there was an open entrance which I easily walked in through.

Peeking into the hallway, I checked for any guards inside the wide space. There weren't any there either. No one was. It was completely empty. Frowning, I continued down the hall, which led to an open door. I walked through it and froze in place with my mouth hanging open.

It was a large room with a beautiful fountain in its centre. There was a colourful carpet hanging on one wall, and the big, beautifully shaped windows were framed by floor-length curtains. It was exactly how my mother described it. Even the throne in the far end of the room was as she described. Covered in coloured silk and large enough to fit three people.

Something poked me in the shoulder. "Who are you? Why are you here? If you came to steal, most of my treasures are too heavy for you to carry. And I may be an old man, but I know how to fight. Well?" Another poke with a dull stick. "Answer me."

I turned and opened my mouth to answer, but the face I was met with stopped me. It looked familiar and yet...strangely not. I almost mistook him for uncle Cerius.

The old man widened his eyes and his hand started to shake along with the staff it held. "L-Lily? Is that you? You're alive?"

"Lily is my mother's name," I said, frowning. Did he know her?

He dropped his staff and came closer, taking my face into his shaking and wrinkly hands. "It can't be," he whispered and let go. "You look a lot like her. A spitting image. Tell me child, is she still alive?"

I nodded slowly. She was in a safe place now, with Medusa and under Hecate's protection. Nothing could get to her there. Athena had assured me of that. "Yes."

The old man teared up and dropped his staff. "She was alive. All these years she was alive. I thought..." He lost balance and almost fell, but I caught him by the sleeve of his robe. "I thought he killed her. The letter. The letter said - and - and - Helios disappeared. I thought she was truly gone." He looked at me and placed one hand on my shoulder. "How old are you, child?"

"Eighteen," I said.

"Eighteen," he repeated, nodding. "Yes, yes. That adds up. But your eyes... You are not Theon's. You can't be." He frowned, then looked down on the floor, shaking his head. "I should have listened to her. I should have let her return to the palace. I was a fool. And I dare accept the title of a competent king. I do not deserve it. I do not deserve it at all."

"How," I paused. "How do you know my mother?"

He lifted his eyes and said, "She's my daughter. The crown princess of Pesok."

~~~

King Serkan of Pesok, my grandfather, sat across from me at a short table, with his legs folded on the plush seating mat beneath him. "...and you were locked in those dungeons all your life?"

I nodded, swallowing a slice of a pear. The table was filled with all kinds of food, served in small plates. From nuts to stuffed grape leaves, there was enough food to satisfy my hunger.

Grandfather dropped his head in his hands. "Your mother was to marry Prince Theon. King now," he suddenly said.

I dropped my fork. "What?"

"I had arranged it with Theon's father, the king of Poseidon at the time. It was the biggest mistake of my life. I only saw the good side of my decision. Pesok would gain a powerful ally. Your mother would be wed to the prince I had thought she fancied. She didn't protest when I announced the engagement..." He sighed. "But I was wrong."

I lost all my appetite. "Did...did they get married?"
~~~

"No." He shook his head. "Two weeks before the wedding, they visited Kingdom Soleil together. King Helios invited every kingdom for a ball. It was a grand celebration. I would remember. I was also there..."

"Something must have happened there," I probed when grandfather went silent, looking off into the distance.

"Yes," he continued. "Lily fell in love with Helios. I should have noticed the signs then. She kept asking me to postpone the wedding to Theon, asking to come back to my palace. Back then I had thought she was only getting overwhelmed with the wedding preparations. I had thought she wanted the marriage."

"She couldn't have possibly wanted to marry that monster," I said sourly.

Grandfather sighed. "I didn't see the monster in him. I didn't see it. I believe that I was blinded by the power he promised my kingdom. And my thirst for power destroyed my daughter's life. I destroyed Lily's life."

I pursed my lips. "Was that why King Theon threw my mother in a cell? Was loving another person the treason she'd committed?"

"Theon felt betrayed. He had fancied your mother and wanted to marry her, but when he discovered her love affair with Helios two days before the wedding...he broke off the engagement. And he sent me a letter."

"A letter?"

"Yes. A letter that announced my daughter's treason against Poseidon. It said that she had betrayed the royal family. Her punishment was death."

"But she didn't die," I whispered, suddenly feeling relieved that King Theon had fancied my mother. It saved her life. Then I remembered Athena's and Alexios's mother, Cassia. "King Theon. He married someone later, no?"

Grandfather nodded. "I had heard of it, though I've never seen her. She was his concubine years earlier. My spy had told me that she looked a lot like Lily. She didn't live long."

I shuddered. Did he marry her because she resembled my mother? Then I widened my eyes. Did he want to marry me because I too resembled my mother? A cold shiver ran down my spine.

"What's wrong? Why is you face so pale, my child?" Grandfather frowned.

"I just...I realized something," I said absently. Though ill-intended, Lady Ursula and Lady Maria may have saved my life by sending me away from the kingdom. If they hadn't done that... My Gods, I was going to be sick.

Grandfather filled a glass cup with water and put it in front of me. "Drink. I realize this must be too much for you. Knowing what happened before your birth." His hand shook as he moved it back to rest on the corner of the table. "To live in those conditions all these years... And I never even knew. I thought both of my children had gone to the afterlife."

I took a sip of the water and met his eyes. "About uncle Cerius...Do you know what happened to him?"

Through the vision he had shared with me the night I met him, I knew that he had burned in the fire that ignited in the Dark Forest. But there there was more. If it wasn't for the fire, he would have died from the wound from a knife that was embedded deep in his abdomen. He had never explained his death. Who killed him? Why?

"Your grandmother, the late queen of Typhon and the mother of my children had an advisor," grandfather began. "I never liked him. He was too young and there was always something brewing in those eyes of his. A thirst for power. I had warned Healea of this, but I believe I was not very convincing with my argument. She didn't listen." He sighed. "I should have tried harder, but I let it go, and he stayed by her side."

After a moment of silence he continued. "Cerius and Lily were separated at a young age. Lily was to be the queen of Pesok, and Cerius travelled to Typhon to take the throne after your grandmother's death. When he became king, that advisor stayed in the royal council. He befriended Cerius and fed him stories about Poseidon's trident. He said that it was in Typhon and Cerius could have the power of the sea if he found it."

"And did he? Did he find it?" I asked.

"I don't know. The last message from my informant told me that Cerius went to the Twin Volcanoes in search of that trident. A day later, Kingdom Typhon was in flames. Some managed to escape -- including the royal advisor," he said.

"Where is this advisor now?"

"In Kingdom Poseidon. He joined Theon's royal council and married a woman from a very powerful family amongst the nobles there. I believe they even have two daughters now, if my memory serves me well." Grandfather stroked his chin. "Ed was his name."

"Ed," I repeated with a frown. "Could it be...Edgar?"

"Edgar?" His eyebrows furrowed. Then he nodded slowly. "Hm, perhaps. I only knew him as Ed."

It is Edgar. You are right.

When I heard that voice in my head again, something became clear. I remembered where I've heard it before and why I recognized it. It was in Hecate's vision.

"Grandfather," I said, "was King Helios a God?"

"I now believe that he was, though I cannot know for certain. The Gods that once walked among us had left Asterin in the hands of humans long ago. Do you know the history of our creation?"

I nodded. "After Asterin was raised from the sea, Poseidon created his own human race on the island. When the other Gods came here, they did the same."

"Yes. That is why our eyes are different. They resemble the eyes of the God that made us. But when people mix their bloodlines, they create their own race and the connection with their Gods is lost, along with the abilities that come with it."

"Like the Sight," I whispered.

"Like the Sight." Grandfather nodded. "You are of a mixed bloodline and yet...you have your Sight. Do you know what that means?"

I frowned and shook my head.

"You are a direct descendant of a God -- his daughter."

"Helios is my father." I realized. That voice in my head truly was my father's. He had called me his daughter, but I didn't believe it. I thought I had heard wrong.

Grandfather patted my hand across the table. "You are a demigoddess, my child. Your mother hadn't told you about your father?"

I shook my head. "My mother had kept a lot from me." I met his eyes. "I don't understand. Why would she keep that from me? I thought we had no family left. I didn't know about uncle Cerius. I didn't know about you. And I certainly knew nothing about my father. Who else is there?" I grabbed his hand. "Do I have any other family? Perhaps a brother or a sister?"

He gave me no response. Instead I heard loud snoring and an empty look in his open eyes. He was asleep.

I shook his shoulder. "Grandfather?"

His head dropped down and he continued to snore.

I sighed and laughed a little. Then I laid him down on a pillow nearby and tried to gently close his eyes. They sprung open and I yelped, covering my mouth quickly. He turned to his side and continued to snore.

"I see now who my mother gets it from," I whispered with a breathy laugh. "Sleep well, grandfather. I will ask my questions later."

Chapter 15: Unexpected Guest

- -

"Your Highness! Take this sunshade! The sun is too strong at this time of day!" Reina, the servant that my grandfather instructed to follow me around everywhere ran after me with a sunshade in hand.

"The heat of the sun does not bother me! You can use it," I called out without turning back. I was still getting used to being addressed with that title. It felt strange the first time Reina called me that, but as the day went on and the more I heard it, it felt more natural. "Now, where is he..."

I had heard a loud whine when I was inside the palace. It sounded a lot like Nephos. I had run out to look for him outside, but he was nowhere in sight. I only saw hills of sand around me and the city far in the distance.

Suddenly another loud whine came from my left. It was very close. I turned my head and saw nothing again. Only an impossibly large hill of sand.

"Nephos, where --" I stopped and took a second look at that large hill and crossed my arms. Tilting my head to the side, I approached it. "Hello Nephos."

What I mistook for sand at first started to transform, changing into white scales of a very familiar and a very large dragon.

Reina finally caught up and panted, out of breath from running after me. "Your...Highness...your sunshade...it's - ahh!" She screamed when she saw Nephos and fell backwards on the sand, staring at him in horror.

Nephos looked at her and bared his sharp teeth.

She screamed again and fainted, dropping the sunshade she's been holding.

The white dragon made a series of sounds in his throat that sounded suspiciously like a laugh.

I sighed and shook my head at him. Then I walked over to Reina, picked up the sunshade she'd dropped and planted it into the sand beside her to protect her from the hot rays of the sun.

"She will wake up soon. I hope... As for you!" I turned and pointed at Nephos with narrowed eyes. "You shouldn't have scared her like that. And why were you hiding from me? I couldn't find you. I heard your whines and couldn't find you. I thought you were in danger!"

Nephos hung his head and looked down on the ground, lightly pushing sand around with his front paw.

"Are you all right?" I asked.

He raised his eyes and nodded, then directed them down again.

"Were you perhaps...bored?"

Without looking up this time, he moved his head up and down in a nod.

I sighed. "I promise that I will come out to play hide and go seek with you later. But please do not startle me like that again."

Nephos raised his head and I was met with his excited eyes. He chirped and shook his tail, sending heaps of sand around us. The sunshade above Reina did nothing to protect her front the sand and now she laid covered in it.

I crouched down beside her and started to wipe it off of her when she coughed and sat up suddenly, hitting her head on the sunshade. "Ow!" She rubbed it. "You Highness, I had the most horrible dream. I thought I saw a giant dragon! It had very large and sharp teeth and it looked ready to atta - aah!" She widened her eyes and fainted again.

I turned my head just in time to see Nephos cover his exposed teeth. "Again? Bad dragon!" I scolded him.

He growled in offence, but then something caught his attention. He turned his head and then immediately dropped down into the sand, his scales shifting back to blend in with the landscape.

I frowned and peered in the direction I saw him looking at and was met with a sight of a camel in the distance. When it came closer, I could make out a rider in white clothes. Half of their face was covered with a scarf, the ends of which hung loosely on their shoulders.

"Reina." I shook her. "Reina, wake up. Someone is coming."

She mumbled something and opened her eyes. I moved the sunshade just before she sprang up to sit again. "Your Highness! I-"

"Yes, you saw a dragon in your dream. Do you see one now?" I asked. She looked around and shook her head, sighing in relief. "But look over there." I pointed. "There is someone approaching the palace. What should we do? You told me to beware of camel riders."

"I did?" She frowned.

"You did, and you never told me the reason why," I said, watching as the rider kept getting closer to us.

"Oh!" Reina smacked her forehead. "A camel rider once stole my silver. It happened to many others too. I try to stay away from them and I thought you should be careful around them as well, Your Highness."

The rider was now only a short distance away. When they stopped in front of Reina and I, I glanced at Nephos. If they tried anything, he would protect me.

I looked up at the rider sitting high on the hump of the camel. The bright sunlight prevented me from seeing the exposed half of their face. I hoped I was looking at their eyes when I said, "If you want silver, we don't have any with us."

They laughed. It was muffled by the scarf. "I have enough of my own."

"That's what the one who stole my silver said, Your Highness," Reina whispered to my ear and glanced at the rider with suspicion.

I crossed my arms. "Why are you headed toward the palace?"

"Why are you here?" the rider asked.

"You must address Her Highness the princess of Pesok with respect!" Reina straightened her back. "Answer her question, you camel rider."

"Princess...?" The rider tilted their head. Then without any warning, they reached down and pulled me up to sit on the camel, in front of them. Locking me in with two strong arms around me, they pulled at the reigns of the camel.

"What are you doing!" I protested and tried to jump off, but couldn't.

"I've been looking everywhere for you, Emilia. Didn't expect to see you here in Pesok of all places."

I frowned and turned my head to look behind me. The rider pulled down their scarf and I gasped. "Alexios? What are you doing in Pesok?"

"Your Highness!" Reina grabbed my foot and tried to pull me off the camel. The animal was walking slowly along the sand which allowed her to keep up with us.

I looked down at her. "Do not worry, Reina. I know him."

She let go of my foot and glanced at Alexios curiously.

We stopped by the palace doors and Alexios jumped off the camel, extending a hand to help me jump off as well. When we reached the guards, they bowed their heads and let us in. Reina quietly followed behind Alexios and I as we walked toward the throne room.

"When are you going to tell me why you are here?" I asked Alexios.

"I have a meeting with King Serkan," he said. As soon as we were inside the throne room, he closed the doors behind us, leaving Reina outside, despite her protests.

"On time as always, Alexios," grandfather said. He rose from his throne and patted Alexios on the shoulder with a crinkling smile of affection.

"I hope you've been well, grandfather." Alexios bowed his head.

"Grandfather?" I widened my eyes and looked between my grandfather and the blue-eyed brute. "We're related?"

The king of Pesok shook his head. "He has called me his grandfather ever since he was a young boy. Since I've always wished for grandchildren, I had taken quite a liking to it."

"I ran away from my kingdom many times in the past. One day I found myself lost in the merchant market in Pesok. That is when grandfather Serkan found me," Alexios added.

"Then we are not related?" I asked. They shook their heads and I sighed in relief.

"Now that my granddaughter found me, I have two grandchildren." Grandfather smiled wide and put his arms around Alexios and I, pushing us together. He let go and clapped his hands together. "Let us have a feast to celebrate!"

"I'm afraid the feast will have to wait. Father captured King Cerius to interrogate him," Alexios said with a purse of his lips.

"You found where uncle Cerius is?" "My son is alive?" Grandfather and I said at the same time.

"He captured the ghost of your son, grandfather," Alexios said to him. "Father had the cyclopes make a device that could capture the soul's essence and trap them in one place." Then he turned to me. "He is being kept in the dungeons where the cyclopes are."

Grandfather fisted his hands. "That bastard. He dares to disturb my son in his afterlife?"

"Why my uncle?" I asked Alexios.

"Do you remember when we overheard Sir Edgar ask your mother about the trident?" he said.

"Yes. He had asked her where 'he' hid it. Are you telling me that uncle Cerius hid Poseidon's trident somewhere?"

"That's what Sir Edgar believes. But he had kept everything from my father. His search for the trident and everything he knew about its powers. But

Rose was there with us too. She had overheard Sir Edgar and I believe she was the one who told my father about it."

"And now he found a way to get his answers from my uncle," I whispered.

Alexios nodded. "He has also found a way to torture him."

I covered my mouth in horror. That's what I was afraid of. King Theon torturing my poor uncle. "How?"

"He gave him back his sense of smell," he said.

I raised my eyebrows. "That is not what I was expecting to hear."

Grandfather frowned. "Cerius is being tortured by smell?"

"He is kept in the midst of cyclopes..." Alexios trailed off. "I got a whiff of one of them and almost hurled my dinner out. I cannot imagine how torturous it is to be surrounded my hundreds of them every single day."

I also remembered that cyclops's horrible stench. Back then I had thought uncle Cerius was very fortunate to have no sense of smell...

"We need to get him out of there," grandfather said.

"Believe me, I tried. It is impossible to penetrate though the group of cyclopes, and even if I had succeeded with that, the device's magic would have stopped me," Alexios said.

I sighed. "Uncle Cerius would have to bear with it until we find a way to set him free."

Alexios nodded. "It is all we can do now. Grandfather, I had also come here for another reason. Has anyone visited you in the last few days?"

Grandfather shook his head. "Other than Emilia, I do not believe anyone has. Why do you ask? Am I to expect a guest?"

"If he hasn't visited you, then he has not yet finished his search," Alexios said. "You would be his last stop before he went back to Kingdom Poseidon."

"Who? Sir Edgar?" I asked.

"Yes. I had come to ensure that he leaves Pesok. I don't want him to stay here longer than Athena had predicted. If I have to escort him out myself, I will."

Grandfather walked back to sit on his throne. "I am ready. Tell the guards to let him in when he arrives. I haven't seen Ed in a very long time. I wish to have a word with him. Reina! Enter please."

Reina opened the doors and walked in, bowing. "Yes, Your Majesty?"

"I will be having my afternoon meal with my grandchildren. Tell the other servants to bring everything here."

"Yes, Your Majesty." She bowed and walked out.

In a short moment, the servants set up a table beside the throne and filled it with the feast my grandfather had ordered. Alexios and I sat across from each other with grandfather seated comfortably on his throne.

As we ate, grandfather told me tales about his adventures with Alexios. From carpet riding on the sand to catching scorpions and making them fight, they've done it all. Alexios kept visiting Pesok to spend time with grandfather as a child to get away from his father, and grandfather was more than happy to host him here.

They had quite a strong bond. One would mistake them for real family with the way they were around each other. Like a real grandson and grandfather pair.

"Grandfather, you shouldn't eat that many chilli peppers, you know that. What will you say to the healer when he visits and finds you with abdominal pain again?" Alexios moved the plate of chilli peppers away from grandfather's reach.

The king of Pesok rolled his eyes and reached for a sliced cucumber instead. "I could have had two more. I know my limits," he grumbled.

"No, you do not," Alexios argued.

"Yes. I do."

"No."

"Emilia, could you push the peppers toward me. I cannot reach them myself. Alexios does not know what he is talking about." Grandfather pointed to the plate of chilli peppers beside me.

I shook my head and pulled them closer to my side. "I think it is better to stay on the safer side. I too do not wish for you to have stomach issues."

Grandfather threw his arms up, slapping his thighs as he dropped them. "Now I have two worrywarts with me. I give up." He looked at me. "Your mother also worried much too often. There is really no need. I am a perfectly healthy man! I could even father a child now if I wanted to!"

I choked on my tea and started coughing uncontrollably. "I don't think -" Cough. "You should."

"Why not? You can help raise you uncle or aunt. Wouldn't that be great?" he asked. Then he looked at the closed doors and called out, "Reina!"

Reina immediately walked in and bowed her head. "Yes, Your Majesty?"

"No." I widened my eyes and shook my head. "No, grandfather. Not her. She's not much older than I am! You cannot be serious."

"Please take these chilli peppers away from the table. I need them out of sight or else I will be tempted to eat them all," the king ordered.

"Yes, Your Majesty." Reina took the plates with her, bowed her head to us, and then left.

I looked at my grandfather, who had his lips pursed and his face was as red as the chilli peppers that were just taken away. Two seconds later, he exploded into laughter, Alexios joining in. They clutched their stomachs and leaned in toward each other in giggles.

I scowled. "Very amusing."

"It was." Grandfather wiped a tear away, his laughter dying down into a chuckle. "You should have seen your face, my child. I would give away all my precious treasures to see it again."

I sighed and picked up a roasted potato, shoving it in my mouth. "You two laugh exactly like the court ladies."

A guard suddenly walked in. He bowed. "Your Majesty, the royal councillor from Kingdom Poseidon is here."

Grandfather wiped his mouth and straightened his posture. "Let him in."

The guard bowed and opened the door. In walked in Sir Edgar. He had a wide smile on his face which faltered when he saw Alexios. "Your Highness." He bowed. "I was not expecting to see you here."

"I had an important matter to discuss with His Majesty," Alexios said. "What are you doing here, Sir Edgar? Did my father send you? I don't remember him mentioning anything about your travels to Kingdom Pesok."

Sir Edgar cleared his throat. "His Majesty King Theon sent me on a secret assignment. He had instructed me complete it as quietly as possible and I must remain unseen. I'm afraid if you inform him of seeing me here, I would fail in my duty. I ask you to please do me this favour, Your Highness." He bowed lowly. "I am only a loyal subject of His Majesty. I wish to serve him well."

"Very well. I will pretend I did not see you here." The crown prince of Kingdom Poseidon gave him a curt nod. "Proceed."

The councillor bowed once more and turned his attention to my grandfather. "Your Majesty, I must speak with you in private." He pointedly glanced between Alexios and I. If he recognized me, he did not show it on his face.

Alexios and I looked at grandfather questioningly. He tilted his head toward the door. "It is all right. Go."

We nodded and walked out of the throne room, leaving Sir Edgar alone with the king.

"He wouldn't do anything to grandfather, would he?" I chewed on my lip nervously.

"Don't worry," Alexios said. "He may look old and frail, but believe me when I say that he can kill anyone in minutes. And Sir Edgar knows that. He won't try anything."

That eased my worries and I leaned my back against the wall by the door, waiting for grandfather's meeting to be over. Alexios did the same, leaning beside me against the wall and tapping his foot.

A servant carrying a tall pile of books walked down the hallway, struggling to see the path in front of him. The books were stacked high over his head, shaking along with his thin arms.

"Let me help you with those." Alexios pushed off the wall and took more than half of the pile, allowing the short man to see where he was going and lightening the weight for him. Glancing at me, Alexios said, "I will be right back."

I nodded and watched them disappear around the corner. A few minutes later, Sir Edgar stormed out of the throne room, startling the guards and servants on the other side of the door. He was muttering something underneath his breath. Then he saw me.

"You must know! She must have told you!" He grabbed me by the neck and pushed me further against the wall. I struggled to get free of his hold, getting frustrated with my lack of strength. "Where is it? Where's the trident? Answer me!"

The guards rushed over and pulled him off me, throwing him down on the ground. I coughed and massaged my neck, watching as Sir Edgar was thrown out of the palace. Leaning against the wall, I tried to catch my breath. "He is crazed," I whispered.

I thought back to the times when I couldn't protect myself. First with Alexios when he dragged me out of the dungeons. Then with the two men hired by King Theon's concubines that left me to die halfway across Asterin. The mountain lions. And now Sir Edgar.

I saw Alexios reappear around the corner of the hallway. Fisting my hands by my sides, I walked determinedly toward him. "Teach me."

"Teach you what?" He frowned in confusion.

"You've trained Nora how to fight at Hecate's sanctuary, have you not?" I asked. I still remembered how the little girl unarmed him with ease.

"I taught all of them how to fight." He nodded. "They know how to handle any weapon and can also fight very well without them."

"I want to learn that too," I said. "Everything they know how to do."

"It took them years of training to master their skills. I have to leave Pesok in three days. You will not be able to learn everything in such a short amount of time."

"Then teach me how to defend myself. I am a fast learner. I only need some guidance." I rubbed my neck, where I felt a bruise coming on. "I need to learn how to defend myself. Will you teach me?" I looked up at his sea-blue eyes.

He held my gaze for a long moment before finally nodding. "Training starts tomorrow."

Chapter 16: Training

Alexios told me to meet him in the library for the first part of our training. He offered no further explanation, only to meet to him there in the morning.

I walked to the grand library that I've seen during the tour of the palace that Reina had been instructed by grandfather to provide for me. It was a beautiful place with carved and painted ceilings, colourful plush carpets, and redwood bookshelves filled with all kinds of books.

I found it odd that Alexios wanted to start training me in the library. I wanted to learn how to fight, not read.

"Are you certain that he said library, Your Highness? His Majesty has excellent training rooms for his guards in the palace. Perhaps you misheard?" Reina said, walking beside me and pushing a cart with a pitcher of water, and biscuits. Despite my protests, she had insisted on bringing it with us in case I got parched or hungry during training.

"I am certain I'd heard him right. He told me to meet him in the library." I nodded.

I saw Alexios leaning against a bookshelf when I walked in. Our eyes met. "You're late," he said.

I raised my eyebrows. "Good morning to you as well. And you never specified the time, so I cannot be late."

"Fair point." He shrugged. He then pushed off the bookshelf and started walking deeper into the room, beckoning me with his hand. "Follow me."

I frowned and followed Alexios as he weaved through the shelves and stopped to pick up a book or two from each one. "Take this." He gave me a pile of five thick books. "And these as well." Another two were added on top. I walked behind him with my arms shaking from the weight of them. "And this."

"Gods, not another one," I huffed and let him add another thick book to the pile. "Is this the first part of training? Am I to carry these books until my arms fall off?"

He took them from me. "No. You are to read them. They each describe the fundamental philosophies of fighting, written by the greatest generals of our time." He put the books down on a table by two chairs. Taking three of the books, he said, "These are for me."

"What will you be reading?" I asked.

"I need to relearn teaching philosophies. It has been years since I trained someone with zero fighting skills." Alexios sat down in one of the chairs and opened his first book.

We read beside each other in silence. The books he had given me to read completely pulled me in, and I did not take a break until I read them all.

Closing my last book, I said, "Now can we start the real training?"

"Your Highness, you should eat something first. You have been refusing to lift your eyes off those books for hours." Reina, who had sat across from Alexios and I with a book of her own, offered me a plate of biscuits. When I took one, she offered them to the prince. "Your Highness, some biscuits?"

"Thank you." Alexios took the plate.

Swallowing my first bite, I looked around the library. "Grandfather did well with this place."

"He did. When I first came here, it was my favourite place in the palace. Still is. Kingdom Poseidon has a grand library in the castle as well, but it could only be used by royals and nobles. Unlike this one," Alexios said.

I turned my head to look at him. "Is it still so? The library in Poseidon."

He sighed. "I'm afraid it is. I had tried to change it. Follow in grandfather's footsteps. But when I went behind my father's back and allowed servants to use the royal library, he did not take it lightly."

"Was that the reason for your punishment?" I asked. "When you were punished to work as a guard."

He nodded. "At first he wanted to punish me by a hundred whips on my back, but when I mentioned that he allowed Rose to use the royal library even though she was a servant, he settled on guard duty."

"You've seen -" I paused to take a breath before I said her name. "You've seen Rose in the library?"

"Many times. I even helped her choose the books," Alexios said. "She had told me that she had a daughter and she took those books for her to read."

"A daughter..." I whispered. She had often told me that I was like a daughter to her, but it was all a lie. And it still hurt to know that. Had she ever thought of me as more than a future bride of her king? More than an assignment?

"All right." Alexios stood from his chair, gave the empty plate from the biscuits to Reina, and picked up all the books from the table beside us. "Let's put these back and go to the training rooms to begin your first real lesson."

~~~

"Let's start with a simple exercise. I want to see how your reflexes work. Then I will teach you techniques." Alexios came up to me with a long scarf and tied it around my waist. "This." He pulled at the scarf. "Imagine that this is your most precious possession, and I will try to take it from you. You must protect it at all costs and block my attacks. Any questions?" Alexios said.

I shook my head and lifted my arms up in front of me. "I'm ready."

"Good." One corner of his mouth lifted into a small smile.

He slowly approached me, then very suddenly shot his hand out to grab at the scarf. I took a step back just in time and he missed it by a hair.

Alexios met my eyes. "Not bad."

He circled around me and attacked me from the back, this time getting hold of the scarf. As soon as I felt his hand, I twisted, hooked my leg around one of his and pulled while twisting his hand off the scarf. It all happened in lighting speed.

Alexios fell on the ground with wide eyes. He pushed off with his hands and jumped to stand. "Where did you learn how to do that?"

"One of the books had illustrations of movements," I said.
~~~

"You mastered that move by simply looking at a picture?" he asked in bewilderment.

I shrugged and nodded. "Is that odd? I always learn better when I see it with my eyes first."

"What else can you do?"

I demonstrated all the movements exactly as I'd seen them in the book. Alexios watched with amazement, ducking once or twice when my fist came too close to his face as I moved.

"You might learn everything you wanted to know after all," he mused. "I had never trained anyone quite like you."

"Is that...a good thing?" I raised one brow.

"We will see." He approached me and began to untie the scarf around my waist. As he worked on that, he said, "Let us take a break and join grandfather for an afternoon meal. I will come up with a new approach for you and we can continue the training soon after."

I nodded. "All right. Let us eat first." When he continued to struggle to untie the knot he had made himself with the scarf, I sighed. "I can do it myself."

I put my hands on top of his to move them away. He didn't budge. "No, I can do it. I tied it. It is my fault that it is --"

"Just move your hands. I can untie it or else we will be here for hours."

"Emilia, I have this. Please stop moving." He looked at me sternly.

I rolled my eyes and released his hands. "All right."

A few minutes later, Alexios gave up. "I don't know how I tied it this tightly."

"Will you let me try now?" I asked.

He nodded and moved away, motioning to the knot. "You won't be able to do it. We might need to have it cut."

I observed the knot and then untied it within seconds. "Here you go." I placed the scarf in Alexios's hand, then walked past him to get to the door. "Now let us join grandfather."

After having an afternoon meal with grandfather, Alexios and I were back in the training room. This time he brought swords, bows and arrows, and a mace. "This is for later," he said. "First we will spar without weapons. There are a few movements that I haven't seen you demonstrate earlier. Let's start with learning those now. Reina, you may enter."

Reina walked into the training room dressed in long pants and a long sleeved shirt similar to mine. She bowed to us.

"I will show you those movements with her. You must watch carefully and learn," Alexios said. I nodded and sat down on the ground, crossing my legs, ready to learn.

He went through simple techniques first and gradually moved on to more complex motions. Reina skillfully kept up with his instructions and sparred with him. I absorbed them all into my mind, ready to try them myself.

"Thank you, Reina. You may leave for now," Alexios said. Then it was time for me to spar with him. "Did you catch everything?"

I got up to stand. "I did."

"Good." He motioned for me to approach and attack first. I chose to start with a simple move. Taking a few steps forward, I tried to punch him right below the ribcage. He blocked it with his arm. "Not bad. What else do you remember?"

I went through the simple techniques with him. It all went well, until I decided to try one of the complex movements. The one that I failed to observe as well as I wished I had when Reina demonstrated it. But I thought I could do it.

I circled my arm around Alexios's neck and hooked one leg around his to kick him behind his knee. I was supposed to let go of his neck as I pushed him, but I missed the right moment and came crashing down to the ground along with him.

Alexios landed flat on his back and I fell on top of him. "You were supposed to let go," he said, breathing hard from all the sparring.

"I know," I said, out of breath as well. "I miscalculated."

"We will work on that move again."

"All right." All the physical training was catching up to my body, which was not used to this much strain. I felt very tired. Tired enough to forget about where I was and tired enough to let my head rest on Alexios's chest.

As I laid there, I heard his fast heartbeat. Must have been from all the sparring he had done today.

He let me rest on top of him, without saying a word. As I caught my breath, my heartbeat slowed down, now beating at its resting speed. I couldn't say the same for Alexios. His was still beating fast.

I lifted my head and looked down at him with a concerned frown. "Are you all right?" I put my hand on his chest, right over his heart. "Your heartbeat isn't slowing down."

He cleared his throat and gently moved me to sit on the padded floor before sitting up himself. "I..." He cleared his throat again. "I must be strained from the training."

I stood up and walked over to a cart in the corner of the room. Picking up a pitcher of water, I poured a glass for myself and Alexios. I walked back to him and extended one glass of water. "Here. This might help."

"Thank you." He took it from my hand and gulped down everything in seconds.

"Better?"

"Better." He nodded. I leaned down to put my ear to his chest to listen for a minute. It was slower than before, but started to pick up again. Alexios took my glass of water. "I need another one."

I frowned and sat back on the heels of my feet. "You should visit the healer later. It doesn't sound right, your heartbeat."

He shook his head and got up. "I am all right, Emilia." After putting the empty glasses back on the cart in the corner, he came back. "Do you think you can continue training for longer or do you wish to rest for the rest of the day and continue tomorrow?"

Though my body was exhausted, I wanted to learn as much as I could before Alexios had to leave Pesok. I didn't want to waste any time. "Let's continue now."

~~~

Alexios stayed in Pesok for longer than he had planned to. After a week of training with him, I could now wield a sword and a mace, and fight in hand to hand combat. I had learned everything with lighting speed. Today I was to learn how to use a bow and arrow.
~~~

"As usual, watch me first as I demonstrate and then you will try, and I will adjust your technique." Alexios went to stand in front of a target with his bow and arrow, behind the mark on the ground. He took his stance, straightened his back, and drew the arrow, aiming it. The arrow went flying when he let go, piercing the very middle circle of the target.

"Could you do that again? I want to see it from the other side," I said, walking around him.

"Watch carefully," he said, repeating his action from earlier. This time I could see the positioning of his hands better. The arrow flew at the target's centre and split the first arrow in half, right down the middle. "Your turn."

Alexios handed me the bow and I picked up an arrow from a tube-shaped case that was filled with dozens of them. I drew my arrow and let it fly. It landed at the bottom of the target, near its edge. I sighed and lowered the bow. "What did I do wrong?"

"Your stance. You need to adjust your angle." Alexios approached me and moved my legs in their proper place. "Straighten your back some more." He pushed at the spot between my shoulder blades. "Now try again."

I fired another arrow and this time it landed farther from the edge, but it was still not close enough to the centre as I'd hoped it would be.

"You're bending your arm when you let go. Keep it straight," Alexios said, pointing at my elbow. I adjusted it. "And your hand should be slightly higher on the bow. Yes, that's good. Wait, no, don't move it more. It's too high now."

He came to stand behind me. "Pick up an arrow and draw it slowly." I did as he told me. He reached around me with his arms and guided my left hand to the right spot on the bow. With his other hand he adjusted my position on the bowstring.

I could feel his breath on my neck, tickling my skin. Turning my head to tell him that he could move away now, I was met with his blue eyes. They were beautifully framed by long and dark eyelashes. As if in a trance, I held his gaze before my eyes slowly traveled down to his lips. Time seemed to be standing still around us as we stood close to each other.

A loud sound of shattering ceramic startled me. Beside a broken pitcher of water laid an arrow. I had let go of the bowstring without even noticing the slip.

Alexios stepped away from me and went to pick it up. Just then grandfather walked into the training room. "How is my granddaughter doing? Ready to take on this old man in a fight?"

I put away my bow and put my fists up. "Anytime, grandfather."

He chuckled. "Very well. I needed a bit of exercise today." He titled his head from one side to another, stretching his neck while at the same time cracking his knuckles. Untying the spacious robe that I always saw him wearing, he shrugged it off. Then he slipped off his shoes, going barefoot on the padded floor.

I had been told that grandfather was one of the greatest fighters in Asterin, but I had never imagined that he would have even more muscle than Alexios. That royal robe hid his true form.

"On second thought," I dropped my fists, "I do not think that I am ready to take you on just yet."

"You will be when I teach you how to use your full powers," grandfather said. "I had been waiting until you became more skilled in combat, and Alexios tells me that you have surpassed his expectations. You are ready now -- to learn how to control the gifts passed on to you by your father."

"And you know what they are?" I frowned.

"You know what they are. You simply do not know that you know. But I will help you discover them."

My frown deepened.

"As you know, Goddess Psamathe had created Kingdom Pesok, and I, as one of her creations possess some of her gifts."

He moved closer to the sandbags that laid in one corner of the room. Opening one of them, he stepped back to stand in front of me. "In combat, combining God given gifts with my human skills make me a dangerous opponent. And it is very important to train both of those abilities before using them together, for your own safety. I will demonstrate something now."

Grandfather lifted his hand and suddenly sand flew in front of my face and I couldn't see anything. A split second later, I saw a fist cut through the dust and fly past my head, a hair away from my right ear. If it had hit me in the face, I would have been laying on the ground, unconscious.

Retracting his fist, grandfather moved the sand back into the open sandbag by a simple flick of his hand.

I gaped at him. "That was incredible! How do you control the sand?"

"It comes naturally. I feel the connection with sand and use it to make it follow my command. Helios is the God of the Sun. You must have a connection with it. Perhaps you haven't noticed it before, but it is there. Close your eyes and try to find that connection."

I closed my eyes and tried to feel something. Anything. With my eyes still closed, I said, "Grandfather, I cannot find it."

"Yes. You can. Think of what you associate the sun with. What makes you think of it? How does it feel to be under its light? Feel it and connect," he said.

I nodded with my eyes closed and took a deep breath. Then I thought about standing under the light of the sun. It was bright -- and warm. Very warm. I imagined what it would feel like to be close to it. I felt its burning hot flames all around me, but it didn't burn my skin. It felt comforting, like an embrace.

I opened my eyes when I smelled something burning. Looking down at the sleeve of my shirt, I saw fire. It was climbing up my arm, fast. Panicked, I slapped at my sleeve to extinguish it.

Alexios ran up to me and ripped off the sleeve of my shirt. "Are you burned?" He checked the skin of my arm. It was completely unharmed.

"The fire only ate away at the fabric," I said. "I didn't feel anything on my skin."

"Are you certain?" he asked.

I nodded. "I am."

He sighed in relief and let go of my arm. "Grandfather, she isn't ready for this yet. What if she had --"

Loud snoring interrupted him. We turned to look at grandfather, sitting cross-legged on the floor and sleeping with his eyes open.

"I can't believe he fell asleep in this moment." Alexios shook his head.

I chuckled and shook my head as well. Then I looked at my arm, where the fire had started not too long ago. It came when I made a connection with the sun. It ignited after I felt its warmth. Its energy. Its hot flames.

I had an ability to create fire.

Chapter 17: A Letter

It was too hot in my chambers. It felt as if the fireplace in the room was burning wood. I frowned in my sleep and pushed my silk covers off my body, but it was still too warm. Opening my eyes, I blinked to adjust to the light. Then I smelled something burning.

My bed. My bed was on fire.

I widened my eyes and jumped off with a yelp, falling onto the floor and backing away from the blackened wooden bed.

Nephos stuck his big head in through my open window and looked at me.

"Did you do that?" I asked.

He shook his head and pointedly stared at me.

"Did I do that?"

He nodded.

I stood and stared at the burning bed. It looked as if it's been on fire for a long time. And I've been sleeping on it without noticing anything.

"How do I stop the fire? I don't want it to burn down the rest of the room," I said.

Nephos chirped and opened his mouth. Then he inhaled deeply, and the flames started to travel from my bed right into his dragon throat. In seconds, the fire was gone.

I exhaled in relief. "Thank you, Nephos."

He nodded in acknowledgment, then pulled his head out from my window and flew away.

"Emilia, I'm going back to Poseidon toda-- Oh Gods." Alexios barged into my room and quickly covered his eyes. He turned around to face the door, his back to me. "What...What happened to your clothes?"

Now that the fire was gone, it was less hot in my chambers and I could feel the morning breeze on my skin. On too many parts of my skin. I looked down at myself and screeched.

The fire ate my clothes.

Strips of fabric hung on my body and left most of it bare. I rushed to my closet and hurriedly put on the first thing my hands could grab. "I'm covered now."

Alexios slowly turned back around, dropping his hand from his eyes.

I pointed to my bed. "I set it on fire in my sleep. It must've caught on my clothes as well. Which is why the..." I looked down at myself. Then I snapped my head up and glared at him. "You should have knocked before entering."

"I did knock. You must have not heard me."

"Or your knocks must have been too quiet," I said, crossing my arms.

"Or you could simply be deaf."

I sighed. "Why do I feel like we've had this conversation before?"

"Because we did. When you barged into my chambers without knocking."

"I did knock!" I argued. I pointed to the door. "Leave please. Before I set you on fire."

"You don't even know how to control your powers." He crossed his arms and leaned against the door. "I am not afraid."

I scowled. Lifting my hand, I thought of the sun's powers traveling to my fingertips. My fingers started to feel warm, then hot, and then fire ignited in my hand. "I know how to throw it," I lied.

"I am leaving." The door closed behind Alexios. I smiled.

"How do I extinguish it now?" I whispered to myself, panicking and shaking the fire off my hand. But it didn't work. Remembering what Nephos did earlier, I opened my mouth, ready to inhale it.

Don't!

I closed my mouth and looked out the window, up at the sky. "What do I do then?"

Return it in.

Father's voice came out fainter every time he spoke to me, as if he was losing his voice, losing the ability to speak to my mind. It was very clear the first time I had heard him. But now, his last three words sounded fainter than a whisper.

"Return it in," I repeated with a frown. "What does that mean?"

There was no answer this time.

"Return it in," I said again, thinking over its meaning. Return it into my hand perhaps?

Closing my eyes, I imagined the flames going back into my skin, seeping in through my pores. When I opened my eyes, the flame had disappeared.

A knock came on my door. "Your Highness, breakfast will be served soon."

"I will be right out, Reina!" I called out and hurried to get ready for breakfast.

~~~

"Grandfather," I said, moving the plate of chilli peppers away from the old man, "you should stop eating them."

"She's right. This is becoming a problem, grandfather. Perhaps I should order the servants to ban those from the palace," Alexios said.

"Worrywarts," grandfather grumbled, rolling his eyes. "Alexios, my orders have a lot more power over yours."

"And mine?" I asked.

"Yours will hold more power when you inherit the kingdom. Right now I am king and I decide what is brought into the palace. And I," grandfather took the plate, "decide when to stop eating my favourite peppers."

"Have it your way," I said, watching him as he ate his peppers with a satisfied smile.

Reina entered the dining room, holding a sealed envelope in her hand. She bowed. "Your Highness, a letter came for you." She gave it to me.

I frowned and opened the blue seal, shaking out the white paper from inside the envelope. As I read it, my eyes widened. I stood up, continuing to read it until the end. "It can't be," I whispered.
~~~

"What does it say?" Alexios asked.

"He found my mother," I said. "He-he knows where she is."

"Who?" Grandfather asked and took the letter from me.

"Sir Edgar. He know that she is in Hecate's sanctuary. He knows where it is. Oh Gods, what if he captured her? What if she is being tortured for the sake of that bloody trident --"

"Emilia, breathe." Alexios stood up and put his hands on my shoulders. I looked into his eyes, my panicked breathing slowing down. "Good. Now think. This could be a trap to lure you in. How could he possibly enter Hecate's sanctuary without Hecate's permission? It is guarded by magic. No one can enter without her permission. The forest around it is a gate and it is protected."

"But how did he know about it in the first place? He knows she is there. How?" I asked.

He frowned. "I don't know."

"I need to go there. I need to make sure that she is all right." I started to walk toward the door.

Alexios caught my arm. "You could be walking into a trap."

"If he cannot enter the sanctuary, he will not be there," I said.

"The cliff. The cliff outside of the forest gate is not protected. He could be waiting there."

"Then I will fight him off. I know how to do it now. I am not helpless anymore. I need to ensure my mother's safety, so I am going, trap or not," I said firmly.

"Then I am going with you," he said.

Grandfather crumpled up Sir Edgar's letter. "That bastard. He has meddled too much with my family. I will not let it go. I am going with you too. Where is this sanctuary you speak of? Near Poseidon, I suppose? My stallions can get us there is less than a week."

"I know an even faster way," I said. "You might not like it."

"I will do anything to protect my daughter. Gods know I haven't done so in the past. If you have a faster way, show us," grandfather responded.

The three of us walked out of the palace after arming ourselves with swords. I lead the way, searching for Nephos. When I saw an impossibly large hill of sand, I approached it. "This is it."

Alexios and grandfather frowned, exchanging a look of confusion.

"If you mean to say that you want me to use sand to transport us, I'm afraid I cannot do it. My powers are limited as I am not a direct descendant of my Goddess." Grandfather scratched his head.

"Please do not be frightened," I told the two of them. Then I turned to Nephos. "Nephos, I need you to fly us somewhere."

White scales started to appear and my father's dragon showed himself.

"Nephos!" grandfather cooed, approaching the giant and scratching his neck. "It's been a long time since I've seen you. I believe the last time was the day you brought Lily home on your back and I nearly joined Helea in the afterlife from all the fear."

The white dragon purred and fell on his back, enjoying the scratches.

I raised my eyebrows in surprise. "You've met him?"

"He's Helios's dragon." Grandfather nodded. "Your mother adored him. I grew to like him too, though after the initial shock of seeing him."

"He can get us to the cliff in no time," Alexios said, regarding the giant with admiration.

After a moment of bonding between my grandfather and Nephos, we all climbed onto the dragon's back. I sat on the base of his neck, Alexios and grandfather behind me.

We flew up into the clouds. Nephos glided smoothly through the sky, flying over the kingdom of Pesok, then what looked to be Kingdom Soleil. It looked beautiful from above. I wished that I could see it for myself one day.

Sooner than I expected, the dragon entered Kingdom Poseidon's territory and flew us over it until we landed onto a familiar cliff near the sea. We'd reached our destination.

I came down first, sliding down Nephos's neck, over his head, and then jumping off from his nose into the green grass below. When Alexios and grandfather climbed off the white dragon, Nephos chirped and flew away.

"He left in a rush. Looks like he has something to take care of." Grandfather watched Nephos's retreating silhouette with one hand over his eyes, shielding them from the sun.

I looked around the vast cliff for any sign of Sir Edgar. He was nowhere in sight. I sighed in relief, but that relief came too early. A moment later the man himself came out from behind a tree, holding a knife to my mother's throat. A young girl stepped out from behind Sir Edgar with a smile on her face.

Agatha.

"Emilia," mother said, "she tricked me into coming out here."

"Agatha?" Alexios frowned. "Why did you do that?"

Her smile vanished upon seeing her prince. She looked away, unable to meet his eyes, and didn't offer a word of explanation.

"She's my precious little daughter." Sir Edgar regarded Agatha with pride. "I had thought she was a useless little thing, but that wasn't the case at all. No. I learned that she is part of this special school that I cannot enter. And to my absolute surprise, Lily is one her teachers."

"Let her go," I told Sir Edgar, drawing my sword. "She knows nothing of the trident. Let her go."

"Then perhaps you know. Has your dead uncle told you where he hid it?" he asked.

"He did. He told me everything about it," I lied. "But I will not tell you where it is unless you let go of my mother."

He lowered the knife. "You know, you came here much earlier that I'd expected. Your mother had just come out from the forest not too long ago. I was planning on taking her to the castle, but then I saw you. It would be a shame to let her go now, don't you think? Right when I finally found her again. And how do I know that you're not lying about the trident?"

Suddenly, Sir Edgar was on the ground and grandfather was throwing fists onto his face. "You bastard!" he snarled. "Don't you dare touch my family."

Agatha drew her sword and brought it down toward my grandfather. I blocked it with my own, the two metal blades clashing loudly.

She glared at me. "Pretty sword. But can you wield it well? You cannot possibly take me on, dungeon girl."

"I beg to differ, you traitor," I hissed, retracting my sword and immediately striking at her.

She blocked it and smiled. "Is that all you've got? That was a weak attempt. I have years of training with my sword. I even named it. That's how long we've been together. But it seems like you've only learned how to hold yours yesterday." She laughed. "I am going to enjoy taking you down."

I rolled my eyes. "You talk too much."

Agatha growled and attacked me. Soon our swords were clashing against each other. When she realized that I handled it much better than she'd thought, she started to curse.

"Not very pretty words for a girl your age," I taunted, jumping over the blade that came slashing at my shins.

"I am old enough to say them!" she screamed, slicing her sword through the air and almost cutting my stomach open, but I didn't let her. I was grateful for all the training I've received. My reflexes became even better with practice.

Agatha tried to swing her sword from behind me. Remembering how I disarmed Alexios during one of our sword fighting lessons, I repeated the same sequence of movements. Rolling back and under the blade, I spun the hilt into my own hand. Then I pointed two swords at her neck.

I quickly glanced to my side. Sir Edgar managed to break free from grandfather's hold, but was soon engaged in a fight with Alexios when the prince stepped in to shield grandfather from his attacks.

My mother was watching everything in horror, shaking with fear.

"Grandfather!" I called out. "Take mother into the forest. Hecate should allow you to pass with her into the sanctuary. Take mother away from here. Please."

Grandfather ran over to my mother and did as I told him to. He guided her into the forest by her shoulders and they soon disappeared behind the shield of tall trees.

Agatha used my moment of distraction to her advantage. She ducked under the blades and swept one of her legs against both of mine, making my knees give in. I stumbled and fell on my side with a huff, dropping the swords, but before she could get her hands on them, I kicked them away and jumped to stand.

She cracked her knuckles, her smile returning. Taking a fighting stance with raised fists, she said, "You will wish that you let me use my sword. Hand to hand combat is my specialty."

"Is that so?" I blew a strand of hair from my face and dug the heel of my back leg into the ground, ready to lunge at her at any second. "Let's see how good you are."

With a loud battle cry, Agatha flew at me with full force. One fist hit my jaw and another right below my ribcage. I gasped for air and struggled to find my breath.

She laughed as she watched me, tilting her head to one side. "Does that prove my abilities to you, dungeon girl? Would you like to call on your ghost friends to protect you now?"

When I finally recovered, I ground my teeth in anger. I could light her on fire and she didn't even know it. People from Soleil were only blessed with the gift of Sight. She must have thought that my only God given power was to see dead souls and their memories. "You truly underestimate me."

"But do I really?" She raised one dubious eyebrow. Beckoning me with her index finger, she said, "Show me a real fight."

I lunged at her, twisting out of every hold she tried on me and blocking every punch. We had traveled closer to the edge of the cliff. I could hear the strong waves crashing against rocks at the bottom.

When she tried to get a hold of my collar, I grabbed and twisted her wrist behind her back. Then I kicked the backs of her knees and brought her face down into the ground, holding her body down by digging my knee into her back.

"Is this real enough for you?" I panted. Sweat dripped down my forehead.

Agatha screamed in frustration, thrashing her body but failing to get out of my hold. Soon she gave up, relaxing her limbs and laying on her stomach with one cheek on the ground.

I let out a long sigh and sat down on top of her. I knew that if I let her go, she would try to attack me again.

"You're heavier than you look," she grumbled.

Suddenly Sir Edgar landed beside us with a cry of pain, and Alexios stood over him with his sword pointed at his neck.

Sir Edgar coughed. "You are making a big mistake, Your Highness. You do not want me as your enemy. I ask you to reconsider whose side you are on. I am one of your subjects and I only have your interest at heart. And His Majesty's."

"Why are you looking for the trident? What makes you think that the dead king of Typhon knew where it was?" Alexios demanded. "Speak. And do not leave anything out."

"I want to gift it to His Majesty once I find it," he said. We all knew that it was a lie. "As for King Cerius... He was the last person to enter the Twin Volcanoes, after his mother. The spirit of God Typhon only recognizes his kin. Only they can enter. I believed that Poseidon had his trident hidden there before he died. All the ancient scrolls I'd read led me to the Twin Volcanoes. I was certain it was there.

"I'd made an agreement with King Cerius. He was to go in and bring out the trident. I'd told him that I simply wanted to see it. That I was fascinated by its history. But when he came out with a long wooden box, he had himself surrounded by guards and did not let me get close to him. Then he traveled outside Kingdom Typhon that same day. When he returned and the Twin Volcanoes erupted and the kingdom was in chaos, I took my revenge on him."

"You could still be mistaken. What makes you think that it was Poseidon's trident inside that wooden box?" Alexios asked.

"What else could it be?" Sir Edgar exclaimed. "It was the trident! And he hid it somewhere! That bloody fire killed everyone who could have known. But perhaps he did tell someone in the afterlife..." He looked at me.

Something shiny glinted in his hand. It blinded me for a moment, the sunlight reflecting from its metallic surface. Then I saw it. It was a knife.

Before I could warn Alexios, Sir Edgar thrust it into his abdomen.

"Alexios!" Agatha and I screamed.

The prince looked down at the knife in his flesh, blood spilling from the wound and staining his clothes scarlet red. Sir Edgar grabbed the hilt of the knife and pulled it out, making even more blood rush out, like a river.

When Sir Edgar stood up and tried to lunge at me with the bloody knife, Alexios grabbed him by the neck to hold him back while one of his hands was pressed firmly against his open wound.

I got off of Agatha and disarmed Sir Edgar, throwing the knife into the sea below. Alexios then twisted and threw him over the cliff, dropping to the ground as soon as he let him go. His face was getting paler with every second, with every drop of blood lost.

I took his face into my shaking hands. "We need to stop the bleeding." Taking off the long scarf around my neck, I folded it. "It will be all right," my voice trembled as I tied the scarf around his abdomen. "We will stop the bleeding and go into the sanctuary. There is an infirmary there, you know. You will be all right. You will--"

Sir Edgar's hand came up from the side of the cliff and grabbed Alexios's ankle. It all happened too fast. One minute he was right in front of me, and the next minute he was falling from the cliff, into the blue sea along with Sir Edgar.

"No!" Agatha sobbed. She crawled to the edge of the cliff and looked down at the angry waves that swallowed the prince and her father. "Alexios, no!"

I watched the waters in hopes of seeing Alexios come up to the surface. I watched for a long time, until the sun started to set, listening to Agatha's pained sobs beside me.

He never resurfaced.

Chapter 18: The Search

When the sun finally set, it was dark on the cliff. And the sea was too dark to be seen. Agatha hadn't left my side. Her crying had stopped and now she quietly mourned the loss of her prince. I had a feeling that he had meant much more to her than her own father ever did.

Medusa came out of the sanctuary many times to bring me inside. This time she was more adamant about my return. "I was planning to threaten to turn you into stone if you refused to come with me again, but you already look like a statue sitting here on the edge of the cliff for hours. Emilia. It is too dark to see now, even if he did resurface. Are you not tired? Not hungry? Your family is worried about you."

"And you, Agatha. I'm afraid you cannot enter the sanctuary as you have betrayed Hecate's trust. And mine as well. But for the sake of our years together, I will have Pegasus take you home. Now up, up, up!" She slapped our shoulders and pulled us up to stand. "Goodness, you girls are heavy," she huffed. "If you put on any more muscle, you could crush people with your weight."

"You could simply be getting old, Medusa," Agatha mumbled half-heartedly.

Medusa's back cracked as she straightened it to stand up. "You are not wrong. Bloody Poseidon," she suddenly cursed. "I wasted all my best years with him. I wish he came back to life so I could kill him myself."

Thunder erupted in the sky.

"Now you hear me, Zeus?" Medusa looked up. "After all these years and all the insults I've thrown at your brother, that was the one that got you angry? I could care less! Your thunders don't scare me."

The sky slowly cleared up.

"Let's go inside, Emilia," she said, rolling her eyes at the sky.

As Medusa and I walked through the forest, I suddenly remembered the book that she stole from the Fates. Perhaps it could tell me if Alexios was alive. "Medusa, could I see that book in the library? The black one with silver threads?"

She pursed her lips. "I know what you want to ask it, but I cannot promise you that it would give you the answer you are hoping for. It might not even give you an answer at all."

"I would still like to try. If it could just tell me--"

"What if it tells you that he is dead? People of Poseidon do have an ability to connect with water, but it would be of little help to him. They cannot use it to heal. That power belongs to Poseidon himself. And from what you've told me, Alexios had a knife wound..."

"I would like to ask the book," I said. "I have to know. We need to find him even if he is..." I swallowed, whispering the next word, "dead."

"I suppose we cannot leave him in the sea. He would need a proper burial." Medusa sighed, then nodded. "All right. Let's go see the book."

Before we entered the library, Medusa took us to a storage room with cleaning supplies. She pointed to a duster on one of the shelves. "Take that one with you. I will take the broom. If you want to get a proper answer out of that book, we need to bribe it."

Armed with a broom and a duster, we stopped by the door that led to the room where the book of the Fates was kept. Medusa took out a key and opened the lock.

"Hello old friend," she said cheerfully. "As promised, I came to clean up here." She raised the broom in her hand, then started to sweep the floors, motioning for me to start dusting the leather cover of the book.

I dusted it off, paying close attention to the small crystal that was embedded on the iris part of the eye that was carved into it. There was a spider web over it and the book was covered in dust, which made me wonder if Medusa had even stepped foot in this room after the last time I was here.

When we finished cleaning, I stepped back from the book. "Could you tell me if Alexios is alive?"

It opened and started to flip through its pages. As if a wind was blowing through them, they all turned one after another. Then it stopped.

Medusa and I slowly approached it and peaked at the open page, watching as black ink started to draw curved lines on the paper. It started with a curved vertical line which connected to another line until it began to form letters. My heart rate picked up in anticipation as each letter slowly appeared.

Once the sentence was complete, my eyes filled with tears and I stepped away from the book.

Medusa pursed her lips. "I suppose I was wrong."

"He is alive," I whispered, wiping my eyes. I looked at Medusa and smiled. "He is alive."

She smiled back. "It appears he is."

Approaching the book once again, I said, "Where is he now?"

This time the book showed me only one word: sea.

"It seems that our bribing has worked. It has never answered this fast before. And with words no less," Medusa said with surprise. She smiled at the book. "I have a question too. Will Pegasus find love?"

The book slammed shut.

"Fine. Don't answer then."

Her snakes hissed at the book as we walked out of the room.

"Alexios is still in the sea. I need to find him," I said as Medusa locked the door.

She turned around and shook her head, putting the silver key in her pocket. "It is much too dark now to see anything. You will not find him. We will begin the search tomorrow morning, as soon as the sun rises. The girls will come then too. We will have more people."

We started to walk out of the library, into a hallway.

"But what if it is too late then? He might be alive now, but what if something happens to him while he's there? We know nothing of his condition. He could be slowly bleeding to death as we speak. I will not sleep knowing that he is out there," I said.

"Emilia." Medusa put one hand on my shoulder. "He has fallen into the sea hours and hours ago. It is a miracle that he is still living. It must mean that he has found a way to survive. That he hasn't drowned. You will only be wasting your strengths if you go out there now. How are you planning to search the dark sea?"

"I..." Nephos was gone. Pegasus had also left with Agatha. There were no boats here that I could use, and the sea was simply too vast for me to search through by myself. The strong waves could have taken Alexios anywhere. "I don't know."

"Have faith in Alexios." Grandfather stepped out of one of the doors in the hallway. "He is a strong boy. A survivor. I know that because I've seen him survive worse situations. He always finds a way. Do not worry, my child." He patted my head. "Now. Join your mother and I for dinner. She has missed you."

~~~

After having dinner with my family and telling my mother about everything that had happened to me since I've left here that day with Athena, I curled up beside her in a bed, in her warm embrace.

Although grandfather's words had offered me some comfort, I was still worried for Alexios. I couldn't fall asleep that night. Instead, I waited for the sun to come up.

When the first rays of morning light reached the windows of my mother's chambers, I got out of bed.

It was finally morning.

I turned my head to look back at my mother. She was still asleep. Seeing her sleep so peacefully, I didn't wish to wake her. Softly kissing her cheek, I quietly walked out her chambers to find Medusa.

She was outside by the statue of Hecate. When she saw me, she waved me over. "I am waiting for the girls. We always gather here first to pay our
~~~

respects to the goddess. Athena should be here in the late afternoon to teach her politics class. She doesn't know about Alexios... I couldn't send her a message as our ways of communication have been compromised ever since Agatha betrayed us. I couldn't risk sending her anything."

"Is Pegasus back?" I asked, looking around the sky to see if Nephos had perhaps also returned. There was no dragon in sight.

Medusa nodded. "He's waiting at the cliff. We also have new boats there. Your grandfather and I stayed up all night building them. Pegasus will lower the boats and everyone to the sea and then the search will begin." She sighed. "I wish Athena could come earlier. Her abilities to communicate with sea creatures would make finding Alexios much easier."

"She can do that?" I asked with wide eyes.

"Yes. She even understands Pegasus much better than I -- his own mother -- do, though he is no sea creature. But I suppose being Poseidon's son has something to do with it."

"Then I will bring her here," I said. "She would want to know what happened and we need her abilities. We cannot wait for the afternoon."

I looked at the statue of Hecate and the sharp point of her sword. It was a portal that led to Athena's chambers. I remembered how the two of us had used it to get to the castle. Looking at it now, it did not look as frightening.

Walking back a few steps from the statue, I started to run toward the sword.

"Wait! What if she isn't in the castle --" Medusa exclaimed, but it was too late. The portal had already pulled me in. Hecate's sanctuary disappeared and I found myself in Athena's chambers within seconds, stumbling a few steps when I got thrown into it.

I looked around the room and found no one here. But then suddenly I heard footsteps approach the door, accompanied by muffled voices. Panicked, I dove under the bed and a split second later, the door swung open.

"-- can you believe it, Your Highness? She should have been dead a week ago. And now she is miraculously in perfect health," Annabelle said, scoffing. "I need to find a new prince to marry... Oh! Could you put it in a good word for me with Prince Alexios, Your Highness? He might be younger than I am, but I don't believe that age should be of concern. With his handsome face and my beautiful and delicate features, our children would look magnificent."

I squeezed my hands into fists.

Athena sighed. "Annabelle, I am very tired. I haven't slept well last night. Could we continue our conversation some other time?"

"Of course, Your Highness! We can continue tomorrow. Rest well, my future sister in law!" I heard the door open and close, which meant that Annabelle was gone and Athena was the only other person here with me.

"Do not," I crawled out from under her bed, "put in any good words for her."

Athena yelped and kicked me in the head. Then she snaked her arm around my neck and lifted my face up. "Who are you and why -- Oh Gods, Emilia!" She let go of me and helped me stand up.

I cradled my head, groaning in pain. "That was a hard kick."

Then I heard a noise by the door and frowned. It sounded as if someone was standing there.

Athena suddenly lunged at me with open arms, embracing me tightly. "I'm so happy that you're alive. I was so worried. When the concubines told me that you ran away, I knew something was wrong. They seemed much too pleased with themselves. Alexios and I looked for you everywhere, but couldn't find you. I started thinking the worst." She squeezed me tighter. "And I apologize for kicking your head... I didn't know it was you. Please do not crawl out of my bed like that anymore."

I returned her embrace with a smile, forgetting about the odd noise by the door. "I will not do that again." Then I remembered why I was here and my smile disappeared. "Athena," I stepped out of her arms and met her blue eyes. They looked so much like her brother's. "I came here to tell you something."

She frowned. "Doesn't sound like it is something good."

I told her everything that happened at the cliff outside of Hecate's sanctuary. When I mentioned Alexios's knife wound and his fall into the sea, Athena dropped down to sit on her bed, losing the ability to use her legs to keep herself standing. "But the book from the Fates told me that he is still alive. He's somewhere in the sea and we are all going on a search to find him. Medusa told me that you can communicate with sea creatures and --"

Athena stood up, regaining her strength. "Yes! We will definitely find him with their help." She took my hand and pulled me in the direction of her closet. "Let's go. Alexios is strong and capable of surviving on his own, but our help wouldn't hurt."

She opened the closet doors and pulled me inside it with her. The portal must have been there, because in a blink of an eye, we were standing amongst a group of girls with Medusa, my mother, and my grandfather with them.

"Now we have everyone," Medusa said. "To the cliff!"

When we made it to the cliff where the boats and Pegasus were waiting, a dark shadow flew over us. I looked up and saw a white dragon. He landed beside Pegasus, pushing him playfully with one paw.

Everyone except myself, my mother and grandfather stood as still as statues, gaping at the giant that stood before them.

"A dra-dra-dragon!" one of the girls squeaked and hid behind Medusa.

Medusa patted the girl's head distractedly, but all of her attention was on Nephos.

Nephos dipped his head down and licked my face. When he saw my mother, he chirped happily, giving her face a smear of dragon saliva with his tongue as well.

"Where have you been?" I asked, wiping my face.

The white dragon motioned to the sky.

"Wait a minute. Is he harmless?" Athena asked me. I nodded. "Are you certain? He wouldn't eat Pegasus if he gets hungry, would he?"

Medusa screeched and ran over toward her son, opening her arms and legs wide in a protective stance and looking up at Nephos. "Don't you dare."

Nephos tilted his head to one side, looking at her with curiosity.

"I promise that he won't ever do such a thing," mother said. "He is not a mindless killer." She turned to the girls. "Girls, do not be afraid. He is a good dragon."

Nephos purred and rubbed his head against mother's arm.

Everyone's expressions turned from fear to curiosity, and some even approached the giant to stroke his scales. Medusa relaxed and leaned against Pegasus, no longer watching Nephos with distaste.

Soon the girls were in the sea, rowing their boats with Medusa leading them. Mother and grandfather were flying on Nephos, and Athena and I were on Pegasus.

"I see dolphins! Pegasus, lower us there," Athena said, pointing to a group of dolphins nearby who were jumping out from water and diving back in with a splash.

As soon as we got close to them, they all approached us, whistling in their dolphin language and regarding Athena attentively. It looked as if they were waiting for her orders.

"I need your help. My brother is somewhere in the sea and I need you to help me find him. You know what he looks like, yes?" she said.

They whistled and nodded their heads.

"Tell everyone else," she added.

They nodded once more and dove into the water, disappearing under the sea.

Next we flew over to a family of blue whales and Athena asked them to help us as well. Then we stopped by a group of orcas, and then a group of sharks.

By the time we were finished, the entire sea was looking for Alexios while we searched for him above water and near all shores and caves. Sea creatures would come up to the surface to tell Athena what they found. It was nothing. No trace of him was in the sea thus far.

I began to worry. "Where could he be?"

Athena sighed. "I don't know. Even the dolphins couldn't find anything and they are very good at finding traces of people. The sharks only found a faint smell of blood, but it led them nowhere. We looked through all the shores and caves I could think of. It's as if he's disappeared."

All of a sudden, a single orca resurfaced and waited for us to approach it.

"That's strange. Where are all the other orcas? I don't ever see them travelling alone," Athena mused, but slowly approached it nonetheless. She listened to the creature and gasped. "She found him!"

"Where is he?" I asked, hope filling me.

Athena listened some more. "She said she will lead us to him. We only need to follow her."

The orca led the way, looking behind her to check that we were following. She took us around familiar caves that Athena and I have already been in, and she kept swimming farther and farther away from Hecate's sanctuary.

I frowned. "Don't you believe this is too far? I have a strange feeling."

"I have that feeling as well, but I also wonder if Alexios was perhaps pulled away by the waves. You did say that they were strong that day," Athena mused.

"That is a possibility," I said with a nod.

We followed the orca until we reached a rocky beach. "She says she saw him here," Athena translated the sea creature's words.

Pegasus landed on the beach and we jumped off him, looking around the rocky landscape. Alexios was nowhere in sight.

Then I saw someone's foot behind a pile of rocks and I pulled at Athena's sleeve, pointing to it. We carefully approached it. When we came around those rocks, the sight before me made me look away as soon as it met my eyes. It was the dead body of Sir Edgar.

Athena gagged and stumbled backwards. "My Gods, did the sharks have a go at him?"

"I don't know, but I certainly do not want to be near him any longer. I wish I could unsee that." I shivered, walking back to the other side of the rocks. "Perhaps it wasn't Alexios that the orca saw here, but him."

I heard a marching set of footsteps and looked up in the direction of the sound. Guards in blue uniforms were marching side by side along the path up ahead. Poseidon guards.

I ran over to Athena and pulled her back behind the pile of rocks where the dead body of Sir Edgar was. I had no other choice. It was the closest hiding spot on the beach. "Poseidon guards," I whispered when Athena gave me a questioning look. "We must be in Kingdom Poseidon now."

We peeked through the small holes in the rocks and watched as the guards marched by. When they were out of sight, we sighed and stood up, only to feel sharp points of metal against the backs of our necks.

"Do not move," someone ordered. "I found them!" he barked out, and the guards from earlier returned, marching toward us.

I gave Athena a side glance, meeting her eyes. She nodded once. "Now!" We ducked and twisted our bodies, disarming the guard behind us and catching him by surprise. I kicked him at the spot between his legs and Athena kneed him in the head when he doubled over in pain. Then we ran toward Pegasus who was waiting for us by the water.

A large, heavy net was thrown over us and we fell to the ground. From the corner of my eye I saw that a net was thrown over Pegasus as well and he struggled to escape it, getting it tangled with each movement he made.

I slashed at the net around us with the sword I took from the guard, but a stomp on my wrist made me drop its hilt and groan in pain. Soon we were surrounded by guards who made a pathway for a man in a crown to pass though and approach us.

"Well, well, well. At last I found you, my beautiful bride."

Chapter 19: Typhon

King Theon's lips curled upwards into a pleased smile as he brought his face close to mine and stared into my eyes. "Perhaps waiting all these years for you to grow up has been a very good decision. You are a mirror image of her -- no, you are even better." My disgust must have shown on my face because his smile dropped and he straightened to stand from his crouched position. "You will grow to love me. I am sure of it. Rose!"

Rose came running to his side. She bowed lowly, not sparing me a single glance. "Your Majesty."

"Bring the dead seals."

She left, returning with a large sac over her shoulder.

"Throw them to the sea. My orca is waiting for her treat. Throw Edgar along with them. She has a big appetite and I have no need for him anymore, that imbecile."

Athena and I watched as Rose fed the orca that led us to this rocky beach.

"Traitor," Athena hissed. "I should have listened to my instincts and stopped following her here."

"But you did, my dearest. You did. And for that I thank you," King Theon said with a chuckle. "I can always count on my stupid daughter to bring me what I want."

"How did you know where I would be?" she asked, turning her head to look at her father.

"I have ears all over my castle, dearest," he responded.

That is when I remembered. The noise by the door of Athena's chambers when I teleported there to tell her about Alexios. There must have been someone listening in at the door. They must have heard everything.

"Father," Athena said. "Let us go. We need to find Alexios. He could be in need of our help."

"Do not worry yourself about your brother. He will survive. He survived every punishment I've given him. Even if some of those punishments were not meant to be his." He looked down at his daughter. "You know that better than anyone."

Athena looked away and down to the ground we laid on. We were still covered with the heavy net the guards had thrown over us. It seemed to grow heavier every minute, pushing us into the rocky ground.

I've thought about burning the net off with fire, but I did not wish to hurt Athena. But even if we somehow found a way to escape from under this net, the guards that stood around us like a steel fence would not let us get past them. Poor Pegasus had stopped struggling a long time ago, letting the net push him down to lie on the rocks, with his wings flat on his sides.

Rose returned from feeding the orca. "It is done, Your Majesty."

"Excellent." King Theon smiled wide and looked down at me. "Now we can bring my bride back to the castle and begin our wedding preparations. Tomorrow you will be my queen."

A loud battle cry coming from above made everyone look up at the sky. Nephos was flying down at lighting speed, with Medusa, my mother and grandfather on his back. Medusa's scream of outrage got louder as they neared the ground. When Nephos landed, she jumped off and ran toward Pegasus, throwing off the heavy net as if it weighed nothing and giving the king of Poseidon a poisonous glare. "I will give your people a statue of you today, Theon. Choose your pose before I do it."

Mother and grandfather ran over toward Athena and I, but the guards that stood around us blocked their way and they were soon engaged in a battle with them. It was twelve against two. The odds were not in their favour.

"Athena, we need to get out of this net and help them," I said, lifting it from my side with a grunt. I wondered how Medusa did it with such ease with Pegasus's net.

"It's impossibly heavy," Athena huffed as she tried to lift it with me. "Any other ideas? We could cut it open...but the guards took away our swords."

I glanced toward mother and grandfather, but I couldn't see them well behind all the guards. "I will light up my side of the net. Be ready to come out with me when I tell you to."

She nodded. "All right. I'm ready. Do it."

I took a deep breath and pushed fire though my skin, transferring it to the thick ropes beside me. The flame spread and burned a hole through the net. When it was large enough, I wrapped my arms around Athena to protect her from the hot fire and we came out.

Medusa ran up to us and threw us each a sword. "I wanted to use up my powers on Theon, but I thought you girls would need weapons." I looked at the two statues of royal guards beside us. Their faces were contorted into surprise, with their mouths open and eyes wide. She'd turned them into stone. "But I will get Theon when my powers recharge. He won't get away with hurting my son. Oh! One more thing before you go. The girls are coming soon to fight with us. I left them when I heard Pegasus's cry for help, but they know where to find us. Now, off you go!"

Athena and I thanked her and joined mother and grandfather in their fight against King Theon's guards. Though they were outnumbered, they worked well together. Not a single scratch on them. The same couldn't be said about the guards...

"Mother, stand behind me," I said as I fought off two guards. "I will protect you."

Mother shook her head, disarming one of them. "No, darling, I am all right. I know that I couldn't do anything when Edgar got hold of me, but I will not let fear overtake me anymore. I've done that for much too long." She disarmed another guard and kicked him. He stumbled and fell on a guard behind him.

"Enough!" King Theon boomed. His face was red with rage. "Lower your weapons! It's an order!"

The royal guards all lowered their weapons, but the rest of us stood holding them up, ready to use them at any moment.

"I said lower your weapons!" He glared at us.

Mother and I stood side by side with our swords raised in front of us. Athena and grandfather stood together, one of their feet on top of a struggling guard on the ground, their weapons pointed at his throat. Medusa stood in front of Pegasus, her snakes raised high on her head, hissing. And

Nephos swallowed a guard, spitting out his armour onto the guards nearby and making them fall over.

"You are not our king," I said.

"I am everyone's king! Asterin belongs to me and you will all obey me!" he shouted.

Medusa rolled her eyes. "He is Poseidon's grandson all right. The arrogance on that one."

"If I had sand around me, I would bury him alive right now," grandfather grumbled.

King Theon's face no longer showed any emotion. He looked as calm as still water, but those cold blue eyes of his had a storm brewing behind them. "Rose," he called her over calmly. "Send for the royal army. The guards seem to be useless here."

Rose nodded once and took out a small device. It looked like a long bent tube shaped like an L. She pointed it to the sky and pressed on something. As soon as she did that, a ball of blue light flew up over us and froze in one place, hovering in the sky.

"They should be here soon," she said, lowering the strange device. I had a feeling that it was made by the cyclopes, just as the one that trapped uncle Cerius was.

King Theon sighed. "I'd wished it didn't come to this, but you leave me no choice. I will have you all punished for disobeying my orders. Though my bride will remain unharmed. We do have a wedding tomorrow after all." He smiled at me.

Mother pushed me behind her and raised her sword. She'd lowered it distractedly when Rose released that blue ball of light from her device. "You won't come anywhere near my daughter, Theon."

"We will see about that, Lily." He chuckled. "When I have your daughter, I will take over Soleil. It must have been very difficult for the people there to live without a proper king. A king that will not abandon them, let alone his own family."

Nephos growled at his words and mother squeezed the hilt of her sword in anger.

"Are you saying that you are the king they need, father?" Athena raised one brow. "I don't believe that you're right. You killed the mother of your children and you abandoned your only son in the sea. You never cared about anyone but your own self. Do you think the people of Soleil would want you as their king? Do you think our people even want you as their king?"

"Athena, that is enough!" King Theon said sternly.

"How dare you speak to your father this way?" Rose stepped in. "I have always despised you, but at least you used to have some manners around His Majesty. Apologize to him. Now!"

"I don't know what has gotten into your head, servant, but you should be careful with what you say to me. You may keep your feelings to yourself. I do not care for them. And don't ever forget that you are speaking with a princess," Athena said, gritting her teeth.

"You say that as if you have a chance at inheriting the throne." Rose laughed. "If it's not Alexios, then His Majesty will simply have another son."

Medusa laughed loudly. "You should have asked the book first before uttering a single word about it. You know nothing. Oh, but do go on. It is quite amusing to listen to you."

Rose pursed her lips. Then she opened her mouth to speak again, but was interrupted by a loud roar that shook the earth beneath our feet. Everyone stumbled as the ground continued to shake for a short moment longer, and then another roar came. It was louder than the first one and it made my skin crawl.

"What was that?" I said, widening my eyes.

"I don't know, but I don't like the sound of it," my mother said worriedly.

Suddenly the sky darkened, black smoke replacing the bright blueness of it, devouring the soft clouds as it spread further and further, until the sun was no longer visible. Its warm golden rays no longer cast to the ground. Only a few made it through the smoke. It was just enough to see our surroundings.

The roar came again, but this time, it sounded closer. Then we saw who the sounds belonged to. A large dark creature circled above us. It was twice the size of Nephos.

"A dragon," I whispered.

"Not quite," mother said, swallowing. "Oh this is not good."

The creature landed in front of King Theon who nearly fainted at the sight before him. It was a black monster with two dragon heads with an almost human one in the middle. His wings also resembled those of a dragon. Only his body was serpent-like, dividing into several thick and slithering tails.

"Where is Poseidon?" The creature hissed and growled all at once as it spoke, snake tongues coming out of its dragon heads. "I smell his blood in you. Where is your ancestor?"

King Theon screamed and hid behind Rose. "Eat her! Not me," he cried.

"She doesn't smell good. Her blood is mixed with the cyclopes." The snake-dragon pushed her away with one tail.

King Theon gave a startled screech and took a few slow steps backwards, raising his hands up in front of him. "Don't eat me."

"Mother," I said quietly, not to draw the creature's attention to me. "Why does that creature look familiar?"

"Because you've seen his illustration in a book. He is Typhon. The father of all monsters," mother whispered, staring at him in disbelief. "He has returned."

All of a sudden, the royal army arrived, advancing toward Typhon on their horses, with their swords raised high. A group of archers remained behind, drawing their arrows and firing them at the monster. Another group started to load their cannons.

"Your Majesty, we have arrived." A man in a special armour for royal generals bowed to King Theon. "More troops are on the way."

"Yes," the king squeaked, then cleared his throat. "Yes, kill that monster!" he said, pointing at Typhon. "Protect your king!"

Typhon laughed. It was a deep and bone chilling laugh that made me want to hide behind my mother as if I was still a little, helpless girl. "You chose war." He moved the entire army out of his way with only one swipe of his tail. "Then war you shall receive."

The ground shook and clumps of smoke came out of it, which then took forms of humans. Burned humans I realized, seeing their marred skin and flesh. An image of the men from Kingdom Typhon, the ones who brought me to Gora flashed through my mind.

I covered my mouth in horror. "These are the victims of the Twin Volcanoes' eruptions."

There were thousands of them. Some staying here to fight off the royal army, but most of them leaving, marching mindlessly toward other kingdoms as per Typhon's orders. "Destroy Asterin. Every part of it. Poseidon hasn't kept his promise."

"Oh Gods, it's happening," mother said.

"What is happening?" I asked.

"The prophesy. It has begun."

Even with most of Typhon's army leaving the battlefield, the grand royal army was outnumbered. They struggled to slay the burned undead. They seemed impossible to kill.

Soon the monstrous serpent-drangon's creations were all over the beach and mother and I were separated from each other and the rest of our group as we fought them off and protected ourselves from being burned by them. I've already witnessed many royal army troops have their skin and flesh burned through by lava with a simple touch from the undead.

"Do not let them touch your skin!" I called out and hoped that Athena, grandfather and Medusa heard me in the midst of this chaos. Mother already knew not to let those creatures near her. She had witnessed those horrific deaths of royal troops with me. It was an awful sight.

"Just cut off their arms!" Athena yelled out from a distance.

One monster reached out to touch my forearm, but I was quick enough to pull it back and slice off its arm with my sword. Seconds later, black smoke came out from the cut off point and a new arm started to form.

"Uh," I took a step back, chewing on my lip in panic. "The arms grow back!"

The monster advanced toward me with a full grown new arm. Its marred face held no emotion and its eyes were blank. Dead. Soulless. Its movements controlled by Typhon's commands with no will of its own.

A feeling of sadness washed over me at the thought of their souls. They couldn't be in peace knowing that their bodies were being manipulated this way after death. It wasn't right.

A smaller sword sliced through the air and the two arms of the undead in front of me were severed in one sharp downward motion. "They grow back slower each time you sever them." Nora swiped sweat off her forehead with her small hand.

"You girls are here!" I exclaimed, as we stood back to back and fought off more of Typhon's creations.

"Yes, we've just arrived. Looks like our help was truly needed. Half of the royal army is dead and I just saw a group of them run away from battle," the little girl huffed, skillfully turning and striking with her sword.

"Ah! That was my favourite dress," Athena complained, ripping off her burned sleeve. She joined Nora and I, and we all stood in a protective circle with our backs to each other. "We really need a plan. And soon. We cannot fight them off for much longer."

"Athena!" King Theon ran toward us, away from a group of the undead that were chasing him. His sword was unsheathed, dangling at his hip in its sparkling gold and silver scabbard. I wondered if he even knew how to use it or if he had simply relied on his royal guards and army to protect him for the rest of his life. "My dearest daughter. Protect your father."

He ducked under our protective circle and stood in it, shaking with fear.

We had no choice but to protect him. There was no time to throw him out as more and more of Typhon's creatures advanced toward us.

From the corner of my eye, I saw Nephos fly toward Typhon who's been watching the battle with a bloodthirsty glint in his eyes, and attack one of his dragon heads.

"Who's the coward behind us? I could only catch a small glimpse," Medusa said when she joined our circle.

"My father," Athena answered, bringing her sword down to sever yet another pair of arms. Nora was right. They did grow back slower each time. But they never stayed severed and that worried me. How much longer could we endure this fight?

Medusa laughed humourlessly. "How unexpected of a king of Asterin."

As we continued to battle Typhon's army, our circle grew. Mother joined us after Medusa did. Then grandfather. And then some of the other girls from Hecate's sanctuary, one by one.

King Theon sat in the middle, on the ground, with his arms around his knees and eyes filled with fear.

"There are too many of them!" grandfather shouted.

"Does anyone have a plan? Anything at all. I cannot endure this much longer. My strengths are depleting," Medusa said.

"Mine too," one of the girls breathed out.

The undead were swarming onto us continuously. There was no time to rest and put down our weapons. With constant swinging of my heavy sword, my arms felt like they were on fire. My shoulders hurt and the smoke around us made it difficult to breathe. We were nearing the end of our endurance and we knew it.

Today could be the day we all die.

"What is that?" Nora suddenly said, looking toward the rising shadow over us. It was already dark with the black smoke covering the sky, but this shadow was new, and it kept growing.

A giant wave of water rose from the sea and up over the beach. It hovered above us, then slammed down onto the ground and swept through it, collecting the bodies of the undead and pulling them with it into the sea.

"I did not image what I just saw, did I?" one of the girls said, coughing out water. We were all splashed by the giant wave but remained unharmed. It only passed through us gently, like a soft caress.

"Look! Over there!" Nora pointed toward the sea where another wave was rising. She had a bright grin on her face, though I didn't know why. I squinted my eyes and tried to see what she was pointing at.

And then I saw him. A man on top of the rising wave, with a glowing golden trident in hand. It was raised high over his head, commanding the waters of the sea.

Alexios.

Chapter 20: Darkness

"Alexios!" Athena exclaimed when she saw her brother descend toward us on a wave of water, with Poseidon's trident in hand. The scarf I'd tied around his knife wound was still tied tightly around his abdomen, stained with old blood.

My heart which was racing from the battle before was now flooding with a sense of relief, calming down into a softer rhythm. He was alive. He survived.

"Son?" King Theon came out of the circle of protection that we'd created around him -- though not for him -- when we tried to protect ourselves from Typhon's undead, lava scorching creatures. He was no longer shaking in fear as he was a moment ago when they swarmed us. Now he looked relieved to see them all gone.

He looked at Alexios with pride. "I knew you would survive. You are my son after all." Athena rolled her eyes. "And you found the trident! Good. You may give it to me now."

Alexios's grip around the trident tightened. "Poseidon has entrusted it to me only. I cannot let anyone else use its powers."

King Theon pursed his lips.

"Poseidon?" Medusa peeked her head over my shoulder. "You saw him?"

"I heard his voice in the sea. It guided me toward the trident and warned me of Typhon's return. I came here as soon as I could --"

Typhon roared in anger and made everyone remember that although his creatures were all washed away, he was still here, undefeated. He flicked Nephos who'd been attacking him mercilessly off with one of his snake tails. Nephos fell to the ground, breaking rocks and making them fly up when his heavy body landed on them with impossible force. He then laid limp, with his eyes closed.

"Nephos!" I cried out and ran to him, but mother pulled me back.

"He is all right. Just unconscious. There is nothing you can do for him now. You will only bring yourself closer to Typhon and I will not let you do that," she said.

"Where is Poseidon?" Typhon growled and hissed. "I sensed his presence on the island. Lead me to him and I will spare your worthless human lives."

King Theon started to shake again. He hid behind Alexios this time. "Tell him, Alexios. I can't die yet. I have too much planned for my life."

Alexios shook his head. "I don't know where he is. I only heard his voice in the water. He could be in the sea, but that is only my guess."

"A mere guess will not do. Prepare to die today, humans," Typhon hissed.

Panicked, King Theon screeched and gripped the shaft of the trident and tried to pull it out of Alexios's hand. "Give it to me! I need it more than you do."

As he pulled on it with more force, the trident started to glow and then it repelled the king with a force so strong that he flew into the black smoke that covered the sky above us. He fell a second later, right on top of Nephos who was still unconscious on the rocky ground.

Typhon suddenly roared with laughter, releasing hisses in between each strangled sound that came out of his monstrous throat. "I will spare that coward. He has amused me. As for the rest of you..." Fast as lighting, three of his thick snake tails whipped across the beach and knocked everyone off their feet. "You first."

Athena screamed as Typhon's tail wrapped around her like a python and lifted her body off the ground. At the same time, clumps of smoke appeared from beneath us and more undead scorchers were created, running toward us with their arms outstretched.

"Athena!" I watched as Typhon brought her closer toward the open mouth of one of his dragon heads. She struggled to break free from his hold. Her arms and legs were all inside the snake tail along with her sword. I took a step forward.

"Wait! I'm coming with you," mother said and ran with me toward Typhon as Alexios splashed the undead out of our way with the trident's powers. When I glanced back, I saw more of them emerge from the ground once again.

Athena's screams snapped my head upward. Her head was now inches away from the dragon head's sharp teeth. I created a ball of fire in my hand and threw it at the dragon head. It screeched in agony and pulled away from her. I threw another fire ball at the tail that held her captive. Typhon hissed and loosened his grip.

Using that to her advantage, Athena pulled out her sword and sliced at the tail, sliding down along with it to the ground. "Gods," she wheezed. "I've never been this scared in my life. Those scales felt awful." She shuddered.

Typhon growled, lowering one of his dragon heads down straight toward me with its mouth wide open and ready to bite my head off. Before I even had time to form fire in my hand to shoot it above me, hot flames that appeared out of what seemed to be thin air struck the dragon face. It screamed in pain and pulled back.

I was so distracted by the horrifyingly sharp and bloody teeth above me, that I did not notice a scaly thick tail circling around me below, wrapping around my legs. When I did notice, it was too late. The wrapped tail tightened around my legs in an instant and circled around the rest of my body in a grip so strong that when it reached my chest, I could only take in the shallowest of breaths.

I heard mother and Athena scream their protests as I was lifted off the ground. The sword in my hand was pushing into my skin and I felt a prickle of pain as it sliced through it, digging in deeper as Typhon's snake tail squeezed me in even more.

The tail stopped moving when it brought me face to face with the monster himself. It was more hideous up close. He had no lips to cover his jagged black teeth. One of his cheeks was missing its flesh, revealing the jaw bone and more jagged teeth inside. The pitch black pits of his eyes had no whites around them. They were burning with anger and a hint of satisfaction as they watched me struggle for breath.

"Child of Helios," Typhon hissed, all three of his heads looking at me. "You are quite the nuisance." He brought his face closer and sniffed once before retracting it back. "Ah. Not yet a master of your full powers. The flame is small within you. I don't need to worry."

He threw me to the side and my body flew like an arrow straight into the pile of rocks that hid Sir Edgar's dead body before he was fed to the orca, close to the sea and far away from Typhon and everyone else. I heard -- and felt -- the bones of my right leg and arm break at the impact.

I screamed in pain as I tried to crawl away from a scorcher that was headed my way. But I couldn't move my broken limbs. It hurt too much.

A silver dragon landed in front of me and growled at the scorcher, attacking it with small fireballs. While it kept the undead away from me, its rider slid down its back and ran over to me.

"Emilia, my Gods. Are you all right? Can you move?" Princess Liana's concerned face looked down at my bloodied body.

"I -" I croaked, my lungs still hurting from the pressure that Typhon's tail squeezed them with. "I think my...my arm and leg." I took in a shallow breath. "B-broken. What are you...how are you...h-here?" I inhaled another small breath. "Hallucination?"

"You are not hallucinating," Liana said. "I am really here. Vunos brought me to the source of the black smoke over Asterin's sky and those deformed scorchers that crossed into kingdom Gora from Soleil. Oh Gods, what do I do?" She sat on the heels of her feet in front of me and bit her lip in worry. "How do I help you? I-I don't know what to do."

"Leave me," I breathed. "H-help the others. I am only a hinderance now."

I winced, speaking becoming more and more difficult. It felt as if my ribcage stabbed both of my lungs with each word that escaped my mouth. The pain of my broken bones along with the burning sting from the wounds on my skin both from my sword and the impact of my landing on sharp rocks was too much to handle.

"I can't just leave you to die!" Liana protested.

"Go," I whispered hoarsely, my throat closing up.

I felt my body giving up. My eyelids felt heavy, drooping over my eyes, ready to cover them and send me into blissful sleep where I couldn't feel all this pain. Not consciously.

"Emilia!" Liana touched my cheek. "Don't close your eyes. Stay with me. Emilia."

My eyes closed and my body went limp. The pain was finally gone.

When I opened my eyes, I was in another place. I've seen it before. In Hecate's memories. Though now there was no more spilled wine nor the golden haired man lying on the floor. Instead he was standing on the balcony attached to these enormous chambers. He was looking down, as if watching something below the clouds.

As I stepped forward toward him, I caught my reflection in a mirror on the wall. I frowned. This wasn't anyone's memory.

I was here as myself.

"Father?" I said, fearing that my lungs would start hurting again, but no pain came, and my voice came out strong and clear.

The golden haired man whipped his head around and met my eyes with his wide ones. They were the same colour as mine. "Emilia?"

Without waiting for my response, he took three long strides toward me and enveloped me in a tight embrace, wrapping one arm around my shoulders and another around my head which rested right near the bottom half of his ribcage.

"Have I died?" I whispered quietly, scared of the answer. If I was here, then I must have died on Asterin.

Father held me at arm's length and looked down at me, shaking his head. "You are still alive, but your soul has escaped your body to come here, to Olympus. To me."

"But why?" I frowned. "Are you going to return with me to Asterin?"

A pained expression crossed his face and he let go of my shoulders. "I can't. Not until Typhon is defeated and the prophesy is fulfilled."

"But you're a God," I argued.

"And that is exactly why I cannot interfere." He ran one hand down his face in frustration. "Hecate told me she had shown you our meeting on the matter. I could not interfere directly. Not if I wanted to keep you alive. And not unless your fate brought you to me. But I couldn't just sit here locked away from the human world by Zeus and do nothing. I found a way to help...indirectly."

"Nephos," I said.

Father nodded. "I sent my best dragon to help you. He had helped your mother long ago, when that -- cow dung of a human that calls himself king now --" He squeezed his hands into fists until they turned white. "When I finally get my hands on him..." He shook his head. "No matter. That is of no importance at the moment. What matters is that now you're here."

I frowned when he suddenly turned his head to look at the sky outside the balcony. "What is it?"

"We don't have much time. Your body is being healed on Asterin as we speak. You could disappear from here at any moment, back into your mortal shell." He clutched my hands in his large ones. "I must do this now."

"Do wha --" I felt a strange tug, as if I was being pulled somewhere. Then my form started to slowly fade. "I think it's happening."

Father clutched my hands tighter and transferred heat into my palms. It kept growing hotter just as the golden glow of our hands kept growing brighter. "You're already being pulled back to your body. I won't have time to tell you everything. I trust that you will know what to do with this when --"

I opened my eyes and was met with sea blue orbs that looked down worriedly at me, and another pair of worried grey eyes stared right back at me when I shifted my gaze to them. I was in the shallow part of the sea, with Liana and Alexios sitting on either side of me.

Liana smiled. "You're back. Can you move at all?"

I tried lifting my limbs and to my surprise, even the arm and leg that were definitely broken before were moving without any pain at all. The cuts on my skin were no longer hurting. I was completely healed, and I had an inkling feeling that it had something to do with the water around me and the man whose blue eyes were filled with relief upon seeing me awake.

"Prince Alexios healed you with the water using the trident's powers," Liana confirmed my suspicions. She squeezed my hand. "I'm so glad you're alive."

I smiled at her, then shifted my gaze to Alexios. Taking his hand in mine, I said, "Thank you."

He brushed his thumb across my knuckles and shook his head. "Do not ever do that again. Ever."

"I won't. Though I didn't have much control over Typhon's -- Typhon!" I sat up, suddenly remembering where I was.

The sky was still blackened with thick smoke, and the scorchers kept appearing from under the ground with Typhon watching our group and what was left of the royal army with malicious joy as they were slowly getting surrounded by them once again. This time there were thousands of the undead.

Alexios lifted the trident in his hand and splashed them all away as he had done many times before. But every time he did that, the scorchers seemed to multiply when they returned.

"My Gods, we need to stop this," I said, standing up, ready to join the battle. "We cannot let this go on."

"Typhon seems to be enjoying our struggle," Liana observed. "He will keep creating those monsters again and again for his own amusement."

I watched as Typhon's face split into a sinister smile when newly emerged scorchers burned through the flesh of an unprepared royal army troop. That smile grew as his screams of agony got louder.

"I have to stop Typhon," I said with an angry grit of my teeth. He has taken too many lives already. I will not let him take any more. No matter what it takes, I will put an end to him once and for all.

I heard a familiar chirp above and then Nephos landed in front of me, his golden eyes reflecting the same fire of determination that was burning within my own. He tilted his head toward his neck, wordlessly telling me to climb up.

Liana whistled to Vunos and the silver dragon flew over to sit beside Nephos. "Vunos and I will help as much as we can."

"Please watch over everyone else. They need you." I turned to Alexios. He nodded.

When I took a step toward Nephos, Alexios pulled me back and locked me in a tight embrace. "Be careful," he said.

I nodded against his warm chest, circling my arms around him. "You too," I whispered.

When I finally climbed onto Nephos, Liana and I flew toward Typhon. He didn't notice our arrival until Nephos and Vunos released their fire to strike him. As soon as he turned his human-like head to look at us, I threw a ball of fire on his face. He hissed in pain, shielding his face with one of his wings.

Liana lifted her hand and squeezed her palm into a first. When she did that, all six snake tails of Typhon were bound to the ground with thick rings of rock cuffing them down. He was no longer able to get a hold of us with those scaly limbs of his.

We continued to attack him with fire from all sides, but I noticed that the parts of him that were struck by flames were recovering soon after they were burned by them.

Typhon roared in anger. "You will pay for this, little humans!"

The ground suddenly cracked open around him as it shook. I widened my eyes as I saw what was about to crawl out of it. More monsters. Much more horrifying than anything I've ever seen. Their red eyes glowed with blood thirst as the crack in the ground slowly opened more and more, allowing their claws to go through it.

Suddenly Typhon screamed in agony and pulled his wing back from a small ray of sunlight that had penetrated through the black smoke above. It left a gaping hole in his wing that did not grow back as it had before, when it was struck with fire.

The monsters in the ground hissed in pain along with their master and pulled back their claws to hide in the dark.

"Darkness fears light," I whispered to myself and looked up at the sky. Typhon had appeared after he covered the daylight with that smoke. Sunlight burned him.

I reached out with my hand to that small sun ray and felt its warmth. I imagined it connecting me to the burning star it travelled from, connecting me to its light, its power. My hand started to glow as it had when father transferred something into my soul in Olympus.

The glow started to spread from my hand to my wrist, then through my arm, then through the rest of me. My body felt as light as a feather as it ignited with heat. I didn't realize that I was being lifted off of Nephos and flying higher, toward the dark smoke above, until I was hovering just below it.

The fire within me kept building, becoming stronger and stronger until it burst through me into a blinding explosion of pure golden light.

I heard Typhon's agonized screeches below and felt him burn under my light, the sounds disappearing slowly along with him, until he was nothing but black smoke which ascended to join the smoke that covered the sky.

I reached up with my hand and touched it, felt it, then made it burn. The fire spread instantly over the smoke until it completely disappeared and revealed the beautiful blue sky it was hiding and the sun that illuminated it.

The darkness was gone.

My body slowly descended toward the ground, and as soon as my feet touched the rocky surface of the beach below, I was attacked with a slimy giant tongue of a white dragon then swarmed with the brave people who had been fighting this battle with me.

"Thank you, thank you, thank you, thank you!" Medusa dropped down on her knees with her two hands clasped together above her head. "Gods, I could kiss your feet right now. I was about to collapse from exhaustion and let those scorchers burn me alive, and leave my poor Pegasus without a mother. He is too delicate to survive in this world without me."

Little Nora ran over and hugged my legs. "You saved us all," she said.

"You saved Asterin." Liana stepped in. "Typhon would have destroyed the island along with everyone in it had he lived to create more monsters."

To the left of us, King Theon had regained his consciousness, sitting up with a scream of panic. "Ahh! I'm too young to die!"

Medusa rolled her eyes. "I'm too tired to turn him into stone right now, but I really want to do it."

I chuckled, then looked at the people around me and smiled. I was able to save their lives along with the rest of the people of Asterin. My heart felt calm and content. No traces of Typhon or his creatures were left behind, as if they were never here. Sunlight covered every surface of the beach instead. They were truly gone. Asterin was saved from darkness.

The prophesy has been fulfilled.

Chapter 21: The Gods

We all sat on the rocky beach, basking in the sun's warm light. Everyone was too spent to move their limbs. Even the troops, the ones who'd survived, from King Theon's royal army sat beside us with their swords struck in between rocks to mark the end of our battle with Typhon and his monsters.

After a long goodbye and a promise to visit soon, Liana had left with Vunos to join her prince in Kingdom Gora. She wished to share the good news with her people.

Mother was leaning her head against my shoulder, watching the sea with me as its waves calmly washed over the rocks on the beach. She had a peaceful smile on her face. That smile faltered when her eyes caught movement in the water, as did mine.

It looked as if a person -- a very tall man was emerging from the sea. His head emerged first, followed by very broad shoulders. Dolphins splashed with joy behind him, bowing their heads. I saw a group of orcas mimic the same action. Even some seals swam close to the beach to offer their respects to him, not fearing their nearby predators.

"Who is that?" Athena asked beside me curiously. "And why is Pegasus galloping toward him?"

"What? Where?" Medusa said, craning her neck to see.

The sea man walked out of the water and onto the beach, greeting an overjoyed Pegasus who's been waiting for him excitedly, flapping his feathery wings. Then the two of them started walking in our direction.

Medusa's mouth hung open in disbelief. She blinked and rubbed her eyes, then blinked some more, widening them when the tall man and Pegasus stood before us. "It can't be," she whispered, slowly rising to her feet.

Pegasus whinnied joyfully and wrapped one wing around Medusa's shoulders and another one around the unfamiliar man's broad ones, bringing them closer.

"Hello, my love," the blue eyed man said in a deep voice. "I've returned."

Medusa shook her head and held her hand up. "Explain yourself, Poseidon. Where were you all these years? And you'll do well to answer me honestly. I see through all your lies."

I widened my eyes and met Athena's equally shocked expression. 'Poseidon?' she mouthed in bewilderment. I nodded. That's what I heard as well.

"In the sea," Poseidon said simply, but continued when Medusa put one hand on her hip, waiting for him to elaborate further. He sighed, looking away in guilt. "Typhon wanted the island for himself and I let him have it. I couldn't step foot in it without his permission. Even gave up my trident as a token of my promise. It was when I was..." He glanced at Medusa before proceeding to speak. "When I was mourning the loss of Asterin... I wasn't myself back then. I couldn't make fair judgements. Once I came to my senses, I had tried to return to you...but Typhon sensed me as soon as I did."

Pegasus let his wings drop to his sides. He walked away with a shake of his head.

Medusa's green eyes started to glow and the snakes on her head began to rise dangerously. "Are you telling me that we all--" she motioned to us "--nearly died today because of your promise to that monster? Over that human's death? And you didn't even lift a finger to help us when he started wrecking havoc on the island? Were you perhaps afraid of him?" she said lowly, poisonous venom hiding behind her calmness, rising to the surface.

"Oh this will not end well," mother said, rising to her feet. "I should pull her away."

Just then a bolt of lighting struck the rocks beside Poseidon and a man in a white and gold tunic appeared. I recognized his white hair and beard as soon as I laid my eyes on him.

Zeus.

He put one hand on Medusa's shoulder and she instantly calmed down, her snakes no longer angry and her eyes no longer glowing with rage.

"That is enough, Medusa," Zeus said. "We should be celebrating Typhon's demise, not blaming one another. Let us forgive and forget."

"Forgive and forget?" Father suddenly appeared, brows furrowed and eyes blazing with fire. "All this time all you truly cared about was your coward brother, didn't you? He was stupid enough to make a deal with Typhon and become bound by that promise, and you pitied him. Was there ever a prophesy? Or did you only want to use my daughter to do everything for you?"

"It was her fate! I would never lie about a prophesy," Zeus said, casting his thunderous gaze upon my father. "It is true that I wanted Poseidon to return to his beloved island and break the deal he was bound by. I would have dealt with Typhon myself had I not been preoccupied with my duties in Olympus. When the Fates informed me of the prophesy, I found a way. Your daughter's fate had already been decided. All I had to do was wait."

"They didn't have to be locked away in the dungeons! You could have let me take them to my palace. Let them live a proper life. If her fate had been decided, she would have defeated Typhon like you wanted! You could have sent me to defeat him."

Zeus shook his head. "I couldn't risk changing the path of her life. Any change could disturb the fate, or even kill her. Did you forget? As for you, you've spent too many years in the human world. Your powers were weakened. I couldn't rely on them."

Father shut his eyes for a moment, taking in a deep breath, then glared at Poseidon. "This is all your fault."

Poseidon looked away. "I know..."

"Zeus is also to blame." Hecate appeared from a shimmering portal that closed behind her when she stepped out of it. "Had he informed us of his plan, we could have helped. Instead he kept us all in Olympus."

"You have responsibilities in Olympus! You seem to have forgotten that we don't only watch over this island," Zeus argued. "There are other human lives we need to care for outside of Asterin."

"He does speak the truth," Poseidon mumbled.

"You've done nothing but sit in the bottom of the sea all these years. You do not get to speak on this matter," Hecate said. Medusa elbowed the goddess and smiled in approval when Poseidon's face contorted into shame.

As I listened to the Gods argue some more, I started to feel lightheaded. All the strength I've felt when my body erupted into light began to leave me. I felt a weakening in my knees and when they couldn't hold me up any longer, I dropped to the ground.

"Emilia!" mother exclaimed, gaining the attention of the Gods. "What's wrong?"

Father rushed to my side. "She must have spent all of her strength in battle. She needs rest."

My parents' worried faces were the last thing I saw before I closed my eyes and fell into the arms of someone behind me.

~~~

A fresh, cold strip of cloth was laid on my forehead and I instantly felt the heat in my body lower. It was building up, and in my sleep I'd worried if I would set the bed I felt beneath me on fire. It wouldn't be the first time.

"You're awake," Alexios said when I opened my eyes.

In my drowsy state, I couldn't help but smile at the prince as soon as I met his gaze. I couldn't forget the moment I'd lost him to the sea. The moment my lungs constricted and my heart felt empty. I didn't get a chance to truly look at him when he'd returned, to tell my heart that he'd truly survived. That it wasn't a dream I'd created in my mind. Wasn't my imagination.

Now that he was sitting in front of me, on the side of the bed, wearing a smile of his own, the emptiness was replaced with warmth. It was different from the warmth I'd felt from fire. Much different. Yet it felt just as comforting, if not more.

I blinked the sleep away and looked around the room. "Am I in your chambers?"

"It was the closest room I could put you in."
~~~

I raised a brow. Athena's chambers were much closer to the west entrance of the castle, but I chose not to mention it. Sitting up in the bed, I threw my legs over the side and planted my feet on the carpeted floor. Peeling off the cold cloth from my forehead, I said, "Where is everyone else? Did the Gods leave?"

"No, the Gods are in the castle," Alexios said. "Your mother left to bring more ice water for you. You were burning up." He put one hand on my left cheek. "Though now you seem to be producing much less heat. That's good."

I may have had my powers under control when I awoke from my slumber, but the burning in my cheeks at this very moment had nothing to do with them.

I locked my golden eyes with his deep blue seas and fell into the same trance-like state I was in during our archery training. All I could see was him, and all I wanted to do was be closer than we were, which is why I found myself looking down at his lips. When I glanced back up at his eyes, I found him doing the same.

Putting his other hand on my right cheek, Alexios slowly drew his face closer to mine until our lips connected.

His soft lips gently moved against my own while one of his hands moved to rest on my back, pulling me nearer. I wrapped my arms around his neck and closed the small distance we still had left between us.

The only reason I parted my lips from his was to come up for air. When I kissed him as soon as we caught our breaths, I could feel him smile against my lips.

A sound of ceramic hitting the ground broke us apart and we snapped our heads toward the door where broken pieces of a bowl laid on the floor along with the water it had held within it.

Mother stood by the open door of Alexios's chambers with her eyes wide. Her mouth opened and closed like a fish, but she said nothing for a moment. "I..I'm just going to...leave you two alone," she said and took two steps back until she hit the doorframe, then turned and rushed out of the room, closing the door behind her.

My cheeks felt so hot that I wondered if it was the horrifying embarrassment I felt at being caught by my mother or if my powers were going out of control. I wanted to disappear at this very moment. Did Alexios have one of Hecate's portals in his chambers like Athena did?

I dropped my head onto his chest. "Oh Gods, I am mortified. Do you think I can ask Hecate if she can erase mother's memory of that moment? Can she even do that? Perhaps she could erase mine as well."

I felt Alexios's laugh before I heard it. His chest shook against my forehead as he laughed at my words. "Your cheeks are very red." He pinched them gently.

I pulled away and scowled, giving him a glare.

He kissed my cheek and stood up, lifting me off the bed with his strong arms. "Do not worry, she only saw us kiss. It could have been much worse."

Now my entire face must have resembled grandfather's chilli peppers, because it felt hotter than the sun.

"Since you're awake and feeling better now, we should join the Gods in the throne room. They've been waiting for us," he said, carrying me to the door.

"Wait," I said, making him halt. "Put me down. I can walk on my own. I also do not wish for others to see us this close. Not now. Not with mother's horrified face still fresh in my mind."

Alexios put me down. "All right. I'll pretend that I'm not completely bewitched by you."

I couldn't hold back my smile. "Thank you. When we walk out this door, we are back to --"

"Your Highness, I heard that you're in your chambers -- oh." Annabelle barged in through the door and frowned when she saw me beside the prince. "What are you doing here? No matter. You may leave." She waved her hand dismissively. "I need to speak with His Highness."

I raised my brows and stayed where I was. I knew perfectly well what she came here to talk about with Alexios. Her delusional wedding plans and their future children. I didn't realize that my hands were in fists until I felt my nails painfully dig into my palms.

"Well? Aren't you leaving? You shouldn't even be here." Annabelle tapped her foot impatiently.

"No," I said. "I'm not leaving." Then I grabbed Alexios's face and kissed him. He grunted in surprise, but responded soon after, wrapping one arm around my waist and kissing me back right there in front of her.

I could only imagine the shock on Annabelle's face before she screamed in frustration and stomped away. I wish I'd seen it.

When I pulled away, Alexios raised a brow. "I thought you weren't ready for others to see us?"

"This...was a different matter," I said.

He smiled and shook his head. "I wonder what you would have done had I not taught you how to kiss."

"Taught me?"

"I can only assume that I was your first. You couldn't have kissed anyone in the dungeons."

"Who's to say that I haven't kissed the guards that brought me my meals every day?" I lied.

Alexios's smile dropped. "What?"

"You heard me." I shrugged and walked out into the hallway, heading toward the throne room.

"Who was it?" He followed me.

"I doubt that you know him," I teased, holding back the laugh that threatened to escape me.

"I know every guard in the castle. Who was it?"

I simply shrugged and kept walking.

"Emilia!"

We reached the doors of the throne room and I opened them, stepping in with Alexios in toe.

Zeus sat on the throne, surrounded by the other Gods, Poseidon, Hecate, and my father. Mother, grandfather, Medusa, and Athena were also within their circle. All their heads turned when Alexios and I walked in.

"Did you gain your strengths back?" Zeus asked me. I nodded. "Excellent. We were waiting for you both. We may now begin the meeting. Theon! You may enter."

A shaking King Theon entered the throne room, bowing once to each God that towered over his height and regarded him with distaste. Father's eyes were filled with more hatred than the rest of them. He looked ready to burn him alive and throw him out of the castle.

"You must know what I brought you here for, yes?" Zeus asked the king. "Take off your crown. You are no longer the ruler of this kingdom."

"Please reconsider! I beg of you!" King Theon dropped to his knees and bowed, touching his forehead to his two hands on the floor.

"It's been decided. Rise if you wish to save the last drops of your dignity," Zeus said. His steel voice left no room for arguments and King Theon silently rose to his feet. "Hecate."

Hecate bowed her head and lifted her hand. The crown on King Theon's head lifted along with it, moving toward the king of the Gods until it dropped into his hands.

"Now, crown prince. Approach the throne. Your coronation will be witnessed by the Gods themselves." Zeus lifted the crown and waited for Alexios to approach him. Only he didn't take a single step forward.

Instead, Alexios dropped on one knee and bowed. "I wish to surrender the crown to Athena. I had never wanted the throne. It was merely the wish of my father."

There was complete silence in the room. Even the wind from outside seemed to stop moving. We all held our breaths for Zeus's response.

"No!" Theon protested. "Alexios is the rightful heir to the throne! The only heir to the throne! I will not let this happen!"

"Silence!" Zeus rose from the throne. "Hecate, send him to the dungeons. In the same cell as Rose. They can keep each other company."

Just as Theon's eyes widened in terror, he disappeared into thin air with a simple snap of Hecate's fingers.

"Now that that's been dealt with." Zeus cleared his throat and stepped away from the throne. "Princess Athena, I believe this seat is rightfully yours. Sit, child."

Athena carefully approached the throne, then took a seat. Her eyes were wide with disbelief as she looked at the crown in Zeus's hands. When she met my eyes, I smiled encouragingly at her. She would be a good queen. A much better ruler than her cruel father ever was.

Athena returned my smile and let Zeus place the crown on her head. "I, Zeus, the king of the Gods and the ruler of the sky, bless your future as the queen of Kingdom Poseidon. May you serve with grace, wisdom, and righteousness. Though your true coronation in front of your people shall take place as well, the crown and the throne of this kingdom is rightfully yours, Queen Athena."

One by one, each one of us lowered ourselves to bow to the new queen of Kingdom Poseidon. Even the Gods paid their respects, bowing their heads to recognize Athena's new reign.

The small ceremony was interrupted by a horrid smell that overtook the entire throne room. It was strong enough to make us all rise and cover our noses.

"I recognize this stench," I coughed and looked to the direction where the smell seemed to be coming from. And sure enough, there they were. The cyclopes. Hundreds of them.

Uncle Cerius pushed through the few of those giant creatures and ran out from their midst, panting for air. "No more! No more of this, you hear me?! I will not be tortured like this! I've had enough! I would rather be whipped a thousand times than endure their stench!"

"Cerius?" Mother approached him, her eyes wide with shock.

"Son?" Grandfather joined them. "Son, are you all right?"

"You...you can see me?" Uncle Cerius looked up at his father and sister, mouth agape.

"Is that the king of Kingdom Typhon?" Alexios asked me.

"You can see him as well?" I said. He nodded. I frowned. How was this possible?

"Of course, my child. Of course I see you." Grandfather enveloped his son in a shaky embrace. His other hand wrapped around my mother's shoulders. "My children," he sobbed. "My precious children. Please forgive me."

My eyes widened when I saw that grandfather's arms did not pass through uncle Cerius. Instead they held onto him tightly as if he was made of flesh and bones -- not a ghostly soul. They could see, hear, and touch him?

Even Hecate, the goddess of magic seemed surprised by my uncle's transformation. "It's a miracle," she said in awe. She turned to the cyclopes. "How did you do it?"

They simply scratched their heads and shrugged. "It's the first time we'd made that device. Must be a side effect," one of them spoke up. "He is not quite alive, but not merely a ghost either."

"I am taking you all back to Olympus," Zeus said to the cyclopes. "You have caused enough trouble in the human world. It is time you resumed your work with the Gods. I don't have nearly as many lightning bolts as I need."

"Please do it now, Zeus. I cannot endure another second breathing in their...scent." Medusa coughed.

Zeus boomed with laughter, then disappeared soon after, along with all the cyclopes.

The door to the throne room slowly creaked open and Pegasus's head pushed through the crack between them, looking around the room and smelling it before walking in slowly. When he entered, a donkey followed him in.

"Pegasus! There you are!" Medusa smiled wide and petted her son's head. "Where have you been hiding all this time?"

Pegasus whinnied in response.

"You went back to the barn again? Oh you poor thing. You must have been so frightened when those monsters came out," Medusa cooed while shooting Poseidon a quick glare. Then she noticed the donkey that has been standing quietly beside her horse son. "You made a new friend?"

Pegasus shook his head and whinnied excitedly. I didn't understand anything, but judging by Medusa's paling face, it couldn't be good.

"A lo... a love...a lover?" she said.

And then she fainted.

Epilogue

"Today is an important day." Mother smiled at me through her reflection in the mirror as she brushed my hair. "You have grown so much, my darling."

I smiled widely in return, enjoying the feeling of having my hair brushed by her after so long.

We were inside the palace of Kingdom Soleil and today was the day of my coronation. Father wished for me to have my ceremony as soon as mother and I stepped foot into Soleil's territory, but I'd refused. I wanted to get accustomed to the kingdom first, meet the people, learn the customs and traditions.

After two months of learning by my father's side as he governed his kingdom, I was ready to take the throne.

Mother put away the hair brush and started to braid my hair. I thought back to the day of my release from the dungeons. It seemed like a very distant memory. Someone else's life. That dark cell without a single ray of sunlight was no longer my home. It never was.

I'd asked mother why she kept everything from me. Why she didn't tell me that she was a princess, that we had family outside of the cell, and that my father was a God.

"When you were born, I'd tried to escape many times. Theon had stopped visiting my cell as soon as he saw you in my arms, and Rose's visits became more frequent. I saw it as my opportunity to run away with you. I'd foolishly thought she was my friend. I should have known that she was preventing me from escaping. She pretended to help me. Even brought a key to my cell. But there were guards waiting for me every time. I couldn't leave the dungeons," she'd told me. "And I had given up trying.

"If you'd known what you know now, you would have wanted to escape. I didn't want to give you empty hope of anyone coming to rescue us. No one had in years." She'd sighed. "But deep down in my heart I had wished that you would one day see the world outside the dungeons, and I wanted you to be prepared for that day. My purpose became to teach you everything you needed to know."

I had understood my mother and I was eternally grateful for everything she had done for me. The knowledge she had gifted me served me well and will continue to serve me as long as I live.

I braided my fingers with my mother's when she put her hand on my shoulder after finishing with my hair. "I love you," I said.

"I love you too, my darling." She kissed my cheek. Then she walked around my chair to admire her work. Tucking in a loose strand of hair behind my ear, she smiled through glistening eyes. "You look absolutely beautiful."

"She is your daughter after all." Father walked into my chambers with a proud smile on his face.

Mother rolled her eyes through a smile of her own, her cheeks tinted red. She always had a blush on her face whenever father was near.

"I hate to interrupt this beautiful family moment, but I need your help," Medusa said, barging in, her voice on the verge of panic. "Donkiass is in pain and I don't know what to do!"

Donkiass was the name she had given to Pegasus's two-month pregnant donkey lover. Though the donkey did not seem to find offence in the name, Pegasus was never happy to hear it. I wondered what Medusa would name their offspring.

"I'll go see what's wrong," mother said before leaving with Medusa.

Father approached me and put his hands on my shoulders, smiling at me thorough our reflections in the mirror. "You have learned everything you needed to know. I'm proud of you, Emilia. Our people are anticipating your coronation, and they are ready to welcome you as their queen."

I smiled. "I am ready to be their queen."

~~~

I sat atop a golden throne, overlooking all the people gathered in the royal throne room to witness my coronation. My golden gown and the royal pendant around my neck shone brightly under a stream of sunlight which entered through the skylight window above the throne.

The people of Soleil stood with their backs straight, each one of them holding a small basket of sunflower petals in their hands. Their golden eyes were shining with joy as they looked upon my silhouette in the light.

Mother, father, uncle Cerius, and grandfather stood just below the first step of the podium with Alexios and Athena smiling next to them. Medusa, Pegasus, and Donkiass were across from them, by the opposite wall of the room. Liana and Prince Leo were also here to witness the ceremony.
~~~

The sunlight was suddenly blocked from above and I looked up to see why. I chuckled when I saw Nephos's head looking down at me, and though I couldn't hear it, the movement of his mouth told me that he was chirping happily.

Father snapped his fingers twice and Nephos moved his head to let the sunlight back in. It was part of the ceremony to be under the light of the sun during a coronation.

"We shall now begin the ceremony," the regent who governed the kingdom of Soleil during father's absence announced, silencing everyone's excited chatter. He now stood in front of the throne.

Members of the royal council walked in through the doors in a single line, walking through the open pathway in the middle of the room. One of them was holding a flat velvet cushion with a rolled scroll on top. Another councillor was carrying the crown.

When they reached the throne, they split into two groups, standing on either side of me. The councillor with the scroll approached the regent and moved back to his position when he took the scroll.

The regent turned to face me, rolling open the yellowing paper. He cleared his throat before speaking. "Are you willing to take the Royal Oath, Your Highness?"

"I am willing," I said. Father had prepared me for the entire ceremony to ensure that I knew what to say and do.

"Do you promise and swear to govern Kingdom Soleil and maintain order and peace within its borders as well as outside, with the rest of Asterin?"

"I promise."

"Do you promise and swear to uphold the laws, administer justice, and protect your people?"

"I promise."

There were more parts to the oath that the regent read out, all of which I promised to uphold. When I finished taking the Royal Oath, the regent rolled up the scroll and a councillor took it from him. The councillor with the crown then approached the regent and held it up.

"Under the light of our blessed sun, under the realm of our Gods, and in front of your loyal people, I crown you, Emilia, as the queen of Soleil," the regent said as he picked up the crown and held it above my head. "May your reign be celebrated for years to come." He placed the crown on my head.

"All hail, Queen Emilia!" father said.

"All hail, Queen Emilia!" Everyone chanted after him and bowed at their waist.

I stood from my throne and started to walk forward, slowly descending the high podium to accept the blessings of my people.

As I walked down the pathway in the middle of the room, I was showered with sunflower petals and loud cheers. I smiled as I made it out of the throne room and walked through the rest of the pathway, lined by more people who could not fit inside.

Glancing behind me, I saw that a long carpet of yellow sunflower petals covered the ground behind me. It kept growing with every step I took.

Soon I reached the end of my path where large open tents and endless rows of long tables for the celebratory feast greeted me.

When everyone gathered and was seated at their tables, servants served the grand feast. I sat at a table overlooking the rest. My family, Alexios, Athena, Medusa, Liana, and Prince Leo were seated with me.

"A toast! To my wonderful niece." Uncle Cerius raised a goblet of wine. "She stayed strong through all the hardships in her life and saved Asterin from darkness. I also wish to express my gratitude for asking Hecate to restore my kingdom, letting my people return to their homes in Typhon. You have made this king very happy. Thank you. May you continue to bring light to our lives for years to come. To Emilia!"

"To Emilia!" Everyone else at the table raised their goblets and drank their wine. Though uncle Cerius did not need food or drink for sustenance, he drank the wine and ate the feast solely for their taste.

The people of Typhon couldn't believe their eyes when they saw their deceased king looking very much alive and well, but they welcomed him back with open arms, even with his very peculiar situation. They were overjoyed when he told them that they could return home.

"You look breathtaking," Alexios whispered, leaning in close to my ear. He and Athena sat to one side of me, while mother and father who were currently speaking with Liana and Prince Leo were seated to my right.

I blushed. Alexios never failed to mention anything and everything he had on his mind. Though what he said just now wasn't outrageous, it reminded me of the words that came out of his mouth when we were alone.

"What are you blushing about?" Athena asked.

Alexios leaned away from me with a knowing smile and continued to eat his food.

Athena glanced at her brother, then back at my blushing face and scrunched up her face. "You know what, I do not want to know."

Across from her, Medusa cackled. "You truly don't."

I choked on my potato and began to cough uncontrollably, reaching for my goblet of wine. Alexios placed it in my hand and I took a much needed sip.

"Are you all right, darling?" Mother turned to me.

I nodded, words failing me at the moment.

"Chew carefully," she said, patting my back before turning back to continue her conversation with Liana and Prince Leo.

"Liana and I have been discussing an alliance between all of Asterin. I know that Soleil had been allied with Poseidon long ago, but what do you think of bringing all kingdoms together and forming a unified council with the rulers of each kingdom?" Prince Leo was saying and it caught my attention.

"A council of Asterin?" I said, interested in this plan. If all kingdoms worked together and shared their knowledge and resources, Asterin would be unified.

"Count me in," grandfather said. "I will gladly take part in this council. Lily will take over after me. Right, Lily?"

Mother nodded. "I will gladly do so."

"Typhon will also participate," uncle Cerius confirmed.

Athena who had also heard Prince Leo's words gave her nod of approval. "Consider Poseidon part of this allegiance as well."

"We can set a meeting and discuss the details of everything later," grandfather said. He looked somewhere to the side, before rising from his seat. "Now if you will all excuse me, this old man has caught the eye of a beautiful lady."

"Father," mother sighed and shook her head in disbelief.

We all watched as grandfather approached an older woman in a beautiful yellow dress and offered her his hand. She accepted it with a smile and followed him to the middle of the dance square where an orchestra was playing music and a few drunken people were dancing their hearts out.

Alexios laughed. "He never changes."

"Your Majesty, may I have this dance?" James suddenly appeared by our table and waited for Athena to give him her answer.

"You may," she said, rising from her seat and following James. She tried to hide her smile, but failed to maintain her indifferent facade when they started to dance together.

"Your Majesty." Alexios offered me his hand.

Just as I moved to put my hand into his, Medusa looked up at the sky and screamed, "Poseidon!"

As if waiting to be summoned, he appeared immediately in front of her. "You called for me, my love?"

"I wish to dance," she said. A hopeful smile emerged on Poseidon's face, but Medusa held up her hand. "This changes nothing."

His smile faltered for a moment, but he nodded, leading her away from the table.

Soon Alexios and I joined everyone else on the dance square, which became bigger when more people joined and servants moved the now empty tables to make space for them.

"When will you tell me which guard it was?" Alexios asked.

I laughed. "Does that still bother you?"

"I am only curious is all. It is not as if I will punish him for being close to you and lock him in the farthest cell in the dungeons to keep him far away from ever seeing you or being seen by me."

I raised a doubtful brow. "Are you certain?"

He nodded after darting his gaze away suspiciously. "Now, will you please tell me?"

"I will tell you on the day of the wedding," I said.

"But that is an entire month away!" he exclaimed. Then he sighed. "I suppose if I waited this long already, I can wait another month."

I rose to the tips my toes and kissed his cheek. "I admire your patience."

~~~

"I lied about the guard."

I watched in amusement as Alexios's face changed from anticipation to a scowl. "I should have known."

"Are you both ready?" Athena's head peaked in through the open door. "The ceremony will begin soon."

"Yes, we are all waiting for you." Nora's small head appeared below Athena's. The girls from Hecate's sanctuary have come as honoured guests.

Alexios adjusted his collar, still not quite amused with his recent discovery. "I am ready."

"I am as well." I swept my hair away from my face and walked out with Alexios, joining Athena and Nora in the hallway of the Pesok palace.
~~~

We entered a beautifully decorated room with very high ceilings, full of other guests. Making our way through the aisles, we took out own seats at the front of the room.

The Gods were among the honoured guests of this wedding. They have gracefully accepted their invitations and spared time from their duties to attend.

Grandfather walked up to the podium and raised his hands, announcing the beginning of the ceremony and silencing everyone. Nephos who's been sitting still behind him with his large body barely fitting inside the room chirped twice.

A soft melody began to play. The two doors of the balcony above the podium opened and mother and father walked out from each one, smiling at each other. They had to separate to descend down the two staircases on either side.

Mother looked beautiful in her white and gold gown, the train of which softly brushed upon each step of the staircase as she moved. Father looked radiant in his white and gold attire. They each carried a white silk ribbon which represented the purity of their love.

When they came to stand together in front of grandfather, his eyes shone with happy tears. "At last, we are here to witness the union between my precious daughter, Crown Princess Lily, and Helios, the God of the Sun. The Gods present with us on this important occasion have blessed this pairing. And today, along with all of us here, they will witness the final ceremony."

Father raised the silk ribbon in his hand and tied it around mother's right wrist. When it was mother's turn, she tied her ribbon around father's left wrist. Then they joined hands, mother's right with father's left. With their free hands they took an apple from grandfather's outstretched hands and raised it to Nephos.

It was a symbolic offering to the dragon, the most magnificent creature in our realm. Once Nephos accepted the apple, he blessed their union.

We all rose to stand as mother and father turned to face the guests, their hands still clasped together. Their overjoyed smiled brightened the entire room and brought smiles to everyone else.

Alexios took my hand and braided our fingers together as I rested my head on his shoulder, watching my parents with happy tears in my eyes.

I never thought it possible to see my mother this peaceful. This elated. There had always been sadness in her eyes for as long as I remembered. Though I couldn't recognize it when I was young, it had never once left her eyes when I finally did see it. But now it was completely gone.

I sniffled and wiped at my eyes, causing Alexios to look down at me with worry. "Are you all right?" he asked.

With a smile tugging at my lips, I nodded. "I am. These are happy tears. I'm simply happy for mother."

He smiled and kissed the top of my head, before turning back to watch the rest of the wedding ceremony.

I thought back to my life in the dungeons. I'd never dreamed of ever stepping foot out of that dark cell. Mother's stories of the outside world and the books I'd read were my only escape from reality. It all changed when the brute beside me forced me out.

I looked up at Alexios, then all around me, at everyone I've met since that day. As I cast my eyes on each person and the giant white dragon, I was reminded of the memories I've made with them. Every frightening moment, every discovery, and every feeling flashed through my mind. I've been through quite an adventure.

It was an adventure I will never forget.